Don't Make Me Wait

Shana Burton

Urban Books, LLC
97 N18th Street
Wyandanch, NY 11798

ISBN 13: 978-1-62286-804-9
ISBN 10: 1-62286-804-8

First Trade Paperback Printing August 2015
Printed in the United States of America

10 9 8 7 6 5 4 3 2 1

Distributed by Kensington Publishing Corp.
Submit orders to:
Customer Service
400 Hahn Road
Westminster, MD 21157-4627
Phone: 1-800-733-3000
Fax: 1-800-659-2436

Don't Make Me Wait

Shana Burton

Dedication

This book is dedicated to my good friends Manuel and Rolando. Thank you for every moment of inspiration.

It is also dedicated to Joshua Malcolm Peltier, my partner in dance, life, and silliness.

Acknowledgments

There are three things I know for sure: salted caramel always makes my day better, my kids have been my saving grace, and I know that God is real! God, thank you for taking my neurosis, my smart mouth, and all of my flaws and creating something wonderful out of it. You are everything! You've blessed me with a beautiful family, amazing kids, great friends, a career that I love, and a man that I love even more! I'm so humbled that you found me worthy of so much of your favor. Thank you for blessing me with this gift and providing an outlet for me to share this gift with the world.

I would like to thank all of the usual suspects. Thank you to my mother, Myrtice C. Johnson, and her sweetheart, Albert Brown, for always being there for my boys and for me. There's no greater feeling than knowing there's at least one person who is always on your side. I am blessed to have two. Thank you to my father, James L. Johnson, for the talks and sound advice. Thank you to my precious babies, Shannon and Trey, for making me a better person. Shannon, I know you're teetering between being a teen and being an adult, but I have faith that you'll navigate through this transition to become an awesome man of God. Trey, I love seeing the young man you're becoming, but can you be my baby just a little bit longer?

Thank you to my friends who continue to support me through this journey called life and to all of the book clubs, reviewers, social media followers, and bloggers who have been down with Team Shana since *Suddenly Single*. I love you all! There's no me without you.

Thank you to my editor, Joylynn Ross, who continues to put up with me while bringing out the best in me as a writer.

A big thanks goes to the real men who inspired this book, Manny Johnson and Ro Harris. Manny, men like you are few and far between, and our friendship means the world to me. Ro, the real "Double A," thank you for sharing your gifts and talents with me. I look forward to watching you become a force in the entertainment industry.

Thank you to my spirit animal, Joshua Peltier. There's so much I want say about you, but it feels like it wouldn't be enough. I don't think I could have finished this book without you. I don't think I want to finish this life without you.

As always, thank you to all of my loyal and fab readers. Please know that I always write with you in mind. I'm so thankful God found a way to connect us. Keep bonding through books!

Happy reading!

Chapter 1

Amari Christopher hadn't smoked in over a year, but at that moment, she wanted a cigarette. Up until recently, cigarettes had been her go-to source of relief when alcohol wasn't available. Then it was prayer. Now, it was therapy, which she hated and only triggered her craving for cigarettes and alcohol even more. Perhaps it was time to revisit prayer.

Her therapist, Dr. Diane Nelson, flipped back a page from the legal pad that she was balancing on her knee. The word-of-mouth reviews verified that she was a thorough but approachable mental health therapist, and Amari's own experience with Dr. Nelson had proven that the fifty-year-old straight shooter could not be easily swayed or beguiled. After all, Amari had unsuccessfully tried to convince Dr. Nelson that a woman with Amari's good looks, money, and connections didn't really need therapy, which provoked Dr. Nelson to inquire, "Then why are you here?" Amari's façade immediately crumbled, and her bravado gave way to a hysterical crying fit that lasted half an hour, during which she blubbered about everything from her first love to guilt over cluttering the environment with her incessant use of water bottles. Summarily, Dr. Nelson promptly scheduled Amari for a minimum of three follow-up counseling sessions.

Surviving the first counseling session didn't completely put Amari's mind at ease, nor did it alleviate her doubts and reservations about the effectiveness of therapy. How could this person, a woman known only as a licensed therapist and her brother's prayer warrior, who knew nothing about Amari, understand? Amari glanced down at the scuff marks slashed across the toe of the therapist's right shoe. She shook her head. The bland, rounded-toe flats, the outdated mushroom wig that framed the woman's stoic face, and the pathetic, cerulean wrinkled flea-market pantsuit her therapist was wearing possibly were all telltale signs. A woman this fashionably challenged couldn't possibly understand the delicate intricacies that wove the never-ending soap opera that was now Amari's life.

Dr. Nelson cleared her throat. "For the majority of our first session, you talked a lot about how fabulous your life is with all of the lavish parties and entertainment industry events you get invited to. You said you loved your job writing for the magazine and that you have finally found the true love of your life. According to you, your life is close to perfect. To be honest, I couldn't figure out why you thought you needed therapy until you were overcome with emotion—"

"You mean my meltdown, don't you?" inserted Amari. "It's okay; you can say it."

"Well, there's a difference between feeling overwhelmed and having what I'd describe in clinical terms as a nervous breakdown. Nevertheless, even before that, something led you to seek out therapy." Dr. Nelson put her notes aside, maintaining intense eye contact with Amari. "So tell me, Miss Christopher, why are you here today?"

Amari weighed the question in her mind. Having accepted that her sanity was on the line, Amari decided to undergo therapy as a last-ditch effort to make some sense of what her life had become. It was true that she had all of the tangible trappings of a good life: a fulfilling career, an enviable shoe closet, and her choice of bedmates any given night of week; those things were nothing more than accessories covering a life that was nearly in shambles. There was only one bright spot left in Amari's life, and it was her love for him that led her to therapy. As much as it pained her to ask for help or show any signs of weakness, Amari knew that Dr. Nelson's counseling sessions may be the only way to save herself and the one relationship that had come to mean everything to her.

"I think I need help," she finally admitted.

"Help," repeated Diane Nelson, then pushed her thickly framed glasses up the bridge of her nose. "That's a very broad statement. Can you narrow that down for me? Why do you think you need help?"

Amari released a slow breath; her eyelids fell with the weight of the secrets she had been harboring, many of which were unconfessed truths about herself. Finally, she was ready to face her demons. Demons, she discovered, weren't pitchfork-carrying imps who lived in the bowels of the earth, but were invisible monsters who lived inside her head.

"I need help because I'm self-destructive," she admitted. "I destroy every relationship I get involved in, but I don't want to do that anymore. I can't." Her eyes bounced from the floor to the person a few feet behind her. "I love him too much to screw this up."

"Why did you want him to sit in on the session today?"

"I thought you said it was okay," voiced Amari. "He's not going to say anything or be disruptive."

"It's fine for me, but I don't want his presence to be a distraction for you. We get into some very personal, intense issues. You need to be in a situation where you feel comfortable to open up and be honest."

"That's why I wanted him here. I want things to be different this time around. I know he may not understand everything I've done or why, but I think that it's important that he knows who I am. I don't want to keep secrets from him."

"Very well. Let's start with what you said earlier. Why do you think you self-destruct in all of your relationships?" posed Dr. Nelson.

Amari glared up at her, thinking, *If I could answer that question, I probably wouldn't be in therapy!* Nevertheless, not even Amari could deny that it was a legitimate question and one that Amari had asked herself after every failed relationship. She didn't have an answer for her therapist any more than she had an answer for herself.

Amari shrugged. "You're the one with all of your degrees plastered all over the wall. Why don't you tell me?"

Dr. Nelson sat upright and scowled at Amari like a parent admonishing a cantankerous child. "I won't tolerate sarcasm, Miss Christopher," she issued sternly. "Now, we have two options. I can politely show you to the door or we can talk, and I can make an honest assessment about the situation and, with the Lord's help, guide you into taking some positive steps in your life. Agreed?"

Amari nodded and attempted to smooth the strands of hair easing out of her messy upswept bun.

"So I'll ask you again. Why do you think you self-destruct in all of your relationships?"

Amari slouched down in the chair. If she could've sunk through the leather seat cushion and the mahogany wood floor in the good doctor's badly lit office, she would have, but as she learned during her first session, that would've been another form of escapism, a tactic Dr. Nelson was trying to get Amari to move past. Sarcasm used as a defense mechanism was another one.

"Miss Christopher, did you hear what I said?" Dr. Nelson asked loudly, jolting Amari back to life.

Amari wasn't ready to respond. Her self-destructive nature was still a sensitive subject and one that she was hoping to avoid for at least two more sessions. She looked down at her knee. It was shaking uncontrollably. She glanced at Dr. Nelson's cherry-finish grandfather clock in the corner of the office, secretly hoping that her second hour-long therapy session was soon drawing to a close. Seeing as how there were at least fifty-eight minutes left, Amari knew it was pointless to try to run out the clock by stalling.

"I think my track record speaks for itself," she muttered at last.

"Relationships can end for a variety of reasons. How can you be solely responsible for a situation that it generally takes at least two people to create?"

"Because I'm the common denominator."

"That's what we're here to talk about, right?"

Amari's pulse quickened. She knew that she was mere moments away from having her life and ego ripped to shreds by the doctor's analysis. Amari exhaled and counted to ten slowly. "I apologize. This is really hard for me, especially when I know that Armand's made me out to look like some kind of oversexed Jezebel. He's in no position to talk, you know! I can't count the number of women he ran through before his so-called spiritual rebirth."

"Your brother never said anything like that, just that you were lost and confused, but his version is just that—*his* version. The only version that matters right now is yours."

Amari had longed to tell someone her side, to make people understand that she was just as much a victim as anyone else involved. But no matter what scenario she spun, she feared that she would still come out looking like the villain.

"I'm sure you're going to believe his side, though," predicted Amari. "Everyone else does. Armand has a way of getting women to believe and do exactly what he wants them to. Just ask his wife or his mistress."

"Is that what happens to you in your relationships with men? Do you feel like you're manipulated into doing or believing things that go against what you want?" Amari didn't say anything. Her therapist leaned back in her chair. "I'll tell you what, Miss Christopher. Why don't you just start talking, and we'll go on from there."

Start talking? Asking her to do that was like asking her to start constructing one of the Seven Wonders of the World. She had no clue how to begin. "Where do you want me to start?"

Dr. Nelson skimmed over her notes. "Toward the end of our initial session, you mentioned someone named Roland. You said he was your first love. You also said he was your first mistake. Why don't you tell me a little more about that?"

Roland. Simply hearing his name invited a variety of emotions. Some were positive; some could be the impetus for an attempted suicide. Roland, being her first serious boyfriend, had taught her everything she knew about sex and love and, later, rejection and heartbreak.

"You want me to talk about Roland?" She cocked her head to the side. "Are you sure we can't talk about someone else? My boss or my last boyfriend maybe?"

"Positive." Dr. Nelson jotted something down in her notebook.

Amari closed her eyes, retracing every moment that led to her sitting in a therapist's office that July morning instead of in her own office at *Rhythm Nation* magazine, where she served as an entertainment editor. No matter how she tried to spin it, all roads inevitably led back to her college sweetheart, Roland Harrison.

"Yes, the first man to break my heart was Roland Harrison," she confirmed. "I'm sure you've heard of him or at least know his type. He had it all: looks, intelligence, money, charisma; a real charmer. And so sexy!" She sighed, almost in a dreamlike state. "Being with Roland was like . . . I can't even describe it. I still get chills just thinking about him." She shook her head bitterly. "I should have known that any Negro that fine was going to be trouble. But it would be petty of me to put all of the blame on Roland. He proved he had a wandering eye, in addition to his wandering penis, when we first began dating during my sophomore year of college."

Amari closed her eyes and let her mind drift back to that previously closed and locked chapter in her life. Strangely, however, she didn't think back to when they met, but rather when she kissed him good-bye for the last time.

"Roland was every woman's nightmare disguised as every woman's fantasy," Amari went on. "He's the reason for me being the mess I am today."

Chapter 2

Eighteen Months Earlier

Roland Harrison was no stranger to controversy or to being the center of attention. The handsome NBA player turned award-winning sportscaster was a magnet for gorgeous socialites, athletes, A-list actors, actresses, and of course, swarms of groupies, who somehow always managed to sneak their way past security. Roland was rarely without the company of beautiful women, and today was no exception as Atlanta's most influential and elite denizens gathered at the historic Biltmore Ballroom for a celebration in Roland's honor.

While throngs of ladies fawned over him, Amari waited for what seemed like an eternity for her moment in the spotlight with Roland. She glanced over at him, decked out in a crisp designer suit with dark subtle waves cradling his skull and his goatee trimmed to perfection. His customary smirk was plastered across his face. It was the kind of grin that let a woman know he was nothing but trouble while simultaneously making him impossible to resist.

At once, the crowd's attention was diverted from the man of the hour to two ladies, presumably spurned lovers of Roland's, who were engaged in a verbal altercation. It appeared that a woman in a ridiculously short red dress thought that the female in the ridiculously tight black dress was lingering around Roland too long, and a shoving match ensued that had to be broken up by menacing men in dark suits. Amari couldn't do anything but shake her head and smile. After knowing Roland for almost twenty years and dating him off and on for many of them, she'd seen it all before. Nothing about this scene was unusual.

Nothing . . . except that this was Roland's funeral.

Once the commotion died down, and the women were ushered out of the room, screaming obscenities at one another, the line of mourners waiting to see the body proceeded forward. Within minutes, Amari was face to face with her dead lover.

She felt a combination of disbelief and crushing heart-ache. Seeing him this way was surreal. Roland, with his swagger and confidence, had always been so full of life. He possessed the uncanny ability to change the energy of a room simply by walking into it. He had the same effect lying dead in it.

"He looks like himself," she murmured, looking down at his lifeless body.

"Thirty-nine and shot down in the prime of his life," lamented an older woman standing in line behind her. Amari sighed, tempted to correct her. According to her sources, it wasn't the bullet lodged in Roland's chest that killed him. Rumor had it that Roland's live-in girlfriend strangled him with the thong she found tangled in their bed sheets before actually shooting him. It was a plausible story. Roland had always been a sloppy cheater. However, with his grieving mother sitting within earshot, Amari decided that this was not the right time or place to mention it.

Amari crooked her neck to kiss Roland's forehead before placing a rose in his casket. Her rose had plenty of company. It was apparent that his other courtesans and concubines had the same idea. He was practically bleeding rose petals.

As Amari said her final good-byes and walked away, Roland's mother, seated in the front row, reached for Amari's hand. Carolyn Harrison had always been kind to Amari. Although Carolyn was in utter denial about the piece of crap excuse for a man she raised, Amari's heart still went out to his mother. Roland had not only been her baby, he was her only child.

Amari stopped and hugged her. "How are you holding up, Miss Carolyn?"

Carolyn nodded, clutching a ball of tissue and fighting back tears. "It's hard, Amari, but it helps knowing that my Roly is in heaven with the Lord now."

Amari gently squeezed Carolyn's hand, thinking, *This poor thing is still in denial.*

Carolyn moved in closer and whispered, "Out of all those women, I think my son loved you most of all."

Amari smiled politely and clasped Carolyn's hand before returning to her seat. As she pressed her way through Roland's myriad ladyloves, Amari wondered if she should've been honored that out of the women Roland was fooling around with before and while they dated and the harem he sheltered afterward, she, apparently, was the one who he loved most of all. She thought maybe if he'd "loved" her a little less she could've avoided those embarrassing trips to the gynecologist to be treated for Chlamydia, bacterial vaginosis, and some other impossible-to-pronounce communicable disease that few people outside of the medical community had ever heard of.

Once she was seated, Amari's mind began flooding with memories of Roland. She recalled falling for him as a college sophomore. When they met, Roland was a junior and the pride of Georgia Tech's basketball team. It was a massive boost to Amari's ego when he asked the shy copy editor of the school newspaper to be his date at his fraternity's founder's day bash. The blow to the ego was equally massive when he dumped her for a sorority princess six months later. Once that fling fizzled out, Roland was back at Amari's doorstep with apologies and roses. A few drinks and well-placed kisses later, he was back in her bed, where he remained until a bevy of unchartered freshmen arrived on campus; then he was gone again. Once he lost interest in chasing them and she grew tired of acting she was no longer in love with him, they found themselves coupled up once more.

One thing Amari had to give Roland credit for was not pretending to be something he wasn't. Though he professed that his heart belonged to Amari, the rest of his body was community property. The fact that he referred to her as his "main girl" as opposed to his "only girl" should have clued Amari in that Roland was not interested in fidelity, but at age twenty she was still both optimistic and delusional enough to believe that she could change him.

College graduation brought with it a job at a small publishing company for Amari, a spot on a struggling NBA development league basketball team for Roland, and Roland and Amari's third breakup. Within a few years, Amari parlayed her job as the acquisitions editor's assistant at the publishing company into a highly sought-after position as an entertainment editor for *Rhythm Nation,* a magazine dedicated to music and pop culture. By then, Roland Harrison was a shining star in the world of sports as a point guard for Atlanta's professional basketball team and a mainstay in the tabloids, known as much for his exploits with models and video vixens as he was for maneuvering his team's defensive plays. Because their worlds often collided, Roland and Amari never lost touch. As adults in their thirties who'd long gotten over their youthful romance, they discovered that a friendship between them could be mutually beneficial. He gave her access to pictures and exclusive quotes. In exchange, she made him look good in the press. For the past seventeen years, he'd been a part of her life. Now he was nothing more than a memory and last week's magazine headline.

The woman who was behind Amari in line took a seat next to her, but Amari was too wrapped up in her own thoughts to notice. She didn't want to cry; Roland wouldn't have wanted that. One thing he always admired about her was her strength and resiliency, but she was brayed with grief.

"Roland, I still can't believe you're gone!" Amari bemoaned, on the brink of tears. "We didn't even get to say a real good-bye."

The woman patted Amari on the back to comfort her. "I know, honey. I never got the chance to tell him good-bye either. He lived next door to me 'til he went off to college. He was such a nice boy; he was so handsome, too. Nothing like those hoodlums running all over the neighborhood now."

Amari shed a tear despite her best efforts not to, but composed herself once she realized the woman had joined her. "Did he make it back to his old neighborhood much?"

She shook her head. "No, not really. Young fellows like that stay busy. But I used to always think it would be nice if he could come back home and talk to the young boys and let 'em know they can be more than street thugs." The woman dabbed the corner of her eye with a handkerchief. "I'm sure he intended to; he just ran out of time."

Amari side-eyed the grieving neighbor. She was positive that Roland had planned to do many things before his untimely passing, but she seriously doubted that mentoring young thugs was one of them. He was way too selfish to devote his time to any cause that wouldn't benefit his brand or his bank account.

Amari refocused her attention on the service as people began to approach the microphone to speak about Roland. His former coaches talked about his unmatched skill on the basketball court while his friends lightened the somber mood by exchanging funny stories about how Roland could always be counted on for laughs and good times. A few teary-eyed groupies recalled how he'd paid their rent and bought them extravagant gifts and vacations, and Roland's television cohost reminisced about Roland's sports commentary and spot-on game predictions. What was noticeably absent from all of the speeches and the eulogy was the lasting and meaningful impact Roland had on anyone's life.

Amari skimmed through the funeral program to see if she'd missed anything. Roland's notable career was written about extensively, but there was nothing in relation to charities he supported or people he'd helped. There was no mention of any causes he championed or even so much as a donated sock to Goodwill. By the looks of it, Roland's life could be summed up in three words: sports, money, and sex. It saddened her to think that there wasn't a single person there whose life was touched by Roland's life in any worthwhile way. Roland's existence was all flash and no substance. He'd lived thirty-nine years, and there was no proof that his life had even mattered, and no amount of sugarcoating from his friends could rectify that.

The worst part for Amari was knowing how much of her own life mirrored Roland's. What had she really done with her life? Yes, she had good looks and an impressive résumé, but that was it. If she died tomorrow, who would there be to wax poetic about all the good she'd done in the world? Who could testify that her living had not been in vain, that she'd done more than take up space and air on this planet? Would there be anything to show for her existence aside from a swanky but empty apartment and a string of meaningless affairs?

Amari knew that this wasn't the life she wanted. In that moment, she heard a small, still voice inside of her urging to make a change. She didn't know how she was going to do it or what that change should look like, but she knew she had to do *something,* and sooner rather than later. She'd already wasted almost thirty-eight years. To waste even another day would be too long.

Chapter 3

After leaving the funeral, Amari returned downtown to her art deco–inspired high-rise apartment. Its exotic woods, geometric motifs, and high-gloss finishes were the perfect backdrop for what Amari had determined would be a "chilled Moscato and Otis Redding" kind of evening. She spent so much of her time listening to and writing reviews for whoever was the new hot artist was for the month that she relished the rare occasions when she got a chance to listen to the music that she actually wanted to hear. 90 percent of the time, her music of choice was the smooth, soulful sounds of Otis.

Amari kicked her way through the ocean of stilettos and dresses blanketing her living room floor. Her foot got tangled in one of the strategically placed cutouts of the daring lace dress she'd worn to a listening party the night before. She scooped up the dress and pressed it against her body. Seeing it was bittersweet. She'd always found the dress to be a bit tacky, but Roland had given it to her as a birthday gift five years ago when he was in between relationships and thought the gesture might garner him a quickie. Her lips creased into a smile, remembering that last "for old times' sake" romp with Roland.

Amari flung the dress aside, poured a glass a wine, and pulled out her tattered photo album. She curled up on the sofa. Otis Redding provided a befitting soundtrack for her memory lane excursion as Amari flipped through the pages of her life captured in photographs. Halfway through sifting through her rebellious teen years, she was startled by a knock at her door.

Amari approached the door with caution, wondering how her visitor made it past the complex's gated entrance. "Who is it?"

A deep voice roared back, "It's me. Open up."

"I've got to change my security code," noted Amari.

She exhaled and unlocked the door, having recognized the gruff voice. On the other side was her twin brother Armand, who, with his deep-set russet eyes, gingerbread complexion, and tightly coiled coif, was the male version of Amari in terms of both looks and, often, behavior.

"Wow. I don't know if this is sweet or sad," said Amari, watching Armand struggle to balance toys, a baby bag, and a bag of fast food in one hand and Amari's one-year-old nephew and three-year-old niece in the other.

"While you contemplate it, can you grab something?" asked Armand in desperation.

Amari reached for her nephew, Trey. "Boy, give me that child before you drop him! Come on in."

Armand released a deep sigh. "Thank you."

"Don't think I'm being selfless. I'm only helping so it'll be one less thing I have to worry about you spilling on my plush carpet and costing me my deposit." Amari sat Trey down and then kissed her niece Jaycee on the cheek. "What brings you by? And it better not be to ask me to babysit!"

"Are you kidding?" scoffed Armand. "I barely get to see my kids as it is. I have to take advantage of every second I get with them. Considering that you're the least responsible person I know, you'd be the last person I'd call to babysit."

Amari poked out her lips. "Remember that next time you and Nia want to go away for the weekend."

"Nia wants me to go away, but not for some romantic weekend with her! She wouldn't mind sending me to hell, though, that's for sure. My never seeing the kids again would just be a bonus to her," lamented Armand, who was in the midst of a bitter split from his estranged wife.

"She's still holding the kids over your head, huh?"

"Nia's still salty about Kim, so she ain't tryin'a cut a brother a break! Now she's talking about bringing in all kinds of lawyers and social workers. The other day, she tells me, 'I was a helluva wife to you, but you didn't appreciate it. Now, I'm going to be a helluva ex-wife and see how you like that!' She's trippin'."

Amari sat down. "She's not trippin', Armand; she's hurt. You were dead wrong for cheating on your wife and just plain stupid for getting caught, but she shouldn't keep the kids away from you because of it. Kids need their fathers. We know that better than anybody."

"Yeah, tell that to the judge—literally! With all of your hotshot connections, I'm sure you've got a judge or two in your pocket or know someone who does."

"I'm afraid that's above my pay grade. But if you need someone to perform at your divorce party, I can hook you up."

Armand sat his daughter down and unloaded all of his baby equipment. "It'll all work itself out. I've just got to have faith in the system and, you know, God."

Amari rolled her eyes. "If that's what you're banking on, you're in trouble, my friend!"

Armand spotted the photo album and picked up one of the scattered pictures. "What's all this?"

Amari made room for Armand next to her on the sofa. "I was revisiting the past." She showed Armand a picture of the two of them as teenagers. "You remember this?"

His eyes widened. "Combat boots and bomber jackets! This was definitely taken in the nineties. I think that was the height of my Jodeci phase," recalled Armand with a laugh. "What was up with my hair though? I'm not sure if that's a fade or a 'fro or both."

Amari laughed. "We've all seen our share of bad hair days! Look." She pointed at a picture of herself in box braids. "I wasn't much better."

"I can deal with your hair, but what were you wearing?"

"I remember that look. You had your Jodeci phase, and I had my rebellious 'grunge meets gangster chick meets hoochie mama' phase." Amari flipped to a picture of her and Roland in college. "Thank goodness by the time I met Ro, I had developed a more practical fashion sense."

Armand could sense that his sister was still unnerved by Roland's sudden death. "I guess this whole thing with Roland has got you feeling all nostalgic."

"Yes." It pained as much as it consoled Amari to talk about him. "It's hit me a lot harder than I expected."

"That's really why I'm here. I know the funeral was today. I figured you might be kind of sad, so I thought I'd come over and cheer you up, bring you something to eat." He passed her the salad he'd brought with him.

She was touched. "That was sweet of you. It was percep-tive as well. I could use an ear right now."

"You're in luck because I've got two of 'em, so talk to me. How are you holding up?"

Amari shrugged. "I'm all right now. The shock of him dying has pretty much worn off. There funeral was kind of weird for me."

"Oh, yeah? What happened?" Armand plunked a spongy ball into his son's waiting hands.

Amari popped open the salad. "It was just depressing, you know?"

"It's supposed to be. It was a funeral, not a rave!"

"No, I mean, the way he lived his life and the way he died. Sure, he was renowned and had a lot of money, but

Roland never really made a difference in the world, didn't positively influence anyone's life. You should've heard the preacher up there struggling to say something good about him. His life was just . . . empty."

"Well, his bed sure wasn't! Actresses, models, desperate housewives; dude's hit list is legendary."

Amari mixed the dressing into the salad. "No doubt if his bed had been a little less crowded, he'd still be alive."

Armand agreed with a nod, keeping a watchful eye on Jaycee as she neared one of Amari's sharp-edged sculptures. "Life is all about choices. Good or bad, we're all a sum total of the decisions we've made."

"Yeah, that was made abundantly clear at the funeral." Amari raised her eyes to meet his. "It . . . it kind of scares me, you know?"

"What does?"

"My life and where it's headed."

"The party life definitely has a shelf life. I realized that after Jaycee was born." He winked at his daughter.

Amari stopped him. "Hold up now. I didn't say I was ready to embrace the recluse spinster life. I'll take the club over being a couch potato any day!"

"I guess you and I got our roles mixed up. I'm the one at home taking care of the kids while you're bed-hopping every chance you get!"

"You've hopped in and out of your share of strange beds too, mister!" she reminded him.

"True and what did that get me except a bunch of crazy broads slashing up my tires and talking trash about me on social media, not to mention a pending divorce?"

"Life has a way of catching up with you," replied Amari, digging into her salad again. "After Ro's funeral today, I took a good hard look at what my future will look like. Yeah, I'm relatively successful, I get to rub shoulders with the rich and infamous, I've got all of the Atlanta

Housewives on speed dial, but is that it? Is this all my life is supposed to be about? Celeb parties and a string of one-night stands?"

Trey rolled the ball to his father, who sent it back to him. "I thought you were cool with that. Shoot, most folks would be. What's changed?"

"I think just seeing Roland lying there dead. I mean, *he's dead,* Armand! Party over, oops, out of time!" she exclaimed, waving her fork in the air. "He lived thirty-nine years, and I can't think of a single person whose life is better because of him. I don't know of anything he did with those thirty-nine years aside from look good, bag groupies, play some ball, and piss a lot of folks off."

Armand agreed. "Yep, that pretty much sums it up!"

Amari tempered her diatribe. "But the cold truth is that I'm no better than he is, not when it really comes down to it."

"Oh, you've been baggin' bad chicks too?" he joked.

Amari huffed and swallowed a mouthful of salad. "You know what I mean."

"So what are you going to do about it?"

"I don't know." Amari considered her options. "Maybe I'll feed the homeless or adopt some orphans," she suggested.

"Feed the homeless?" Armand laughed and continued rolling ball to his son. "Mar, you don't even give spare change to the panhandlers you pass on the street! And how are you going to adopt some orphans if I can't even get you to watch your blood niece and nephew for more than an hour?"

Amari brooded. "I'm just waiting for them to get a little older, Armand. I told you that."

"I've never even known you to keep a plant alive for more than two weeks. You think somebody is going to trust you with an actual human?"

Amari grudgingly conceded. "Okay, maybe adoption isn't it, but I want to do something!" She started back eating her salad. "I want my existence to have meaning and purpose."

"What makes you think it doesn't?"

She thought of another idea. "You think I should attend one of those wellness retreats? You know, the ones where you get in touch with nature, find your center, and figure out the meaning of life."

Armand sneered. "I don't know about all that, but if you want to figure out God's purpose for your life, I suggest—"

Amari cut him off. "Don't say it!"

"Why not?"

"Because I already know what you are going to say, and I don't need another lecture from you about going to church."

"Hey, all I'm trying to do is help you."

Amari bristled. "When are you going to realize that religion is something crooks and prudes thought up to keep people from getting laid and to convince idiots to give all of their money to the church?"

"I thought getting laid and getting idiots to give up all their money is what you do," mused Armand.

"Very funny." She playfully elbowed him. "Besides, I haven't done that since college."

A chuckle from Armand followed. "You should at least think about coming to church with me. Since all this craziness started with Nia, church has been my saving grace in every sense of the word."

"But I'm not you, Armand." She chewed and swallowed her salad. "Yes, I'm glad you found God and Jesus or whatever it is that you think you've found in that church, but all that religion stuff is for fanatics and blue-haired old ladies. I just don't think it'll work for me."

"Neither is what you're doing. I know you want more out of life than to keep sluttin' around, trying to find validation in schlongs and dollars."

Her jaw dropped. "Sluttin' around? You better be glad I love you, li'l brother."

"I love you too, but, hey, I've got to call it like I see it."

"And what you see when you look at me is a slut?" charged Amari.

"No, what I see is a woman who doesn't know who she is or what she really wants. Going to church and getting in touch with God might help you discover your purpose. Judging by the way changing Trey's diapers gets the best of you, I think we can assume mothering and adopting orphans ain't it!"

Amari caved. "Okay, I admit that kids and diapers may not be my thing, but I don't need some preacher who's just as flawed as I am trying to tell me how to live. And I don't need a God I can't see, hear, touch, taste, or smell controlling my life. I have a degree, money in the bank, and a contact list people would kill for. Anything I can't figure out, I can pay someone to tell me."

"I know that's what you think. Heck, a few months ago, I would've said the same thing. But when Nia packed up the kids and left, I had to accept that what I was doing wasn't enough. I knew I had to do something different."

"Yeah, but it's still not working. She served you divorce papers, and you're on a visitation schedule to see your kids."

"She filed, but the divorce isn't final yet. God has the final say."

"You mean the judge has the final say, which could come any day now."

"I'm still believing in God for a miracle and praying for my family's restoration. Even if it doesn't happen, I know how to cope now. I can rest assured that God has my back and that I'm gonna be all right either way."

Amari wrapped her arm around her brother. "You'll be all right because your five-minutes-older sister has your back!"

"I know you do, but there's nothing like the peace of knowing you don't have to fight your battles alone and knowing that you have a church family and a Heavenly Father fighting and praying for you. That's what becoming a member of Greater Hope and being under the pastor's leadership has done for me."

"Well, hooray for you, Armand," she retorted with lackluster inflection and lowered her arm. "But what I see when I look at you is a man still clinging to a dead marriage when the writing is spray-painted in gigantic fluorescent letters on the wall. You need to deal with that and focus on how you're going to pay this woman on your bartender's salary and stay a part of these kids' lives. You can't use God or religion as an excuse to not realistically deal with your situation."

"And you can't knock it 'til you try it!"

Amari shook her head. "Try what? Being dumped and a paycheck or alimony payment away from poverty? No, thank you! If that's what they want to teach me at church, I'll pass."

"It's not God's will for His people to be broke, busted, and disgusted. That's not what our church teaches. Come on. What's it going to hurt to go to one service to appease your baby brother? Truth be told, I could use the help getting these two up and out the house tomorrow morning."

"Tomorrow?" Amari balked. "Geesh, don't I get some time to think it over?"

"It's a couple of hours out of your life, Amari. I bet you spent longer than that putting your outfit together today."

"I can't argue with you there, but church? All that enforced whoopin' and hollerin', Bible totin' and quotin'. That's really not my scene. You know I like to sleep in on Sunday mornings. Saturday nights usually wear me out!"

Armand gave her the once-over. "You know you're one birthday away from being the old chick in the club, right?"

"We're the same age, homeboy! Thirty-seven is not old, and who said it was the club wearing me out on Saturday nights?" quipped Amari.

Armand groaned and scooted away from her. "Okay, we have just entered the Land of Too Much Information."

She laughed. "Are you searching for the quickest exit?"

"If it's the one that leads you to church with me in the morning."

Amari whined, "Armand."

Armand rose and picked up his son. "Just think about it, all right? Service starts at ten."

She handed him the baby bag. "I'll think about it, but I won't make you any promises."

"You can't because tomorrow isn't promised to any of us. You can't take time for granted, Mar, or assume anything. Look at Roland. Don't you think he would've made different choices if he'd known his number was about to be up?"

Amari's eyes alighted to the photo album still turned to Roland's picture. Time and choices were two things Amari had always assumed she'd have more than enough of. She still had choices, but for the first time, she wondered if there would be enough time.

Chapter 4

"So it was Roland's passing, not the relationship itself, that impelled you to make a change," deduced Dr. Nelson, her pen triggered to jot more notes when prompted.

"He lived and died, and his life made a difference to no one," answered Amari. "I knew I didn't want to end up like that. I also knew that if I kept living the way he did, I would."

"What kind of difference would you like to make, Amari? How do you want to be remembered?"

"Not as some party girl who writes celebrity fluff for a glorified tabloid. I want to feel and experience meaningful things. I want there to be a void in the world when I'm no longer in it. I want my life to have meant something." She paused. "More than anything, I want to love and be loved."

"You think Roland died without finding real love."

She nodded. "That includes loving himself."

Dr. Nelson tilted her head. "What about you? Do you love yourself, Amari?"

Amari hesitated before responding. "I want to, but I don't know if I'm there yet," she admitted.

"You said you love this new person in your life. How can you love him when you don't even know if you love yourself?"

"Loving him makes me want to change and love myself," affirmed Amari.

"Why is loving yourself so hard for you to do?"

Amari released a deep sigh. Her knee began trembling again. "I'm not really a good person, Doc. I'm selfish and self-centered. I've hurt people in order to have my way. I don't always consider the other person's feelings. I'm thirty-eight years old, and I'm a complete mess. What's there to love?"

"There's some good and bad in all of us. Have you tried focusing on the things you like about yourself instead of what you don't like?"

She sucked her teeth. "No, not really."

"You said you're not a good person. What does a good person look like to you?"

"I don't know. I guess someone who puts others first, a person who people admire and respect."

"Amari, no one is perfect. Even people who give their last to other people have issues. You have to love your-self despite the imperfections. That doesn't mean you shouldn't strive to be a better person, but it does mean you have to learn and accept yourself as you are now."

Amari's eyes fell downcast. "I don't know if I know how to do that."

"Do you think your struggles with self-worth have anything to do with your upbringing?"

Amari shook her head. "You people always go right for the inner child Oedipus/Freudian complex, don't you?"

"I wasn't going for anything. I'm only here to help you sort things out, not just regurgitate theories. However, childhood is often a good place to start."

Amari squirmed in her seat. "I had a normal childhood, nothing special."

Dr. Nelson raised her pen. "Define 'normal.'"

"You know, normal," Amari hedged, anxious to avoid delving into the issue any further. "I was born in Baltimore, but we moved to Georgia shortly afterward. We weren't rich, but we survived. I had friends, I went to school, mostly stayed out of trouble. I guess I can thank my twin brother for that. My brother Armand and I are extremely close. We've always had each other's back. Overall, my childhood was pretty mundane, so we don't have to go into depth with all that."

"Would you say you had a happy childhood?"

She paused. "Pretty much."

"Tell me about your parents."

Amari grimaced. "Why? We're here to talk about my relationships."

"That's what we're doing. You and your parents have a relationship."

Amari released a coarse laugh followed by a terse, "No, we don't." She shook her head and clammed up, realizing she had revealed more than she intended to. "My parents and I are fine. We're not particularly close, but I'm okay with that."

Dr. Nelson persisted, "Are you really?"

Amari swept the question aside. "It's a long story, and we really don't have time to get into all of that. I'm paying you by the hour, remember?"

"I think it's important to evaluate your relationships with both of your parents."

Irked by Dr. Nelson's refusal to let up, Amari shot back, "And I don't, so let's agree to disagree about that!"

"Amari, we've talked about this. Avoiding the issue doesn't make it go away."

Dr. Nelson was worse than a dog with a bone; Amari knew she'd have to resort to acrimony to get this therapist off her back. "We're here to make sure I don't make the same mistakes going forward, not rehash mistakes my parents made. If it's okay with you, I'd rather move on and talk about something else. If not, maybe it's time for me to look for a new therapist, one who actually knows what she's doing!"

Dr. Nelson jotted down more notes.

Amari relented. She knew Dr. Nelson was a consummate professional. More importantly, Amari knew she wasn't going anywhere despite her threat to do so. "Look, I'm not one of these people who blame their parents for being screwed up. This is something that I've brought on myself," acknowledged Amari. "I accept that. My parents had nothing to do with it."

"Then why don't you want to talk about them?"

"It's a sensitive subject, that's all. And before you let your imagination and note-taking run wild, no, my parents did not abuse us. They weren't crazy stage parents who tried to live out their dreams through us or anything like that," she clarified. "Things between us are just complicated."

"Why? There has to be a reason. You said that you had a relatively normal childhood. You weren't neglected or abused. I assume they took pretty good care of you."

"Yeah, my mom did take care of us to the best of her ability. She made sure we had food and a clean place to stay, but she was young, you know? She was barely out of teens trying to raise two kids alone. She didn't have all the answers."

"Was your father in the home?"

Amari shook her head. "He wasn't around much, but that's not entirely his fault. Nor does it mean he didn't care about us or love us."

Dr. Nelson appeared to be absorbed in thought as she listened. "How did not having him around make you feel?"

Amari stood up to stretch her legs. "You know, Doc, I'm not really into the whole 'let's talk about our feelings' thing. I prefer to deal with the facts. Besides, what does how I felt when I was a kid have to do with now?"

"Not having a father around as a child can lead to all kinds of issues that deal with trust, rejection, abandonment, a lost sense of identity—many of the things that may have led you to my office."

"I just don't want you to get the wrong impression of him. My father wasn't a bad person."

"I'm not here to make any judgments on your father. The point is to determine if that loss has affected the way you feel about yourself, and in turn, the way you behave in your relationships."

Amari turned away, distracting herself by reading Dr. Nelson's wall plaques. Anything to keep from dealing with the issue at hand.

Dr. Nelson went on. "I know reliving all of this can be tough, but sometimes facing it is the only way to get through it and tackle the root cause. We can't deal with it if you don't talk about it."

Amari slowly faced Dr. Nelson again. "My father not being there had nothing to do with him being a deadbeat parent or anything. When we moved to Georgia, he stayed behind in Baltimore at my mother's insistence. I think being around him would've just been too painful for her."

"Why?"

"There were reasons they couldn't be together, circumstances beyond his or her control."

"What were the circumstances?"

Amari didn't say anything.

"Amari, we won't make any headway if you continue to shut down like this. I want to help you, I really do; but you've got to trust me. Otherwise, we're just wasting each other's time."

The smart aleck in Amari wanted to tell Dr. Nelson what she could do with her wasted time. Then she looked back at the person seated behind her. He didn't say anything, but his reassuring smile helped her remember why she was there in the first place.

Amari exhaled and returned to her seat. "My mother was given away by her birth mother when she was a baby. My mom was only a few weeks old when her biological mother dropped her off at the hospital. My grandmother, who was working as a nurse at the hospital, was the one who found my mom. Even though my grandmother and my grandfather desperately wanted children, they had given up hope of ever conceiving a child. They had been trying for years and, by that point, my grandmother was well into her forties. So when an abandoned baby showed up needing a loving home, she and her husband were happy to oblige. The Christophers adopted her and raised her as their own."

"Are you and your grandparents close?"

"We were, but they died."

"Oh. Sorry to hear that."

"Thank you. They were good, 'salt of the earth' kind of people, probably the closest thing to angels I'll ever meet," Amari wistfully recalled.

Dr. Nelson looked down at her notes again. "Did your mother know that she was adopted or who her biological parents were?"

"My mother was aware that she'd been adopted. My grandparents never kept the adoption a secret, but no one had any idea who my mom's real parents were."

"Was she ashamed or struggled with rejection as a result of being adopted?"

"No. In fact, my grandparents used the fact that she was adopted to let my mom know how special she was because she'd been chosen, not an accident like so many other kids. My mother, on the other hand, always made it quite clear that my brother and I were sources of shame for her and the entire family."

"Why would the two of you be a source of shame?"

"My mother was unmarried and twenty, for one. No one really thinks twice about single mothers having babies today, but it wasn't quite as accepted then. It was tough on the whole family, made even more complicated by the fact that she was expecting twins."

"Oh," replied Dr. Nelson, understanding. "Is that why she left Baltimore, to escape the stigma of being an unwed mother?"

"That was part of it. The other part was who my father was."

"Why was that an issue? Was he married or an older man?"

"He was a relative," filled in Amari.

"I see." Dr. Nelson delivered a minimal reaction and appeared to be unfazed. "Molestation would explain why she felt shame, both toward you all and herself, especially if it was never addressed properly."

Amari shook her head. "My mother wasn't molested. She was in love."

"It's not uncommon for molestation survivors to feel a strong emotional attachment to their abusers—"

"She wasn't molested," repeated Amari. "My parents were in love. I told you my mother didn't know who her biologically parents were. She saw the Christophers as her family and never bothered to track down her real parents. It wasn't an issue until she began dating my father."

"What happened to make it an issue then?"

"After they started dating, my father used to tease her about how much she looked like his Aunt Terry. No one took it seriously; it was more of a running joke between them. Then one day, when my mother was about three months pregnant with Armand and me, my father invited her to a family cookout. His aunt was there, and he introduced them. My mother said that as soon as she saw Terry the hairs stood up on the back of her neck. I imagine it must've been eerie for my mother seeing a woman she'd never laid eyes on before who had the same dark face, wide eyes, and full lips that she did." Amari took a moment before continuing. She rarely revealed to anyone what she was about to say next, and there was a queasiness stuck to the pit of her stomach. She hated this feeling, hated thinking about her parents, and hated having to explain how she and her brother came to be.

"Long story short," Amari went on, "I guess they started putting the pieces together. It wasn't long before they figured out that my mother was the daughter my father's Aunt Terry had left at the hospital when she was a teenager. Terry and my dad's mother are sisters."

Dr. Nelson's eyes widened. "So you're saying—"

"Yes," confirmed Amari. "I'm saying that my parents are also my cousins."

Chapter 5

Eighteen Months Earlier

Amari began questioning her last-minute decision to join her brother at his church the second she pulled her Range Rover into the Greater Hope International Church parking lot. As much as she loved Armand, the thought of disappointing her brother wasn't nearly as sobering as the near-death experience Amari had the night before. A late-night run to Starbucks to satisfy a sugar craving that only a caramel cappuccino could fulfill nearly resulted in Amari being mowed down by a speeding Corvette as she crossed the street in the rain. She wasn't sure if the driver didn't see her or if she underestimated how fast he going. Either way, it was by the grace of God the driver was able to swerve moments and inches before flattening her in the middle of Peachtree Street. Following that harrowing experience, spending a couple of hours in the presence of the Lord didn't seem like such a bad idea after all.

Amari stepped out of the car, weighed down by a sense of dread as she set her six-inch perforated sandals on the pavement. There was a crisp autumn chill in the air, but Amari was perspiring like it was the middle of July. She hadn't seen the inside of a church since her grandmother's funeral fifteen years prior and had only visited once or twice on Resurrection Sunday before that. She wasn't sure how she'd be received, but she doubted that it would be with open arms. She didn't belong there, and she knew it. It would only be a matter of time before everyone else figured it out too.

Once Amari reached the entrance of the church, she took a deep breath, put on a brave face, and pulled open the door to the vestibule. She was greeted by an usher as soon as she stepped in.

The usher, clad in a beige Greater Hope polo shirt and khakis with a smile that appeared to stretch every available facial muscle, gripped Amari's hand and said, "Namaste."

Amari shied away from the usher. She didn't know this woman and wasn't comfortable having her invade her personal space. Unsure how to respond to the "Namaste" greeting, she retorted, "Um, okay, whatever."

The usher slipped her an offering envelope. Amari took offense to the presumptuous gesture. She had no intention of filling the church's coffers with her very hard-earned money. "I'm not here to give," Amari warned her before declining the envelope. "I'm just visiting."

The usher didn't break her smile. "No problem. Follow me, and I'll help you find a seat." The usher opened the doors to the sanctuary.

"I'm looking for my brother, Armand Christopher," said Amari, peering over the heads of the congregation in search of Armand and the children. "Do you know him? Tall, handsome, two kids in tow."

"Let me walk you to the front, and we'll see if we can find him."

Amari spotted her brother seated on the third pew. "No, I think I see him. Thank you."

Amari sauntered down the aisle, turning her nose up at the people waving their hands and praising the Lord with the same exhilaration and zeal she usually reserved for sporting events and sex. She shrank away from two women as they joined the choir in a jubilant rendition of

"We've Come This Far by Faith," led by a woman whose commanding alto voice forced Amari to stop and take notice. She paused momentarily to look at the lyrics on the screen hovering over the pulpit.

Before the words had a chance to sink in, Armand caught sight of Amari and signaled for her to join him. She brushed past the curious onlookers as she maneuvered her way through the row of parishioners to squeeze in next to her brother.

"You're late," hissed Armand, momentarily breaking from singing to admonish his sister. "I thought you were going to come by and help with the kids this morning."

"Do you know what a miracle it is that I'm even here at all? I would've swung by your place on the way here, but I ran into Traffic. That's why I'm late."

"Was there an accident?" he asked, concerned.

"No, not an accident. Traffic; he's a deejay I met at a club last week."

Armand shook his head in disbelief. "His name is Traffic?"

"That's his stage name. His real name Travis Johnson. I stopped to get gas on the way over and bumped into him. We chatted it up for a few minutes." Amari drifted into her own world. "My goodness, if you could've seen the way his basketball shorts were riding just low enough to scope his—"

"Shhh!" Armand brought his finger to his lips. "Mari, please! We're in church!"

Amari's potty mouth earned her a cold glare from the church member seated next her.

She sulked. "I forgot. Sorry." She looked around the pew. "Where are the kids?" she asked, seeing no evidence of her niece and nephew.

"They're in children's church. Now can you just be quiet and enjoy the service?"

Amari gazed out at the people surrounding her and felt both isolated and exposed. The members seemed to all be in on the same secret, caught up in praise and worship of a being she had no real knowledge of. They even dressed differently. It was then she began to second-guess her choice of attire. While she was dressed head to toe in designer labels, she realized that her body-hugging sheath dress probably wasn't the most appropriate option. It did nothing to hide her curves, and its Venetian red hue made her anything but inconspicuous. She drew her arms close to her body, suddenly feeling insecure.

She leaned over to Armand. "I think my dress is too short. What do you think?"

"Amari, contrary to what your ego believes, you are not the most important person in the room right now. God is. Nobody in here is even thinking about you or that loud dress you rolled up in here wearing."

"So you do think it's inappropriate," she inferred, tugging on her dress.

He glanced over at his sister. "Leave it alone. The dress is fine."

"But I have on a thong," she whispered to him, flustered. "Is that allowed?"

Armand squinted his eyes, baffled. "Are you serious?" He noticed her fanning herself with her hand. "You all right?"

"Yeah, it's just hot in here. Don't they believe in central air or are they trying to give folks a glimpse of what hell is gonna feel like?"

Armand was amused watching his sister become unglued. "I think I'm finally beginning to understand where that 'sweatin' like a hooker in church' simile came from."

She huffed. "Well, what do you want me to do, Armand? I hate panty lines and going commando at church just felt wrong."

He was confused. "Yet hooking up with some random deejay before coming to church felt right?"

"People in church aren't really sexually active, are they?" she asked in a hushed tone. Amari's eyes darted across the sanctuary. "I feel like everyone is looking at me, like they can smell the fornication me!"

"Will you relax? The average person probably thinks that distinctive aroma is your perfume. Only you, me, and the Lord know differently."

She glared at him. "You know this isn't helping, don't you?"

"We're at church. Here, you're with family. Nobody is judging you."

"Please, everybody's judging! People do it without trying." Amari spied a couple seated in front of her sharing a Bible. "Ugh, I don't have a Bible! Now they're really going to think I'm a heathen! Who shows up at church without the handbook?"

"More people than you think." He pointed toward the pulpit. "That's why the church bought that big ol' screen to post the scriptures. Lighten up, Amari!"

"Okay, good to know." Amari pulled her cell phone out of her purse and began tinkering with it.

"Are you trying to find a Bible app?" asked Armand.

"No, I needed to check my e-mail right quick." The act was met with a biting look from her brother. "Don't look at me like that. Work doesn't stop just because it's Sunday, you know."

"Considering that this is the day even the Lord rested, I have to beg to differ."

Amari scrolled through her unread e-mails. "Then why is the pastor working, Armand? Did you ever think about that?"

Armand exhaled sharply. "No, but I do think this is the last time I'm inviting you church with me."

After the praise and worship faded out, a minister approached the pulpit. "Welcome to another glorious day that the Lord has made! Let us rejoice and be glad in it! On behalf of Pastor Joshua Campbell, First Lady Frieda Campbell, and the entire pastoral staff, we'd like to welcome all of you and thank you for joining us for another beautiful Sunday here at Greater Hope International Church. If you haven't greeted your brothers and sisters in love this morning, let's take a few moments to do that now. Amen?"

The congregation responded with a rousing, "Amen!" The choir broke into an up-tempo number, and the churchgoers began scattering from their seats, greeting one another with handshakes and hugs.

Armand tapped Amari on the shoulder. "I'll be right back. I think I see someone I know."

"Armand, where are you going?" she asked in a loud whisper.

"I'll be back!" he insisted, walking away. "Go fellowship. Mix and mingle."

Amari, unfamiliar with the church's procedure, stood in place with her arms clenched close to her body, hoping no one would approach her.

Seconds later, someone asked her, "Is this your first time?"

Amari whirled around when she heard a male's voice behind her. "Excuse me?"

A man in a gray suit flashed a set of perfect teeth, putting her at ease. He asked again, "Is this your first time here at Greater Hope?"

"You caught me off-guard with that question. It's been a long time since a man has asked me if it's my first time doing anything," she ruminated. "But, yes, this is my first time here."

He laughed a little. "I figured it was. I pretty much know all the familiar faces around here." He outstretched his hand. "Hi, my name is Mandrel Ingram."

"I'm Amari." She extended her hand into his, sizing him up. He was tall, looked to be around her age, and had a subtle, cool edge about him. His buff complexion, almond-shaped eyes, and pouty mouth weren't hard to look at either.

"It's a pleasure to meet you, Amari."

"Are you the one-man welcome wagon here?" she asked.

"Not exactly, just being friendly. So what brought you to worship with us today?"

"My brother invited me."

"Who's your brother?"

Amari pointed to Armand, who was making his way back to their pew. "The tall one over there with my eyes and that aquiline nose."

"Oh, you're talking about Brother Christopher," replied Mandrel, recognizing him. "I can definitely see the strong resemblance between the two of you. I don't know him all that well, but he seems like a good dude as far as I can tell. A devoted father and family man."

"He's the best. I think my presence is embarrassing him, though. He just informed me that this is my last invitation to his church."

"Well, it's my church too, so your next invitation is on me. How about that?"

She grinned. "Works for me!"

"Who's the oldest between you two?"

"I am," boasted Amari, "by five minutes."

"Oh, you're twins?"

"Yep, double trouble," replied Amari.

"It must've been cool growing up together and having someone to share your childhood with."

She gave a nod of affirmation. "It was. What about you? Are you an only child?"

"I might as well be. I've got an older brother and sister. They've got about sixteen years on me. I was what most parents refer to as a surprise."

"Don't feel bad. We were surprises too. In fact, I believe you can use the word 'surprise' to explain how half the world's population got here."

He unleashed a hearty chuckle. "You're probably right."

Armand approached them and shook Mandrel's hand. "What's up, man?"

"It's all good. I was getting acquainted with your lovely sister over here."

"Don't worry," Armand cautioned him. "Her bark is worse than her bite."

"She's not so bad," remarked Mandrel, then winked at Amari. "Enjoy the service."

"I will, thank you," said Amari. "Nice meeting you."

Mandrel waved and dashed off.

"You're making friends, I see," teased Armand.

"That's better than making enemies, right? Lord knows I've made enough of those!"

"It would be hard to make an enemy out of Brother Ingram. He's a good dude."

"And unlike my dear brother, he actually invited me to come back to church again," added Amari.

Armand sighed. "He'll have to repent for that later."

Amari made it through the rest of the service without embarrassing herself or her brother. She surprised herself by remaining awake for most of it. She even tuned into the sermon every once in a while. Not enough to offer a decent summation, but enough to know that Ephesians 6:16 promises that the shield of faith will protect her from the fiery darts of the wicked one—whatever that meant.

"Wait here," instructed Armand as they made their way toward the parking lot once church let out. "I'm going to run over to the children's building and get Jaycee and Trey. You stay here and try not to get in any trouble while I'm gone."

"Will you just go?" Amari shooed him away. "And hurry up. I'm hungry!"

While Armand fetched the children, Amari caught up on her missed text messages. She was in the midst of replying back to a very explicit text from Traffic when Mandrel startled her again.

"You know, you have a bad habit of sneaking up on people," she said, hoping he hadn't peeked the risqué message she'd just sent back to Traffic.

"I don't think it's people," countered Mandrel. "I think it's only you."

"Some people find that kind of behavior creepy." She cast a half smile to let him know she was kidding. "Lucky for you, I'm not one of those people."

"The last thing I want to do is creep you out. Otherwise, we'll never get you back here. Then Greater Hope will go down in your mind's history as that church with the creepy one-man welcoming committee."

She put her phone away. "How about 'the creepy one-man welcoming committee with the great smile'?"

He grinned. "I'll take it. So did you enjoy the service?"

Amari nodded. "It was nice. I was pleasantly surprised."

"I'm glad. I hope you plan on making this a regular stop on Sunday mornings. It really is an awesome worship experience."

She shook her head, politely turning down the offer. "I'm not really a 'church on Sunday' kind of girl."

"No one is until they start attending. Take it one Sunday at a time."

"Well, we'll see. This isn't how I typically spend my weekends."

"Since you don't spend your Sundays in the house of the Lord, how do you usually spend them?"

"Meeting my deadline or screaming at my staff writers for not meeting theirs. I'm an editor-slash-writer."

Mandrel was impressed. "A writer, huh? That's cool. Do you freelance?"

"Sometimes. Have you heard of *Rhythm Nation?*"

"The Janet Jackson album?"

"No, silly, the magazine. I'm the entertainment editor."

"Wow, check you out!" he exclaimed.

"I love it. I'm not rich, but the job comes with a lot of perks money can't buy."

"I'm sure it does. Fancy parties, backstage access, hanging out with celebrities . . ."

She nudged him. "Not to mention all the cool T-shirts I get from work!"

They both laughed.

"What about you? What do you do?" asked Amari.

"I'm a cabbie."

Amari blurted out, "Seriously?"

"Yeah, I own a whole fleet of taxis," touted Mandrel.

"Oh, really?" Amari batted her eyes, immediately switching into flirt mode. She was impressed by words like "I own a fleet," which usually came with a sizable bank account attached.

"Well, 'fleet' may be stretching it a bit. I have three cabs. I'm not sure what the official number is to legally declare that it's a fleet."

Amari turned off the charm. Three cabs wasn't worth the effort.

Mandrel reached into his pocket and pulled out a card and handed it to Amari. "In case of emergency."

Amari read the front of the card: "Man of Wheels Taxi Cab Company. Whenever you need a ride, we'll be parked outside."

"I've always been a huge Superman fan," explained Mandrel. "He's the Man of Steel. I'm the Man of Wheels."

Amari snickered. "It's cute."

Mandrel's brow furrowed. "It's a little more than cute. It's my livelihood."

"That wasn't a put down. I thought it was catchy, that's all." Her gaffe was met with silence. Amari diverted the awkward moment with another question. "So is cab driving your passion? Is it what you've always seen yourself doing?"

"Not really but my creditors prefer to get paid in monetary value, not passion, so I have to adhere to my options."

"I couldn't do that," Amari disagreed. "If I'm not happy and fulfilled in a job, I quit."

Mandrel cleared his throat. "I guess some of us have to be a bit more financially responsible than that."

"I'm financially responsible," she informed him, "but I also stay true to myself. Freedom before finance."

"That sounds like it could be the catchphrase for a credit card company."

"I'm a woman of many talents," boasted Amari.

"I don't doubt it." Mandrel's eyes were glued to her like gum to the bottom of a shoe.

A nervous energy passed between them. Before they could explore it further, Amari caught sight of Armand carting his two children and heading toward the car.

"There's my brother. I better go. My niece and nephew are a little impatient. It's not a good idea to keep a couple of hungry toddlers waiting."

"Believe me, I understand. Don't let me hold you up," insisted Mandrel. "Come back to see us again. You've got my card in case you need a ride."

She held up the card. "I'll keep it handy. It was nice meeting you, Mandrel."

"Nice meeting you too."

Armand looked up to see his sister approaching his car. "Hope I didn't keep you waiting too long."

Amari smiled. "It's cool. I had good company."

"Yeah, I noticed," he replied snidely, securing Jaycee in her car seat. "As soon as I get these two strapped into the car, we're out of here. It looks like they worked up an appetite in children's church, and I don't think those cookies and juice boxes they were handing out are gon' cut it!"

"You need any help?"

"Nah, I got it." As Armand fastened the belt over Trey's car seat, he motioned his head toward Mandrel, who was still in the parking lot conversing with another woman. "I saw you talking to ol' boy. What's up with that?"

Amari rolled her eyes. "Absolutely nothing. He was only being friendly."

"Friendly or flirty?" asked Armand, smirking.

"Friendly! Besides, he's not my type." Amari glowered. "He's too white bread. I'd get bored."

Armand closed the car door to the back seat. "Maybe a guy like that is exactly what you need. He's single, you know."

"Is he?" Amari considered the possibility for a moment before nixing the idea. "Then he's probably gay."

"He's not gay, Amari."

"Well, weird or boring or horrible in bed or some other defect. If no one else wants him, I certainly don't."

Armand opened the driver's side door. "Sometimes it ain't about what you want. It's about what you need."

"Yeah, and what I need right now is some serious grub!" She placed her hand over her stomach. "I'm starving."

"What you need is a good man who can pay for it! I ain't got no money to be spending on you, girl! You have champagne tastes; I've got beer money." Armand climbed into the car and cranked the ignition.

"Dinner is on me," volunteered Amari. "That's another strike against Mandrel. He's a cab driver. There's no way he can afford me!"

"I didn't know you were for sale."

"Trust me, baby brother, what I'm working with over here is priceless!" quipped Amari. Then she realized that she still had Mandrel's business card in her hand.

"What's that?" asked Armand, following Amari's eyes down to the card.

"Mandrel's business card. I was going to throw it away, but I think I ought to hold on to it a little longer." She dropped the card into her purse before walking to her car to trail Armand. "It never hurt anyone to have options."

Chapter 6

Almost two weeks later, Amari was on her fourth drink, her third cigarette, and down to her last nerve at the palatial estate of a music mogul. She sat at the bar half-listening as Clint East-Hood, a relatively unknown rapper who had finagled an invitation to the mansion party, clamored for an "Artist on the Rise" interview with *Rhythm Nation*'s top dog in entertainment.

"Like I was saying," he blabbered on, "I can do it all. I can act, rap, dance. Shoot, I'll even do a reality show! I'm just trying to get put on, and all I need is that one big break. If you give me this spread in *Rhythm Nation,* I can shut this whole city down, for real!"

"So you said," muttered Amari, sliding her martini-soaked olive off the toothpick before popping it into her mouth. The olive was decidedly more interesting than the man in front of her or the party, for that matter.

"All right, then, so what's up?" entreated Clint, panting like an excited puppy. "Can I get a card or number, an e-mail or something? Let's make this happen!"

Amari frowned. "Have you heard the expression 'don't call us; we'll call you'?"

Clint East-Hood's face fell. "So what you sayin'?"

"I thought it was obvious."

Amari's eyes glazed over as Clint East-Hood began launching into another segment of his sales pitch. She wondered how many more drinks it would take for her to be even the slightest bit interested in what he was saying.

Clint chatted away and thought he was finally making headway when a quicksilver smile spread over Amari's lips, only to be let down again when he discovered that he wasn't the chosen beneficiary.

Amari stood up to greet her smile's recipient. "Jamal, baby, it's so good to see you!"

Jamal Warner was a talented music producer with whom she occasionally indulged in romantic interludes. He could always be counted on for his discretion, bedroom acrobatics, and the most potent marijuana.

Jamal wrapped his arms around Amari's waist. "I knew it was only a matter of time before I spotted the most beautiful woman in the room."

Clint East-Hood became star struck after recognizing Amari's companion. He gasped. "Jamal? Hey, you're Jamal Warner, aren't you?"

"The one and only," cooed Amari, locking her arms around him.

"Ay, man, I'm a huge fan of your music!" enthused Clint. "I'd love to get you to produce a track for me one day."

"Thanks," Jamal replied coolly. "And you are?"

"He was just leaving," replied Amari, striking Clint with an icy glare.

"Oh, is Jamal with you?" asked Clint, finally tuning in to how affectionate they were with one another. "Is she your ol' lady, Jamal?"

"Of course," replied Jamal, then leaned into Amari's ear and whispered, "At least you can be for the next hour or so."

Amari was stoked. She couldn't think of a better way to liven up the party than to sneak off for a spine-tingling tryst with Jamal. Her lips erupted into a slow smile as she addressed Jamal. "What did you have in mind? Or do I have to ask?"

Clint interjected himself into the conversation again. "Ay, so what's up with the track and the interview? Y'all can tag-team it, and, Jamal, in the article, you can be like, 'Yo, Clint East-Hood is a dope new artist I'm working with. Everybody needs to support this brother.' Then ol' girl can write it up like, 'You know he's got to be dope if Jamal is rockin' with him because he only works with the hottest rappers!' I can just blow up from there."

Amari was so wrapped up with Jamal that she had forgotten that Clint was still in the vicinity. A scowl registered on both Amari's and Jamal's faces. "You're still here?" barked Amari and hurried Clint away. Clint stormed off, but not before calling her an expletive and telling Jamal that his last two tracks were whack.

After Clint made his dramatic exit, Amari didn't give him a second thought. She retrieved her drink and devoted her full attention to Jamal. "Thanks for coming to my rescue."

"Was that clown giving you a hard time?" asked Jamal.

"No, I meant rescuing me from boredom. This party sucks." Amari took a gulp of her martini. "I was about to leave until you showed up."

"Leave? Are you kidding?" squawked Jamal. "Look around. It doesn't get any hotter than this in Atlanta!"

Amari complied. With a few exceptions, everyone there had hit records, successful clothing lines, record labels, and various accolades under their belts. She was definitely among the crème de la crème of the industry. It just didn't excite her like it used to.

"It's always the same thing. Same party, same people. Everybody flossin' their overpriced cars and jewelry. Fake smiles, fake boobs and butts, and even faker friends. Wannabes like that idiot Clint desperate to fit in. It feels like we're at an affluent high school or like we're trapped in a rap video stuck on replay." She downed the last of her drink and moped. "I don't know. Maybe I'm getting too old for all this."

"I don't know what your problem is," griped Jamal. "There's more money in this one house than most people see in their whole lifetimes. Everybody is turned up and having a ball. You're the only one here not having a good time, pretty lady. But I've got something to cure that," he hedged and delivered a mischievous grin.

Amari smirked. "Is the cure in your pants or in your pocket?"

"Both." Jamal reached for her hand. "Come on; let me show you a little bonus room I scoped out a little while ago. Let's just hope it's still uninhabited."

Amari set her empty glass down on the bar. "I've been drinking, so you know I can't be held accountable for my actions."

Jamal sneered. "I know I've had more to drink than you, so I can't be held accountable for mine either."

Amari stumbled a little as she slipped her hand into his.

"Whoa, careful now!" He helped her stagger back to her feet. "You good?"

She brushed her hair back and gazed up at him through half-closed eyelids. "I'm great."

"Yes, you are." He planted a soft kiss on her lips. "The best I ever had, in fact."

Music blared from all directions as Jamal led Amari through a maze of partygoers and rooms decked out in ostentatious artwork and glitzy fixtures.

"Come on," bade Jamal when Amari, dizzy from all the alcohol she drank, slowed down to catch her breath.

Amari slid off her slinky metallic heels, hoping her walk would be made easier without having to move around on stilts. "Where is this room you were talking about? Where are we going?" she asked as they bounded up another flight of stairs.

"Right here." Jamal placed his hand on the doorknob of a secluded bonus room on the top floor of the house. "They call this place the Upper Room."

Once Amari stepped into the dimly lit room, she understood how it earned that nickname. The stench of long-gone cigars, cigarettes, and weed still permeated the air and clung to the walls as tightly as the colossal Bob Marley paintings did.

"Alone at last." Jamal directed Amari toward the curved leather sectional in the center of the room.

"How did you even know about this place?" asked Amari as she sat down.

"Let's just say I've visited once or twice." He eased onto the sofa, contouring his body to fit as closely to hers as possible. His eyes drifted over Amari's sparkling silver romper. "You know you're looking good tonight, right?"

"Yeah, me and every other chick here! I'm surprised you noticed."

"Don't you know if there are a thousand ladies in the room, you'll stand out from all of them? You've got these gorgeous eyes and radiant skin . . ." He traced her face with his finger as he spoke. "Beautiful, voluptuous lips and body for days." He let his hand fall to her legs. "You've got these smooth, thick thighs. How could a man not notice you?"

Amari beamed. His lines weren't original, but it all sounded poetic to her inebriated ears. "So is that what you meant when you said you had something for me? Flattery?"

"And this." He reached into his pocket and tossed a dime bag of marijuana onto the coffee table in front of them. He pulled out a flask from his sports coat. "I brought this in case the weed in your system starts getting lonely."

"Wow, you don't miss a beat, do you?" she asked before knocking back the whiskey the flask contained.

"What kind of music producer would I be if I did? Now, bring your luscious lips over here," commanded Jamal.

Amari set the flask down and wallowed in his amative kiss. Jamal's wet lips, not content to just remain on hers, began traveling down her neck the same time his hand slid its way from her thigh through the bottom of her romper.

Amari felt warm and sexually awakened as Jamal explored her body with his mouth and fingertips. It was familiar territory, and he was a skilled traveler. She melted in his hands.

Without warning, the amorous feeling she'd just had turned into nausea as her head started to spin. Amari's mouth felt watery, and she had the urge to heave.

She spread her fingers across Jamal's chest to stop him from going any further. "Jamal, wait. I don't feel so good."

He peeled off her hand and kissed it. "Don't worry." He lowered her body down on the couch. "You're going to feel like a champion in about five minutes."

"No, I'm serious." She shoved him off of her. "I think I'm about to be sick."

Jamal sighed and thrust the flask to her. "Here, drink something to take the edge off."

"You can't be serious!" She swatted the bottle out of her face. "That's what got me feeling like crap in the first place!"

"Well, let's roll the weed," he proposed, growing impatient with her.

Amari leaned back on the sofa with her eyes closed. "Jamal, I don't want to drink, and I don't want to smoke. I think I just need to chill out for a minute. Can you turn on a fan or something?"

"This is some bull," murmured Jamal. Not yet deterred, he stroked her thigh and dropped his voice to a near whisper. "You don't have to do anything. Lay there and let me do all the work, and you know firsthand how I put in work."

Amari exhaled and addressed him with a foreboding tone. "Jamal, I swear if you come anywhere near my honey pot right now, I'll scream!"

He copped an attitude. "Who do you think is gonna hear you up here?"

"Then I'll kick or bite!" she threatened. "Don't test me!"

Jamal moved away from her, but made no effort to hide his frustration. "Dang, Amari! How you gon' get a brother all excited, then punk out? You're too old to be a tease, and I'm too old to be dealing with blue balls!"

She let out a deep breath. She was burning with anger and queasiness. "Will you just shut up and find me a cool towel or something?" demanded Amari.

"How am I supposed to know where they keep the towels around here?"

Amari was now incensed. "You know where they smoke weed, but you don't know where the bathroom is? There must be at least twenty of them in this place! It shouldn't be that hard to find one."

Jamal muttered something under his breath and charged toward the door. Amari wasn't sure if that meant he was getting the towel or leaving her to fend for herself. After fifteen excruciating minutes alone in the room, she concluded it was the latter.

Amari wanted nothing more than to drag herself home and crawl into bed, but between the liquor, her churning stomach, and a throbbing headache, there was no way she could even pretend to be in any condition to drive.

Afraid to make any sudden moves and risk throwing up, Amari groped the sofa and coffee table, fumbling for her purse in the darkened room. Her hand found its way to the black sequined wristlet, and she fished out her cell phone. She scrolled through her phone and called her brother. It rang once before exiling her to voice mail. There were only two other contacts in her phone she could call in case of emergency. One, her college roommate, was spending the week in New York; and the other, her secretary, wasn't answering the phone. It was then that Amari wished she'd made more friends.

Amari rummaged through her purse hoping to find at least a lone aspirin at the bottom of her bag. Her fingers landed on a card. She pulled it out and shone the light from her phone on it. She flipped it over. It was the card Mandrel had given her at church for his cab service.

"Yes!" she cried out, elated to have a ride home. She kissed the card. "Maybe there is a God!" She quickly dialed the number listed on the card.

A man picked up after the first ring. "Man of Wheels. What can we do for you?"

"Hello, um, is this Mandrel?"

"Yep, speaking. How can I help you?"

"Hey, this is Amari Christopher. I don't know if you remember this, but you met me at the church a couple of weeks back."

There was a pause. She crossed her fingers, hoping that he hadn't forgotten her.

"Yeah, yeah. You're Armand's sister, right?"

She cheered up. "That's right!"

"Hey, how's it going? If you're calling for a ride to church, I'll be more than happy to accommodate you this Sunday."

"Actually, I was hoping to get a ride a lot sooner than that. You see, I'm kind of in a situation," explained Amari, willing him to fill in the blanks so she wouldn't have to admit to being too hammered to drive home.

"Okay," he prompted her, waiting to hear more.

It was apparent that she'd have to fill in the blanks for him. "I'm at this party," she went on, "and I can't really drive myself home, not without endangering lives."

"Ohhh, I see," he said, realizing her dilemma. "We're honored that you chose us, and we're happy to be of service. What's the address? I'll send one of my boys right on out."

Amari wasn't thrilled about the prospect of being in the company of yet another male who might try to take advantage of her. "I don't mean to go all *Color Purple* on you, but I can't be riding in the car with no strange man! I'm in a very vulnerable state right now."

"I'll come pick you up myself, how's that?"

"That's perfect." Amari gave him the address.

As promised, Mandrel was outside waiting for her within thirty minutes.

"Thanks for coming," said Amari, thrilled to see a familiar face in the darkness of night after getting lost no less than ten times trying to find her way out of the manor.

Mandrel opened the door for her, gawking at the lavish estate in the background. "I think I'm more interested in staying. What is this place?"

She climbed into the passenger's seat. "Some bigwig record label owner's not-so-humble abode. I wasn't all that impressed."

"My goodness, woman, if that doesn't impress you, I know my 2,500-square-foot home will downright depress you!" Mandrel closed her door and slid into the driver's side.

Amari reclined the seat. "I never thought I'd be saying this, but it's not the size that matters."

"I think men everywhere just breathed a sigh of relief," he deadpanned, buckling his seat belt.

"Let me be more specific." She raised a finger. "It's not the size of the *house* that matters; it's the people and the love in it."

"I couldn't agree with you more."

"I can't thank you enough for coming to get me," said Amari. She stretched out in the seat with her eyes closed. "I was starting to feel like I didn't have a friend in the world."

"You always have a friend in me and in Jesus." Mandrel took a moment to look at her head-on. "No offense, but you look somewhat . . . haggard. Is everything all right?"

"This is the look of a freshly purged stomach. 'Vomit chic,' if you will. I think I threw up everything I've eaten in the past five years."

"Dang, girl, when you party, you party!" He cranked up his Ford Escape hybrid. "So where to, Miss Christopher?"

"To the bed in my apartment or the nearest vacation spot, whichever one comes first."

"Seeing as how I don't think we'll pass by the Caribbean on the way, you'll probably need to give me your address."

"Do you know where Overland Park is?"

"Yeah, that's a pretty swanky address."

"Well, it's quiet and it has a bed and a clean toilet. That's about all I require right now."

Amari slept for the rest of the ride home. She awoke to Mandrel gently rousing her and lifting her from the seat. He helped her get stationary on her feet.

"I got it from here," she told him and adjusted her outfit, which had crumpled and rolled to reveal more than she wanted it to. "Thank you."

"I'm not convinced, and I couldn't face your brother in church Sunday if I left his sister out here like this. Let's go."

Amari leaned on Mandrel for extra support as they stumbled to her building's elevator and up to her fifth-floor apartment.

"You didn't have to walk me in," insisted Amari for the third time before collapsing onto her living room sofa.

"I know that, but as your cab driver, it's my job to make sure you get to your destination safely. You asked me to make sure you got into your bed, right?"

"I did, didn't I?" She bolted up as another thought entered her head. "Wait, you're not here for sex, are you? I mean, you're cute and everything, but it ain't happening! Not tonight anyway."

Mandrel was disappointed that she thought so little of him. "What kind of man would I be if I tried you like that, especially when you're barely coherent?"

"You'd be most men," answered Amari, having a flash-back of Jamal.

"But I'm *not* most men. Now, where do you keep the tea?"

She kicked off her shoes. "Oh, do you want something to drink? I think I've got some soda and juice in the fridge."

"It's not for me; it's for you. A cup of hot tea should hit the spot."

Amari was impressed by the gesture. "That's so sweet of you; thanks. The teabags are in the kitchen, top shelf of the cabinet. Better yet, let me grab them for you."

Mandrel stopped her before she could get up. "I got it. You sit back and let me take it from here."

Amari was happy to let him take the reins. "Are you always this nice or are you just pitying me right now?"

"A little bit of both," Mandrel called out to her from the kitchen. "You want me to bring you some of this aspirin you've got in here? You may want to take something. You're going to have a nasty hangover in the morning."

Amari shook her head. "This isn't my first rodeo, cabbie. Bananas, hot water, honey, and lemon are the best cure for a hangover."

Mandrel stepped aside so she could see him. "I don't know if I'm in awe or concerned that you know that."

She laughed. "When you're on the scene as much as I am, you learn a thing or two."

"Apparently."

Five minutes later, Mandrel brought the tea to Amari and joined her on the sofa.

"Thank you." She sipped the tea.

"Is it okay?"

"It's perfect." She waited before speaking again. "I'm glad you came and got me, Mandrel, though I can't say I'm happy you had to see me like this. It's not exactly my finest hour."

"There's nothing you need to be embarrassed about. In my line of work, I see it all," he assured her. "Besides, I'd much rather you call me than drive in this state. You did the right thing."

"Still, though. Wild parties, getting wasted . . ." For the first time, Amari felt ashamed of her behavior. "I can't imagine what you must think of me right now."

"I don't think any more or any less of you than I did an hour ago."

"Was your opinion so low that there really isn't anything I can do to make it worse?"

"Come on now." He elbowed her. "Why would you even say something like that?"

"Mandrel, you seem so straight-laced and moral, and all I am is some party girl who was too drunk to drive home."

He recoiled. "Is that all you really think you are?"

Amari set the teacup down on her coffee table. "Given the fact that I was drunk at a party and couldn't drive home, I'd say that's a pretty accurate description."

"Don't you think you're more than the person you were tonight?"

"Oh, I was this person last week too!" she added.

"I'm serious, Amari. Not including what happened tonight or last week, tell me who you think you are."

She glowered. "What kind of question is that?"

"It's one I think you need to give some serious thought to. I believe life becomes a whole lot easier when you know how to answer that question."

"Mandrel, I can barely tell you what my name is right now!" Amari evaded giving him a direct answer. This was not the time for a metacognitive interrogation. "Let's save that question for another day, like tomorrow. I may need you to drive me back over there to pick up my car."

"That's fine. I'm happy to oblige."

Amari picked up the cup and took another sip from her tea. "What about you? Who is Mr. Mandrel . . . Ingram? I think that's what the card said."

"Yes, it's Mandrel Ingram. Your memory is still in check, so you're not that drunk." Mandrel sat upright and answered in a way that blended sincerity with confidence. "First and foremost, I'm a man of God. Beyond that, I'm a servant, a father. I'd like to think I'm a good example and someone who gives the Kingdom a good name."

"Sounds like you're practically a saint," surmised Amari.

"Not by a long shot. I just try to do what's right."

She nodded. "So you've got a kid, huh?" She sipped her tea again.

"Yes. I have a son named Dallas. He's eleven."

"Then I'm assuming that you have a baby's mama somewhere, too."

He corrected her. "I have an ex-wife. She was my high school sweetheart."

"I think they're called high school sweethearts for a reason," deduced Amari. "Most of those relationships reach their peak in high school. I've rarely seen them work beyond that."

"Where were you with this helpful hint when I needed it twenty years ago?" joked Mandrel. "We gave it a good run though. We got fifteen years and one great kid out of it."

"Are they here in Atlanta?"

"No, she and my son live in Tampa. She moved back to her hometown after the divorce."

Amari propped her feet up on the coffee table. "Is it hard being away from him like that?"

He released a deep breath. "Hard doesn't even begin to describe it," admitted Mandrel, "but I try to make it work. I go down to Tampa a few times out the month. Matter of fact, I was down there last weekend. We hung out, shot some hoops. I usually bring him up here when he's out for the summer, but it doesn't replace being able to see him every day."

"I get it." Amari reflected on her own fatherless childhood. "My dad lived out of state too. I would've done anything to have him closer to me."

"What about you? Do you have any kids?"

Amari scoffed. "Did you seriously just ask me that? I'm like the poster child for birth control!"

"Don't you want kids someday?"

"I don't know." Amari mulled it over. "I mean, it's one of those things that's a nice thought, but I think having a kid would slow me down too much, you know? I like to get up and go when the mood strikes. I like to travel. I like to party and sleep in and be plain selfish with my time and energy and money. You can't do that when you have a child."

"That's true, but being a parent is an incredible experience, Amari. No party or vacation can compare to being with my son and watching him grow into a young man. There's nothing like it."

"You sound like my brother. He's a great dad, and he'd do anything for his kids. Don't get me wrong, I love my niece and nephew, but when I look at the way he has to struggle with them, I want no part of that life."

Mandrel was taken aback. "That's a little selfish, don't you think?"

"I think it's more selfish to bring children into this world you don't really want." Amari downed the last of her tea. "Believe me, I know what that feels like."

"I suppose you're right. There has to be no worse feeling for a child than to think he or she isn't wanted." He noticed her empty cup. "Can I get you something else?"

"No, you've done more than enough for me as it is. Thank you."

"You're most welcome." He rose. "Now that I see you're okay, I think I'll head back out. I'm still on the clock, you know."

"Wait, I didn't even pay you!" Amari gasped. "Oh, my God, is the meter still running? I've probably run up a month's rent by now!"

"Don't worry about it." Mandrel cupped his hand over hers briefly before releasing it. "This one's on the house."

"You don't have to do that. You've already been incredibly generous as it is, and you've gone above and beyond the call of duty tonight." Amari scooped up her purse off of the floor and began digging into it for cash. "Let me at least pay you for the gas it took driving out to the sticks and back."

Mandrel stopped her. "No, I insist. Consider it me paying it forward. Of course, that means you have to show the same kindness to someone else that I've shown to you," he stipulated.

"Then let me be kind to you," bargained Amari. "Let me take you out for lunch or drinks one day next week."

"You don't have to do that."

"Well, you won't let me pay you for tonight, and I refuse to be anybody's charity case. Let me do this. I know a great spot where we can go have drinks and listen to live music."

Mandrel hesitated accepting the invitation. "Amari, I don't drink, so—"

"Okay, then lunch. Better yet, brunch next Saturday at eleven at the Egg and I. How does that sound?"

He finally conceded. "Brunch it is. Thank you."

Amari shook his hand to seal the deal. "Great, I'll see you next Saturday."

"Or maybe Sunday at church," ventured Mandrel.

She cracked a half smile and let go of his hand. "You'll see me Saturday."

He chuckled. "All right, you get some rest."

"I will." She walked him to the door. "Good night."

They both hung back a second, then leaned in for an awkward hug. Amari was the first to break away. "Good night."

"Sleep well."

Amari locked the door behind him. She couldn't help being moved by his kindness. Perhaps it was her alcohol-infused haze, but she also couldn't help thinking he could be more than a cute designated driver for her.

She chided herself for even going there. "Amari, girl, he is sooo not your type! He doesn't drink, he doesn't party, he's got a kid, and he probably lives in the church. What do you want with a dud like that?" She put it out of her mind.

As Amari dressed for bed, her phone pinged, signaling that she had a text message coming through. She reached for her phone. The message was from Mandrel.

Glad I was able to come to your rescue tonight. Call me anytime.

She smiled into the phone. Perhaps Armand was right. She knew Mandrel definitely wasn't the kind of man she wanted, but that didn't mean he wasn't the man she needed.

Chapter 7

"Let's talk about his text message for a moment," suggested Dr. Nelson. "Mandrel indicated that he'd come to your rescue if you ever needed him. Were you bothered by that?"

"No, why would I be?" she asked slowly, unsure of where Dr. Nelson was going with this line of questioning.

"A lot of women, especially ones who thrive on being independent and self-sufficient, don't like the idea of a man thinking he has to rescue her."

"I didn't look at it that way because, as far as I'm concerned, he did come to my rescue. Who knows what would've happened if I had tried to drive or if some pervert had found me passed out at the party?"

Dr. Nelson readjusted herself in the chair. "Tell me, Amari, do you feel like you need to be rescued?"

"Yes, sometimes," she admitted.

"Rescued from what or whom?"

"Myself mostly."

"You don't think you're capable of saving yourself?" posed Dr. Nelson.

Amari squinted her eyes, processing the question. "Is anyone really capable of doing that?"

"I think that depends on several factors: a person's desire and determination for a change, access to resources, spiritual beliefs. But it's different for everyone. I think you've made a positive step by deciding to seek therapy. I think it proves that, given the right tools, you're very capable of saving yourself."

Amari exhaled. "I guess we'll find out, won't we?"

Dr. Nelson skimmed through her notepad. "So you'd taken an interest in this young man Mandrel?"

Amari cut in. "I don't know if I'd call it that, at least not at that time."

"Then what would you call it?"

She thought it over. "I knew he was a nice guy. I just wasn't sure if he was the man for me."

"From what you've told me, he seems like a pretty good guy. Kind, attentive, committed to his walk with the Lord. What is it about those qualities that didn't appeal to you?"

"I can't explain it." Amari sighed, frustrated that she couldn't put what she wanted to say into words. "I don't know. He just seemed so together and perfect," she said, speaking with her hands. "It's hard to be with somebody like that."

"Did you find that intimidating?"

Amari nodded. "A little, yeah."

"Why? You're successful, smart, and attractive. Why would a woman in your position be intimidated by a cab driver?"

"There was something about him, a quality that I didn't have; nor did I think I could ever possess it."

"What quality is that?"

Amari considered her answer before saying it aloud. "Innate goodness."

"You don't think you're a good person?"

"I think I have good moments, but I can't say for sure that I'm what you'd call a good person."

"Interesting." Dr. Nelson continued making notes. "What does a good person look like to you?"

Amari looked back at the male figure behind her. "Him."

"How do you feel when you look at him?"

Amari was silenced. It was one of those questions that was impossible for her to answer with one word. Just thinking of this person, whom she loved with everything in her that had the capacity to love, evoked such a deluge of feelings that Amari found herself on the brink of crying.

Dr. Nelson picked up on Amari's change in mood. "Amari, are you all right?"

This was why she hated therapy! There were too many feelings she didn't want to acknowledge, but she knew Dr. Nelson wouldn't stop until she'd been gutted open and left emotionally raw and exposed. She could feel the swell of emotion rising inside of her, but she didn't want to risk another possible meltdown, so she responded with a conventional, "I'm fine."

"Are you okay to go on? Do you need a minute?"

Amari composed herself. "No. What was the question again?"

"How do you feel when you look at the young man behind you?"

She sucked in and expelled a deep breath. "The same way I always feel when something or someone great comes into my life." Amari turned somber again. "I feel like I don't really deserve it, like I'm not good enough."

Dr. Nelson spoke to her gingerly. "Who told you that you were good enough?"

A cache of people began to pass through Amari's mind: her mother, Roland, her father, Mandrel—all people who she failed to measure up to.

She addressed Dr. Nelson's question. "Nobody has to tell you something like that. You just know." Her lips quivered, an indicative sign that she was losing the silent war she'd waged against the tears threatening to fall from her eyes.

Dr. Nelson lifted a tissue box from her desk and handed it to Amari. "What's got you so upset?"

Amari could feel her tears rising to the surface. "I feel like this is my last shot to get it right, and I just don't want to disappoint him. I know if I screw this up, I'll end up losing him too, and that would kill me," she confessed. "People who don't know me very well pretty much think I have it all together, but that whole haughty attitude thing is just a front. Even now, I'm scared to death."

"What are you afraid of, Amari?"

"I'm afraid of letting anyone get too close," acknowledged Amari. "I'm afraid I'll hurt them, but I'm just as afraid that they'll hurt me."

"Sometimes, getting hurt is inevitable and unavoidable. The important thing to remember is that most people don't hurt you on purpose. None of us are perfect, and people make mistakes, but you have to be able to look past a person's mistakes and into that person's intentions. You have to ask yourself, 'Was this person trying to hurt me?' I guarantee the answer is usually no."

"That's that therapy talk," said Amari, wiping her eyes. "It sounds good in theory, but doesn't work as well in practice. Most people never get past the other person's mistakes no matter what the intentions were."

"Is that what you're afraid of? Making a mistake with him and not being understood or forgiven for it?"

Amari nodded. "How can I not make mistakes? I am one."

Chapter 8

Eighteen Months Earlier

Amari was on her fifth wardrobe change. She looked in the full-length mirror, scrutinizing the framed reflection staring back at her.

She swayed from left to right in the mirror, trying to capture a view from every angle. After much deliberation, she concluded that the leopard print stamped on the dress was too busy and the lace that trimmed it was too sexy. The length also bothered her. Amari's grandmother used to joke that dresses should be like essays: long enough to cover everything but short enough to be interesting. Her dress was neither.

Amari groaned and peeled the dress off. She started digging through her closet again, hoping a long-discarded outfit would magically appear and look amazing on her. Unless she found the perfect ensemble within the next ten minutes, she was definitely going to be late for brunch with Mandrel.

It wasn't that she was nervous about seeing him again as much as it was that she felt as if she needed to impress him. The first time Mandrel saw her, Amari was a fish out of water at church. The second time, she was drunker than Cooter Brown. She simply wanted Mandrel to see that she was a normal yet stunningly beautiful human being after all.

After another twenty minutes of vetoing outfits, Amari settled on a color block sweater dress. It was casual enough for brunch and showcased her figure without being overtly sexy. She paired it with her favorite boots and dashed out of the apartment.

Amari was thankful that traffic was forgiving that day, and she was able to make it to Egg and I in record time. She even had a minute to spare. When she arrived, she panned the room for Mandrel. She didn't see him. Amari looked at the time. She expected absolute punctuality from a guy who was able to make it clear across three county lines within thirty minutes to pick her up from the party.

"Hello, welcome to Egg and I," announced the restaurant's hostess. "Are you ready to be seated?"

"Umm, give me one second." Amari checked her phone to see if he'd called to say he was running late. He hadn't, so she decided to call him instead.

Mandrel began apologizing the moment he answered the phone. "I'm sorry to keep you waiting, but I'm pulling up right now," he said.

"That's fine. I'll go ahead and grab a table and see you when you get in."

The hostess led Amari to a table for two near the center of the restaurant. "Your waiter will be here in a second. Enjoy."

The hostess scurried off, and Amari peered around the corner to see if she could spot Mandrel. He should've been walking in at any moment.

A waiter approached the table with menus and introduced himself. "Are you dining alone?" he asked before setting down the extra menu.

"No, my date is just parking the car. He'll be in any second now."

As the waiter droned on about the day's specials, Amari kept her eyes on the lookout for Mandrel. It had been several minutes since they'd spoken. How long did it take to walk from the parking lot to the door?

The waiter left after taking her drink order. Amari tried calling Mandrel again.

"Hey," replied Mandrel. "I'm in here, but I don't see you. Where are you sitting?"

"You can't miss me. I'm right smack in the middle of the restaurant."

Mandrel was quiet for a few seconds. "Are you sure? I just see a couple with three kids."

Amari looked around to see if she saw the family he was referring to. "I don't see them. Come around the corner. You can't miss me."

Amari hung up the phone and browsed the menu. By the time she had settled on having the spinach, bacon, mushroom omelet, Mandrel still hadn't arrived. Now she was perturbed. She called him again.

"Dang, Mandrel, where are you?" she screeched into the phone.

"Amari, I swear I'm here looking for you. I've walked around this restaurant at least four times, and you're nowhere to be found."

"What are you wearing?" she asked. "Maybe it'll be easier if I come find you."

"Jeans and a striped button-down. It's navy blue."

This time, Amari stood up to look for him. There was not one man there in navy blue. "I still don't see you."

"What *do* you see?" he asked.

"I see a waitress with big red hair carrying an order to a table. Do you see her?"

"No. I see a black guy with dreads."

Amari spun around the see if she could find him. She saw a tall man with flowing locs. "Is he about six feet?"

"No . . . Actually, that was just a very unattractive woman. She's kind of stumpy and chunky. Do you see her?"

"No. Either both of us need glasses or we're looking at two different things."

"What do you see now?" queried Mandrel. "A woman just walked in with a terrier stuffed down in her purse."

"Is that even sanitary?" Amari grimaced and looked around the corner. "I still don't see you or a woman with a dog, for that matter."

"Keep looking. One of us is bound to find the other sooner or later."

Amari proceeded to make another round through the restaurant. She didn't see anything that Mandrel had described to her. "I don't understand this. How could you possibly be lost? This place is the size of a matchbox!"

"Yeah, if I didn't know better, I'd swear we were being punk'd."

As Amari returned to her seat, it occurred to her that maybe she *was* being punk'd by Mandrel. He was probably gaslighting her for his own amusement. The thought of being made a fool of sent her into a tailspin.

Amari chucked her cloth napkin on the table, her blood boiling. "Mandrel, you're not even here, are you?"

"Amari, I swear to you that I'm in this restaurant. I've got three waitresses looking for you."

"Yeah, right." She rolled her eyes. How stupid did he think she was? "What kind of grown-behind man sits around playing these teenage games?"

"I'm just as confused as you are, Amari, I swear!"

She'd had enough. It was one thing to make her the butt of a cruel joke. It was quite another to needlessly drag it out. It would've been more humane to just stand her up the old-fashioned way. "I can't believe I wasted my time and energy on a jerk like you. Lose my number!"

With that, Amari turned off the phone. She was tempted to walk away, but she refused to let Mandrel's juvenile antics ruin her appetite, especially once the waitress returned with her delectable meal.

Amari spent the next twenty minutes replaying everything that had transpired between her and Mandrel. She couldn't understand what he had to gain by trying to pull one over on her. Had it all been an elaborate ruse to teach her a lesson about drinking and riotous living? But that didn't make any sense either, especially since he had several opportunities to lecture her about her reckless lifestyle the night he picked her up from the party.

She speared the omelet with her fork, angry with herself for falling for his good Christian boy smokescreen. He'd seemed so nice; so much for him being a standup guy! None of those guys truly existed. She'd accepted that fact years ago.

"Amari!"

She looked up upon hearing the sound of her name. It was Mandrel dressed in blue jeans, a navy striped shirt, and completely out of breath. The hostess escorted him to her table.

Amari pushed her plate away and huffed when she saw him. "I was just leaving." She turned to the hostess. "Can I have the check please?"

"Certainly," said the hostess then walked away.

"I'm so sorry," began Mandrel, trying to catch his breath. "But I wanted you to know that I came."

"Yeah, after gassing me up and keeping me waiting for half an hour!" she argued. "Now, if you really want to make amends, pay this bill and never call me again."

"I'll do that, but first I wanted to give you this." He set a folded paper napkin on the table and opened it so that Amari could see what was written on it.

She twisted her face into a scowl. "What is this?"

"It's a note from the manager at Egg and I on Huff Road. See?" He pointed to handwritten words scribbled in the center of the napkin. "He wrote this to verify that I was there."

Amari took a closer look at the napkin. It had Egg and I's second location stamped on the bottom of it along with a note from the manager that said:

Please forgive him. He was here and had the whole staff looking for you!

The date and time were included.

Amari smacked herself on the forehead. "I totally forget there are two locations. I'm so sorry for lashing out at you like that."

"No, I'm sorry! I should've double-checked the address." He pulled out the adjoining chair. "Is it all right if I sit down?"

"Of course! Please sit." Once he was seated, she apologized again. "Mandrel, I'm so sorry. This is all my fault."

Mandrel pulled his chair closer to the table. "Don't apologize. It was an honest mistake."

"No, now I'm apologizing for all of the nasty things I was thinking about you before you got here." She smiled, feeling the vindication that only comes when a woman realizes that she had not been stood up or that she is not delusional after all. "I'm glad you made it, though. I was getting kind of lonely without you."

"You? Nothing is quite as pathetic as looking like a man who's just been stood up. I think the couple at the table next to me wanted to offer me their infant son as a conciliation prize."

She laughed. "The important thing is that you're here now."

"Yes, I am." Mandrel was as relieved as she was. "Do you really have to leave?"

Amari looked at her watch as if she had somewhere else to be. She didn't have plans, but there was no need for Mandrel to know that. "I guess I can stay a little longer."

Mandrel opened up the menu. "Thank you for being so cool about the whole mix-up."

"I'm cool now; I was plotting your demise ten minutes ago!" jeered Amari.

"Your forgiving heart is appreciated. And for the record, there is no way I would've turned down the opportunity to have brunch with the woman whose smile I haven't stopped thinking about since we met."

Amari blushed like a schoolgirl. She was amazed at how quickly her anger had dissipated. It was almost as fast as their outing had gone from a friendly brunch to feeling like a real date.

"So what are you in the mood for?" He stopped reading the menu. "Oh, wait, you've already eaten, haven't you?

"It's okay. I don't mind staying and keeping you company while you eat."

The waiter returned to take Mandrel's order.

"Are you sure you don't want anything else?" asked Mandrel after placing his order.

"Yes. Gotta watch my figure."

"Are you kidding me? You look great!"

"Thank you."

"I'm serious! Women pay long money to look like you and to have your curves. Your body is perfect. I love a woman with a little meat on her."

Amari beamed, so rapt by his compliments and enticing gaze that it took a second for his words to sink in and for her to realize that he'd just referred to her as meaty.

"Wait, what?" She blinked rapidly. "So you think I'm fat?"

"No, I find you very attractive," he disclosed. "I mean, obviously, you're not skinny, but—"

"Obviously?" she interjected, ready to declare war on him.

"No, not like that!" he stammered. "I just meant that you're sort of . . . full and voluptuous all over."

"So I'm full-figured?" Amari asked in accusation, stung because she prided herself on maintaining what she thought was a svelte size-ten figure.

"Yes! I mean, no! I mean . . ." he skittishly replied and closed his eyes, desperate to dislodge the foot that he'd just crammed in his mouth. "Aww, shucks, Amari, you have a big booty! It's the kind of shape I like."

"Huh?"

"I mean you, though, not your booty!"

Amari broke the tension with laughter. "It's okay. You're human. It's all right to look as long as you don't gawk."

Mandrel blushed over. "I can't help it. I'm a butt man," he confessed, embarrassed. "Always have been, always will be. I just don't want you to think that all I'm interested in is a slammin' body because it goes way beyond that."

Amari wrapped a thread of hair around her finger. "So I interest you, huh?"

"Absolutely," he asserted.

Amari propped her elbows on the table and rested her chin over her hand. "What else are you interested in? What do you look for in a woman, aside from a big ol' juicy backside?"

Mandrel took her teasing in stride. "You're not gonna let that go anytime soon, are you?"

"Nope," she replied, smug. "Now, how do you like your women, Mandrel?"

"You make it sound like I'm choosing how I want my steak cooked."

She reworded the question. "All right, then, what do you look for in a woman? What kind of traits do you like?"

"So you want to know what I like in a woman, huh?" He took her question into account. "For starters, I like a woman who knows what it means to be a woman."

"What does that entail, being barefoot and pregnant?" she asked half-jokingly.

"Not at all. It means knowing how to carry yourself like a lady. I don't like a woman who talks too much or who thinks she knows everything."

She stiffened again. "So basically you're not looking for a woman who has an opinion," surmised Amari.

"No, I'm looking for a woman who will give me a chance to express my opinion before throwing in hers," he explained, taking a dig at her assumptions.

She sat up straight, glaring at him. "A lesser woman might have taken offense to that," she retorted.

"Thank God you're not a lesser woman," quipped Mandrel.

"Well played, my friend." She relaxed a little. "Go on."

"Like I said, I think she ought to know how to be a woman. Contrary to what you might think, I admire a woman with her own mind and who makes me think and look at the world differently. I need that contrast and her wisdom. I also like a woman who's mild mannered."

"That's a code word for weak, isn't it?" pressed Amari.

"Not at all. A weak, insecure woman couldn't deal with a man like me. By mild mannered, I mean having a sweet, gentle spirit. I need a woman who doesn't have to yell to get her point across or have a foul attitude or use profanity. I like a woman who people notice, but she's not trying to be the center of attention."

Amari nodded slowly. "Interesting."

Mandrel leaned in closer to Amari. "The main thing, though, is she has to have a relationship with God. If she has that, I think everything else falls into place."

"How so?"

Mandrel expounded on his theory. "If she loves God more than she loves me, she'll be sensitive to the things of the Spirit. I don't have to worry about her cheating or being deceptive or doing anything to hurt me because her spiritual side won't allow it. It would go against her nature."

Amari rolled her eyes and mumbled something inaudible.

"Did you say something?"

Amari parted her lips to repeat it, but decided to hold her tongue. "It was nothing."

"You clearly said something," maintained Mandrel. "I take it you don't agree with what I said about being a Christian woman."

"Not at all." Now ready to be candid, Amari stated, "No offense, but I think that's bull!"

He sat back, eager to hear her take on the issue. "Why is that?"

"Just because a person has a relationship with God doesn't mean he or she is not going to screw up," reasoned Amari. "People who love God lie, cheat, and steal all the time. Religion has nothing to do with it. The reason people do or don't do something is because they want to, not because of some God complex."

"I'm not talking about religion," clarified Mandrel. "I'm talking about a relationship with God."

"If being in a relationship with an actual person who I can see, touch, and be accountable to isn't enough to make me do the right thing, how is being in a relationship with someone I can't undoubtedly prove even exists going to change that?"

Mandrel was thrown. "Wait a minute, are you saying you don't think God exists?"

"No, I just said that I don't believe He has any bearing on decisions people make. I haven't killed anybody. It's not because God told me not to; it's because I don't want to go to jail nor do I have the right to take another person's life. I donate clothes to Salvation Army and help old ladies across the street, and it's not because God told me to do that either. I just enjoy helping people. God doesn't enter the equation."

Mandrel's eyes bulged. "Wow!"

"Wow what?" snapped Amari.

"I just . . . I didn't know you felt this way," he replied, still stunned.

"Well, you said you like a woman with an alternative view of the world," she reminded him.

"Yeah, an alternative view, but what you're talking about is a whole other alternative belief system."

Amari sat back with her arms folded across her chest. "I'm open-minded enough to concede that I could be wrong. Opinions are like past mistakes: everybody has more than one! Who's to say which one of us is correct?"

"The Bible, God's own words," testified Mandrel. "I think that's the final authority on everything."

"God didn't write the Bible, Mandrel. People did. And look how many times it's been translated and distorted or misinterpreted. The Bible stopped being a truly reliable source a long time ago, assuming it ever was one."

Blown away by her views on religion, Mandrel shook his head. "I don't know if the way your mind works is intriguing or scary."

The waiter returned with Mandrel's food and turned to Amari. "Can I get you anything else, ma'am?"

"No." She changed her mind. "On second thought, I'd like a mimosa please."

"Coming right up." The waiter made his exit.

"Drinking at noon?" muttered Mandrel before praying over his food.

"It is legal, you know?"

Mandrel shrugged his shoulders. "Yeah, it's legal but . . ."

"But what?" she hurled, infuriated over how judgmental he was. She mocked him: "A real lady doesn't drink?"

Mandrel drove his fork into his lobster scrambler. "I'm not saying anything."

"So you don't like that I drink, you don't like that I actually have an opinion, and you don't like my beliefs about God. Is there anything about me you do like? Aside from my behind, I mean."

Exasperated, Mandrel exhaled and set his fork down on the plate. "This is not the date I had in mind."

"Now *that,*" she pointed a finger at him and sniped, "is something we can both agree on!"

Mandrel surrendered with his hands, attempting to assuage her. "No, no, no, I think you're taking that the wrong way."

Amari wasn't pacified by his words. "Of course I am. Misinterpretation: add that to the list of things that you don't like about me."

"I never said I didn't like you, Amari."

"No, you didn't. You just said that you don't approve of the way I act, the way I drink, or what I believe," she itemized.

Mandrel took in a deep breath. "I don't like where this conversation is headed. I think we should start over."

"I couldn't agree with you more." Amari gathered her purse and jacket. "Let's start from the part where I was leaving."

"Amari, wait," pleaded Mandrel.

"And waste another minute of my valuable time with you?" Amari tossed the cash for her meal on the table. "I don't think so!"

Amari marched out of the restaurant, still heated from the exchange with Mandrel. He was way too smug and self-righteous. She only wished she had left before he got there. Better yet, she wished that she'd never invited him to brunch; then he wouldn't have confirmed her worst suspicions. In reality, his behavior didn't turn out to be all that big of a surprise. For once, however, she wished she had been wrong about a man being a complete and utter jerk.

Chapter 9

"It was horrible!" rehashed Amari, recounting her brunch with Mandrel to Armand over the phone. "Definitely a strong candidate for worst date ever! I can't believe I thought he was such a nice person."

"I think you're blowing this way out of proportion. Honestly, Mar, I haven't heard anything that the man said or did that was so wrong," replied Armand.

Amari ripped open a bag of potato chips. "In addition to being a self-righteous, overzealous religious fanatic, he treated me like I was the Antichrist. After, of course, salivating over my big booty, all under the guise of claiming to be a so-called Christian!"

"Come on now, I know this dude. He's not that type."

"Armand, I know Mandrel is your church member and all, but I'm your sister," she pointed out. "You're legally bound by DNA to take my side in this."

"I'm always on your side. I just think you're being a little hard on the brother."

"I don't! No one should profess to be this pious Christian and put yourself on some sort of pedestal when you really belong down here with the rest of us." She crammed a handful of chips into her mouth.

"Being a Christian doesn't mean being perfect. Nonbelievers don't own the right to be the only douche bags in the world."

"Well, if acting like Mandrel is what going to church and being a Christian is all about, y'all can keep it."

"Don't judge all Christians by one man, and don't judge Mandrel off of one bad date. I really think he's one of the good guys."

"Yeah, and apparently he thinks he's too good for me. I'm not surprised. You Christians tend to think you're better than the rest of us anyway."

"As much as I'd love to hear you bash Christians, I've got to go. Nia is on her way over."

"Dropping the kids off or picking them up?"

"Neither. We're going to dinner."

"Really?" Amari perked up. "So is this a date?"

"*Date* is pushing it. We're trying to get along better for the kids' sake. We thought that it would be good for them if we still did things together as a family."

"Oh, that's wonderful, Armand. I know that'll mean a lot to Trey and Jay."

"It's another unpleasant trait of us Christians. We choose peace over war whenever possible."

Amari rolled her eyes. "Yeah, yeah, yeah. Have fun but don't get your hopes up. Remember, it's just dinner, not a reconciliation."

"Gotta start somewhere, right? I'll check you later."

No sooner had Amari hung up the phone did it ring again, this time to alert her to open the entry gate to her apartment complex.

She answered the phone. "Hello, who is this?"

"Amari, it's me." He paused before identifying himself. "It's Mandrel."

She cringed. "What do you want?"

"I just want to talk, that's all. Five minutes."

"I think we said everything we needed to say."

"Maybe you did, but I didn't. Just five minutes, I promise."

She debated whether to allow him entry. Although he'd been a donkey at brunch, she couldn't deny how pleasant he'd been prior to that. She concluded that it wouldn't hurt to at least hear him out.

"I can only guarantee two minutes. Come on." She buzzed him in.

Amari barely had time to give herself a quick once-over in the mirror before Mandrel was knocking on her front door. She opened the door. The first thing she noticed was the contrite look on his face. She was still on thirty-eight hot with him, but it was awful hard to stay mad with him pricking her heart with his sad puppy dog eyes.

"I apologize for stopping by unannounced like this," began Mandrel.

"I can't imagine that we have anything else to talk about," said Amari, leading him into her living room.

"I have a few things I want to say to you. I only ask that you hear me out. Once I've said what I came to say, I'll leave. You never have to see me again if you don't want to."

Amari folded her arms across her chest. "Okay, start talking. Say what you came to say then leave. The sooner we get to the part about never seeing you again, the better."

Mandrel was taken aback by her attitude. "Dang, I guess I really did mess up any shot at a friendship with you, didn't I?" Amari didn't look at him or respond. "When I got home, I realized I may have come on too strong or come off as too rigid, but I'm not that guy. I try to live by a certain standard, but I do laugh. I can have fun, and I'm sorry you didn't get to see that person. I was judgmental and a bit of a blockhead, and I hope that you'll forgive me."

"No, Mandrel, I'm the one who's sorry. I was completely wrong about you, but it's cool, though. I see you for what you are, so if you only came by to offer me some crappy apology or a long, drawn-out explanation, don't. There are no hard feelings. I just think it's better if we each go on our separate ways."

"That's not all I came to say." He reached into his back pocket. "I came up with a list."

She sat down. "A what?"

"I did what you suggested. I made a list of all the things I don't like about you."

Amari's mouth dropped open. Shock soon gave rise to anger. "You're telling me that you literally sat down and made a list of the things you hate about me, and you expect me to sit here and listen to that foolishness?" spat Amari, gesturing with her hands as she spoke. "Save your breath and save yourself from getting cussed out so bad that even your grandkids will need therapy!" She stood up. "Your two minutes are up. Let me show you to the door."

"Actually, I made two lists," he revealed quickly as Amari ushered him toward the door. "One with things I don't like, which was around seven things."

Amari fumed. She was moments away from erupting. "Mandrel, you've got two seconds to get your list, your sanctimonious attitude, and your low-budget outfit the heck out of my house!"

Mandrel went on, ignoring her threats. "I also made a list of the things I do like." He handed her a slip of paper. "That list was closer to a hundred."

Amari paused then snatched the paper from his hand. She unfolded it; the corners of her mouth upturned into a smile as she read what he'd written. "Her lips; her smile." She snickered. "Her sass; her energy; her style; her brutal honesty." She let the list fall to her side, uncertain as to whether she should be flattered or still pissed off. "Okay, Mandrel, what's going on here?"

"Nothing. I'm just a man who wants to get to know you better," proclaimed Mandrel. "I don't want anything more from you than the opportunity to do that."

Amari lowered her defenses. "Why? You made it pretty clear at brunch how you felt about me."

Mandrel sidled closer to her. "I don't think I did," he revealed, delivering a look so intense that it made Amari's heart race. "If I had, you would've known that I haven't stopped thinking about you since the first second I laid eyes on you in church."

His revelation temporarily silenced her. Amari cleared her throat and broke from their stare down. "You should've said that instead of cataloging my list of flaws."

"Amari, nothing about that date went as I hoped it would, from the restaurant mix-up to you thinking I was calling you fat. It was a rough brunch."

"Rough? Let's call it what it was. It was a catastrophe!" decreed Amari.

"Catastrophe is a little strong. I'm thinking more along the lines of a disaster," he joked.

"Oh, you're funny now?" Amari smirked. "Where was that sense of humor when we needed it a few hours ago?"

"Baby, it would've taken the Kings of Comedy, the queens, the court jester, and the whole *Def Comedy Jam* crew to rectify that situation!"

Amari laughed aloud. "It was pretty bad, but it wasn't just you. My snarky attitude didn't help at all."

"Your attitude doesn't bother me. You're feisty. I like that."

"Oh, really? What number was that on your list?"

He winked at her. "I think that was number nine."

Amari exhaled, becoming serious again. "All right, Ingram, so what are we doing here?"

"For starters, I'd like to take you out again. A real date this time, where I pick you up, we go to the same restaurant, and I leave my criticism at home along with my foot-in-mouth syndrome."

"A real date, huh?" She thought it over. "What if it doesn't work out the way you want it to?"

Mandrel held her face in her hands, penetrating her with a fixed gaze. "What if it does?"

Chapter 10

Dr. Nelson repositioned her glasses. "How did that whole exchange with Mandrel make you feel?"

"I felt a lot of things," recalled Amari. "I was excited, happy . . . a little scared."

"Why were you scared?"

"Mandrel is not like any of the other guys I've dated. To be honest with you, at the time, I hadn't seriously dated anyone since Roland. It was just sex with drinks before and afterward. Real dating was kind of like unchartered territory for me."

"Even though you had misgivings, you still decided to forge a relationship with Mandrel, correct?"

Amari nodded. "It seemed like the right thing to do at the time."

"You said, 'at the time.' What changed as time went on?" asked Dr. Nelson.

Amari paused. "I did."

Dr. Nelson scribbled something in her notebook. "How so?"

She took a moment to reflect. "It wasn't anything big at first. Small, subtle changes here and there."

"Was that the first time you changed for a man?"

"Yes."

"Why do it for him? What was it about him that inspired you to change?"

"There was something about him that made me want to be a better person," divulged Amari. "No other man had made me feel that way."

"So you changed in order to please him," presumed Dr. Nelson.

"Yes, but then I started changing in order to please Him." Amari lifted a finger toward heaven.

"How does God fit into this picture?"

"Well, there was no way I could date Mandrel and not go to church. And there's really no way to go to church every Sunday and not learn anything. It didn't take too many Sundays for me to figure out that God wasn't pleased with how I was living my life."

"You don't think God accepts you as you are?"

"I didn't at the time. Then again, I didn't accept Him either."

Dr. Nelson nodded. "Do you think the changes you made in your life after meeting Mandrel affected you positively or negatively?"

Amari bit her lip. "You know, when I first met Mandrel, I was cold and unfeeling. In a lot of ways, I'd cut myself off from the world emotionally. Back then, I didn't think that I was capable of caring about or genuinely loving a man again until I met him. Deep inside, I was still a scared little girl who was afraid to let anyone love her. That's the reason I gave up hope of ever having a sincere loving and lasting relationship with anyone. I no longer feel that way. I suppose that counts as a positive effect."

"You didn't think you were capable of real love?"

"I believe it was more like thinking I wasn't worthy of it. I didn't receive it, so, with the exception of my brother and his kids, I didn't give it to anyone else either."

"And now?"

Amari took a deep breath. "Now, I'm starting to feel like I deserve authentic love. For the first time, I think I'm ready to see what that feels like."

Seventeen Months Earlier

Amari flung the door open and threw her arms around Mandrel's neck. "Hey!"

He kissed her on the cheek and released her, admiring the snug turtleneck and maxi skirt she was wearing. "You look great!"

"Thank you."

"I've noticed you've been dressing a little more conservatively the last couple of times we've gone out," noted Mandrel, following Amari into her apartment. "I like it."

"Well, I thought about what you said a couple of weeks ago about being confident and sexy without revealing too much. Initially, I was somewhat vexed about it, like, 'How dare he insult my outfits! Nothing in my closet costs less than three hundred dollars!' But then I had to admit that some of my wardrobe should've been left in the closet of my twenties. At thirty-seven, I should be a little more refined in my clothing choices, so I decided to take your advice and leave some things to the imagination."

"I think that's a great idea. Hey, no need to advertise it if you ain't selling it! You're living proof that it's possible to still be chic and sexy without showing 'em all your goodies! You ready to go?"

Amari poked a pair of dangling earrings through her ears. "Yeah, just give me ten minutes to put my makeup on."

"If you need ten more minutes, it means you're not ready, doesn't it?"

Amari opened her compact and began coating her eye lashes with mascara. "Only if you're being technical."

Mandrel wrinkled his nose, looking down at the tubes of lipstick, mascara, and lip liner scattered on the coffee table. "What do you need that stuff all over your face for anyway? I think you're more beautiful without it."

"I don't." She pressed her lips together to evenly distribute her lipstick. "Besides, every girl knows you never leave the house without at least putting on a little lip gloss and mascara."

"Okay, well, put that on and forget that other crap. I want to be able to see Amari, not"—he picked up her tube of lipstick—"NARS."

She exhaled and put away her compact. "The things I do for you."

Mandrel turned Amari around to face him. "See? That's much better, no makeup needed." He swept a strand of hair away from her face. "Sometimes I think you sell yourself short regarding how beautiful you really are. That's a mistake that most women make. Besides, the Good Book says a woman's beauty should not come from outward adornment. It should be that of your inner self, the unfading beauty of a gentle and quiet spirit, which is of great worth in God's sight."

Amari copped a playful attitude. "I know I'm beautiful. The makeup just ensures that I'll be devastatingly gorgeous in man's sight—my man in particular."

"Sweetheart, we're going to the movies. You don't need to go for 'devastatingly gorgeous.' Beautiful will suffice for tonight."

Amari was hoping he'd see her as more than just beautiful that night. She wanted to be sexy. They'd been dating for three weeks. He'd taken her to a concert and had dragged her to church with him for the past three Sundays. They'd gone dancing at a stepping class the week before, and that night, he was taking her to see a romantic comedy that she'd been pestering him about. After the movies, she was hoping that he'd take her to his bedroom.

"You know," she drawled seductively, "that movie is only going to last a couple of hours. It starts at seven. It'll still be early when it lets out, and you have the night off. What did you have in mind for afterward?"

Mandrel shrugged his shoulders. "I don't know, a late dinner, maybe?"

"Or we can go back to your place and watch TV," she suggested, then added, "with the TV off."

He chuckled. "Now what fun would that be?"

"Don't underestimate me, Mr. Ingram. I know how to bring the entertainment."

"Do you now?"

She smiled and nodded. "I, um, did some shopping after work today."

"Oh, okay. What did you buy?"

"This." Amari scooped up a shopping bag lying on the sofa. "It's for you."

"For me?" He was surprised and confused to receive the Victoria's Secret bag. Mandrel opened it and pulled out a black Chantilly lace teddy. "Baby, I'm flattered, but this isn't really my style. I'm more of a jeans and T-shirt kind of guy."

"It's for me to wear, silly rabbit, and for you to enjoy watching me put on . . . and take off."

"So I guess I don't have to ask what you have in mind for after the movie tonight," supposed Mandrel.

"I think we both know what I have on my mind," she said, tantalizing him. "I hope it's on yours too."

Mandrel exhaled and stuffed the lingerie back into the bag. "Amari, I thought we talked about this."

"We did, like, three weeks ago. You said you wanted to wait to have sex." She moved toward him. "I say we've waited long enough."

"Yeah, wait for marriage, not until your next shopping spree."

"Marriage?" Amari shook her head and tried to stifle her laughter. "I don't think you're being realistic about that."

"That's been my reality for the past two years."

"Okay, but marriage, babe? Who knows when that's going to be? You could be administering self-love for another ten years! I think two years is long enough for anybody. You're due for a reward, and I'm due for one too. For me, waiting three weeks is the equivalent of waiting two years."

"That's not how it works, Amari. I made a promise to myself and to God to wait until I get married, and I intend to keep it."

Amari placed her hand on her hip. "Mandrel, I know you love God and everything but come on. I know you miss having sex too. Admit it."

He capitulated. "I'm not gonna lie. It's been tough at times, especially when I know I'm missing out on seeing you wearing that." He pointed to the negligee. "But that's when I go to God in prayer and ask for strength."

"I don't understand you. Why do you need to pray for the strength to resist when I'm giving it to you free and clear?"

Mandrel tried to make her see it from another perspective. "All right, say we do it. We go back to my place after the movies, make love, then what?"

"If it's good, we do it again!" she jibed.

"But what comes after that? Sex is fleeting. Don't you want something that'll last? Love is eternal, and we can have that without sex."

"We can also have it with sex, Mandrel. I honestly don't see the big deal."

He gave up. "We're in different places with our spiritual walk, I guess."

Amari's temper flared, as she was not one to handle rejection well. "Oh, I get it. So now we're back to me not being holy enough for you, right?"

"No, it's not even about that. Baby, I've rushed into relationships sex first. In the moment, we loved the idea of sex, but we didn't give ourselves the chance to build a foundation of love, respect, and sanctity. I'm trying to get to know you, Amari. I want to know everything about you before we take that step, and I want our relationship to be based on love, not lust."

"What about what I want?"

"As much as I care about you, Amari, I can't put your wants above God's will. Just as important as that is that I'm trying to build something real with you. I don't want our hormones to mess this up."

She'd never been turned down for sex before, but knowing why he did made the pill easier to swallow. "You really do care about me, don't you?"

He lifted her chin and looked her in the eyes. "Are you just now figuring that out?"

Amari was encouraged by his words. This was new for her. No man had ever offered her more than laughs and a good time. "So . . . so you think we might actually have something real here?"

"I do. I've been searching for someone like you my whole life. Now that I've found you, I want to do everything I can to protect what we have. Even if it means not letting you have your way with me!"

He pulled her into a loving embrace. Amari relished being in his arms. It was wonderful to be with a man who sincerely cared about her, made excruciating by the fact that she couldn't touch him.

For now anyway.

Chapter 11

It had been two weeks since their last date because work, Mandrel's visits to his son, and Amari's hectic social calendar had kept them apart. The only solution for the moment was to combine her love life with her work life, so Amari invited Mandrel out to hear a new artist she had to interview and to follow up the performance with dinner.

"Thank you for coming out tonight. I know the club really isn't your scene, especially on a Tuesday night."

Mandrel pulled open the door to South City Kitchen and allowed Amari to pass through ahead of him. "It wasn't so bad."

"Are you serious? That guy was terrible! No substance, no artistry, just noise over a beat. I hate you had to sit through that."

"This is how you earn a living, so do your thang! The crowd looked a little young, but, hey, I was young once too."

"You're still young," declared Amari as they made their way inside. "Forty isn't exactly retirement age."

"No, but it is the youth of old age."

"I prefer to think of it as the old age of youth."

After greeting them, the restaurant's hostess led Mandrel and Amari through the densely packed crowd and found them a table.

Once they were settled, Amari began venting about the drudgery of her job again. "That is the part I hate about my job. I don't even know how this clown managed to get connected enough to score an interview and feature in the magazine. He only has one song out, and it's mediocre at best. He's an utter disgrace to hip-hop and music in general, but talent is optional to make it in show business these days. With the right imagining consultant and a catchy beat, anybody can be a star."

"Have you ever considered writing about any gospel artists? If you're ever looking to highlight one, we've got singers with unbelievable range at Greater Hope."

"I would love to spotlight different kinds of music and real talent, not this auto-tune, braggadocios crap record labels keep spitting out, but my name isn't at the top of the masthead. What she says goes."

Mandrel challenged her. "Are you afraid to take a stand for the Kingdom?"

She frowned. "Who said anything about taking a stand? I'm there to write and edit, not champion anybody's cause. If I put one of your choir members in the mag, I'd have churches lined up from here to Mayberry pestering me for an interview."

"Would that be so bad?"

"Not if it was a gospel magazine but we have to cater to our demographic."

"Judging by the crowd tonight, I assume your demographic is young men and women rocking oversized chains, sagging pants, and who cuss every other word."

"Precisely."

"What happened to freedom over finance?"

"Finances won out. Hopefully there will be some real talent at the music showcase I have to cover in a few weeks."

"Oh, yeah? Where is it?"

"It's in Asheville, North Carolina. A bunch of independent artists are converging there for some kind of music festive or summit, something like that."

"You driving up there?"

"I guess. The magazine doesn't spring for airline tickets if it's less than a five-hour drive."

"If you want some company, let me know."

Her mood lightened. "You'd go with me?"

"Yeah, I don't want you driving that far alone."

"It's an overnight trip. Can you take off like that?"

"Amari, I have three other drivers. I don't have to call in. I'm the boss."

A waitress in a low top and miniskirt walked up to the table. "What are you folks drinking tonight?"

"Water with lemon for me. Thanks," ordered Mandrel.

"I'd like an electric lemonade." Amari glanced over at Mandrel. "On second thought, make mine a water with lemon too."

"Amari, you could've ordered whatever you wanted," Mandrel told her after the waitress departed.

She shook her head. "I don't need to drink. I need a clear head to write this article tonight."

"I must admit, I do like seeing you sober."

The waitress returned and set the glasses of water on the table. She placed a glass of Kir Royale down in front of Amari.

"Hold up, I didn't order this." Amari handed it back to her.

"It's courtesy of that gentleman at the bar," explained the waitress.

Amari turned to see who was responsible for ordering the drink for her. It was Traffic. He waved when she looked up at him. His presence made her nervous. He was an escapee from her old life that she didn't want popping up in her new one.

The waitress took their dinner orders and scurried off.

"Who sent over the drink?" asked Mandrel.

"Nobody," muttered Amari before gulping down her water. It gave her excuse not to talk and, more importantly, not to answer any questions.

"He's somebody. He bought you a drink, didn't he?"

She brought the glass down from her lips. "He's a deejay I know, but there's nothing going on between us."

"I didn't say there was."

"I was simply reassuring you," she contended.

"Reassuring me about what? I wasn't questioning the status of your relationship. I just asked who he was."

She was testy. "And I told you."

"Why are you so defensive?" probed Mandrel.

"I'm not," she lied. Amari didn't know why she felt both guilty and defensive, especially since neither feeling was warranted. "I just feel like there are some questions I don't think you have the right to ask me."

Mandrel was taken aback. "Excuse me, the right?"

"Yes, there are certain questions you shouldn't ask unless you're in a relationship with someone."

He retreated with his hands up. "Won't happen again."

"Thank you." Amari waited a few seconds before speaking again. "Would it really matter to you if he was someone special to me?"

"Do you mean if the two of you were dating?"

"Dating, sleeping together, whatever."

"Possibly," he replied. "Would it matter if I were seeing someone?"

"Yeah, but what could I do about that?" she asked. "It's not like we're an official couple or anything."

Mandrel seemed hesitant to broach the subject of their relationship status. "Do you want to be an official couple?"

She swallowed hard. "I don't know. Do you?"

He laughed a little. "You know we just met a month ago, right?"

"Actually, it's closer to two months now," she informed him.

"Pardon me, two months."

"Mandrel, I'm not asking you to be exclusive with me. You can date whoever you want."

"I'm dating the person I want. The only person I want."

She tried to douse her smile. "That's good to know."

"But I'm forty years old. I'm not out here dating just to have something to do. I'm looking for a wife."

"Oh?" She sat erect. "So what does that mean for us?"

"It means I'm not trying to play games or waste my time or yours. If you're not looking for anything long term, I need to know."

"I hadn't really given it any thought," admitted Amari. "To tell you the truth, I haven't had a lot of serious relationships."

"When was your last one?"

She thought back. "Five years ago, maybe, but I can't even really say it was serious. More like long-term casual dating. I've been consumed with work since then. Dating hasn't been a priority."

"What about now? Can you see yourself with me long term?"

Amari nervously wrung her hands together in her lap. "Sometimes. What about you?"

"I like you, Amari, but I'm sure that's been obvious since the day we met. At the same time, I don't want to rush it. I still see some potential red flags between us."

She looked him up and down. "Like what?"

"I think the foremost important thing is your salvation."

She shrugged her shoulders. "What about it?"

"I can't marry a woman who hasn't given her life to Christ."

Amari was annoyed. "What does that even mean?"

"It means having accepted that Jesus died for your sins and allowing God into your heart."

The waitress came back and set the plate of shrimp and red mule grits down in front of Mandrel and the order of smoked risotto for Amari. Amari barely listened as Mandrel prayed over their food. She was still chewing over his salvation stipulation.

"You do know I believe in God, don't you? I'm not a total infidel."

Mandrel stirred the tomato gravy into his grits. "There's a difference between believing in God and accepting Christ as your Lord and Savior."

"I believe that Jesus died on the cross and rose again," she told him. "Isn't that what Easter is all about?"

"That's what Resurrection Sunday is about. Easter is about celebrating spring and eggs and whatever else stores can get you to spend money on. Salvation, on the other hand, is free."

"So how does that work?" asked Amari. She began dicing up her food. "I see people coming down the aisle at the end of church service when they invite people to join Greater Hope, but where do they take them? Is it some secret room where they make sacrifices? Do they make you sign something?"

He chuckled. "You watch too much TV. They go over Roman's Road and lead you to Christ. There's no signing or taking blood oaths."

"Is that it? Is salvation your only requirement?"

"That and being faithful. I can work around everything else. I can't deal with cheating though."

"You don't ask for much. What do I get in return?"

He brought her hand to his lips and kissed it. "For you, baby, nothing less than the whole world."

Chapter 12

"I believe you're up to six, young lady," announced Armand, as he refilled his sister's drink at his bar, Mand Cave.

Amari sipped her martini. "This is not my sixth drink, Armand! It's only the second one."

"I was not talking about your drinking habits. I was referring to two days ago at church. It was the sixth Sunday I've seen you at Greater Hope."

She dismissed his acknowledgment of her church attendance. "You keeping tabs on me now?"

He waved at a group of twenty-somethings filing out of the bar. "Of course! You know it hasn't gone unnoticed that you're often in the company of a certain church member, either. That's not from me; that's information coming straight from the gossip ministry."

"So that's what this is really about, isn't it? You lured me here under the guise of unlimited martinis, but it's really a fishing expedition. You want to know what's going on between Mandrel and me."

"If there's tea, you might as well go on and spill it."

Amari shook her head. "I swear I've never seen anything as nosey as church folks!"

"You can't blame folks for being curious. Brother Ingram is a hot commodity at Greater Hope. He's single, got a good job and a good head on his shoulders. There are women there who have been thirsting after him for years, and you roll up in your short dresses and sky-high shoes and steal him away from the thirst traps! They don't know you well enough to ask you what's going on, so they bombard me with questions."

"Well, you know I don't mind ruffling some feathers and inspiring envy." She took a few sips from her drink. "And it's like you said: they had years to get at Mandrel. I got him in one Sunday without even trying. Obviously, they're dealing with a man who knows what he wants, and it wasn't any of those hatin' heifers at the church."

"Are you and Mandrel official now? Do I have to start calling y'all Mamari or some other corny hybrid name?"

"Not unless you have an immediate death wish!" she threatened him. "As for whether or not we're officially a couple, it depends on how you define the word 'couple.'"

"I think what matters is how you and Mandrel define it."

Amari grunted under her breath. "If we're going by my definition, then we're definitely not a couple!"

"What's going on?" asked Armand, concerned.

She sighed and took another sip.

"What?" pressed Armand.

"All right, before I say anything, I have to warn you that we're about to enter the Land of Too Much Information again."

Armand groaned. "When do you not drag me into that dark, dismal place kicking and screaming?"

"This is true, but I don't want it to be said that I didn't prepare you."

"Consider me forewarned."

"Good. Now back to your question about us being a couple." She took a pause. "A couple to me is two people who verbally commit to one another."

Armand agreed. "Okay, that's a good working definition."

"It is also two people who engage in intimate acts exclusively with one another."

"Yeah," he answered slowly. "Is this the part where this conversation is going to start getting weird for me?"

"It might," she cautioned him. "Mandrel and I have been seeing each other for about two months now. We enjoy each other's company; we get along well. We don't argue or take each other for granted. I know that Mandrel cares about me, and I don't think he's seeing anyone else, but there's still a problem."

"What?"

She huffed and blurted out, "He won't sleep with me."

Armand squint his eyes in disbelief. "You're pulling my leg, right?"

"No, and it's so frustrating!" vented Amari, balling her fists, nearly knocking over her drink. "I mean, I can't even remember my last orgasm."

Armand moved the glass out of her way. "Wow, you managed to find a new dimension of TMI that I wasn't even aware of until this moment," he replied. "What I meant was that I hope you're not giving him a hard time about staying celibate."

She reached for her drink again. "Armand, I couldn't give Mandrel a hard time if I wanted to."

Armand shook his head. "And we're back to that weird dimension."

"This isn't the time to judge me!" she argued. "I'm being sincere right now."

"Sincere about what, Mar?"

"My concerns about this relationship. Does being a Christian give him the right to withhold sex from me? Is this some sort of test to see if I'm worthy?" she asked. "What if we get serious and he asks me to marry him? Does he really expect me to marry someone I've never even French kissed, much less ever slept with? "

"Of all of the things you could be worried about, this is what you've chosen?"

"Don't do that!" Amari shot back.

"Do what?"

"Try to slut-shame me! You wouldn't tie yourself someone who's a Popsicle in bed any more than I would! And I refuse to apologize for being a woman who enjoys a good roll in the hay."

"Amari, if that's how you roll, that's your business, but Mandrel doesn't have to have sex with you if he doesn't want to. In reality, he shouldn't have sex with you. He can't go around fornicating. He's a saved man."

"So does that means he has to save it for marriage too?"

"It means he should."

"Shouldn't I get a say in that decision? It affects me too."

"You have choices just like Mandrel does. Nobody is forcing you to be with him."

"I didn't say I don't want to be with him. Shoot, the fact that I want to be with him in every way is the problem!" she exclaimed.

"I think you're putting too much emphasis on what's in that man's pants and not enough on what's in his heart. Sex shouldn't make or break your relationship."

"Armand, do you know how many relationships fail because of sex or lack thereof?" She answered her own question. "Plenty! You don't have to look any further than your marriage to know that."

"I didn't cheat because Nia wasn't having sex with me. I cheated because I was selfish and thought I could get away with it." Armand began slicing limes for garnishment. "It had nothing to do with what Nia was or wasn't doing."

"Oh, don't get all 'holier than thou' on me. I get enough of that from Mandrel. You know as well as I do that practically everyone over the age of eighteen is having sex. It's a natural part of life."

"Saying something is natural only means that it's carnal. It's what your flesh wants, but you're supposed to control your body, not the other way around. Once you get saved, you're led by the Holy Spirit. Unless the Lord approves, you're not supposed to do it."

She sucked her teeth. "Whatever. I think this whole notion of sex being strictly for married folks is absurd. Sex is simply an expression of love and physical attraction. It should be open to anyone who has the maturity to handle it and the money for prophylactics. Religion shouldn't have anything to do with it."

"You need to take that up with the policy maker."

"I would if anyone could point Him out to me."

"Mar, you're stumbling and falling at the same time—you're trippin'!" Armand took stock of his sister. "Do you really like Mandrel?"

"I think I do," admitted Amari. "I believe we could have something special."

"Then forget about sex. You finally have a good man, don't blow it. No pun intended."

She tossed a few peanuts at him. "You're chock-full of jokes today, aren't you? What about you? Are you celibate?"

Armand smirked and swept the peanuts into his hand. "All that ain't your business."

Amari raised her eyebrow. "Like that's going to stop me from asking."

"It's different for me. I'm married."

"You were married when you slept with another woman."

"And that's why my wife wants a divorce, so there's something to be said for keeping it zipped up. Listen, Mar, if this dude cares about you and the worst thing about him is that he's trying to do right by the Lord, you'd have to be a special kind of stupid to let someone like that go."

"I know, and I could agree with you if it was just about sex, but it's not. We don't just not have sex. We don't do anything."

Armand was perplexed. "What do mean?"

"Our relationship is so G-rated that it could be a reality show on the Disney Channel. There's no touching or kissing other than a cheek or forehead kiss. We don't cuddle or any of that stuff."

Armand wiped off his cutting board. "Why not?"

"He says if he gets worked up, it'll be too hard to turn it off, so he doesn't put himself in those situations."

Armand nodded. "Makes sense."

"Yeah, for him, but what kind of relationship is that for me? There's practically nothing in terms of affection. I did more with my fifth grade boyfriend than I do with Mandrel. I need passion. I like to know that the guy I'm with is attracted to me and can't keep his hands off of me."

"You have to respect what the man is trying to do, though. He's serious about his walk with God. That's to be commended."

"Yeah, we'll see," hinted Amari.

Armand wrinkled his brow. "What's that supposed to mean?"

"I have an out-of-town assignment for work coming up in two weeks."

"What kind of assignment?"

"I'm supposed to cover some holiday music revue in Asheville, but the point is Mandrel agreed to go with me."

"And?"

"And it's an overnight trip. In the mountains. With a gorgeous woman. In the honeymoon suite," relayed Amari. "It'll be dripping with romance."

"Wait a minute. So he agreed to shack up in the same bed with you in Asheville?"

Amari averted eye contact. "Not exactly."

"That's what figured. What lie did you tell Mandrel to get him to go along with this?"

"It's only a lie if you get caught. I told him I was getting two rooms, but somehow I only remembered to reserve one, and it's the ultra-romantic honeymoon suite. Between the fireplace, the king-sized bed, the hot tub, and the sexy little number I'll be wearing, Mandrel won't be able to resist me."

"Amari, don't be a hindrance to that man. Let him have his relationship with God without your interference."

"I'm not trying to mess with his relationship with God. I'm trying to improve his relationship with me."

"By backing him into a corner and forcing yourself on him?"

She slumped down into the chair, pouting. "It's not like that."

"The man is trying to respect you, which is a heck of a lot more than Roland, Traffic, and all of those other Negroes have tried to do. Please let him. Respect yourself."

"I have self-respect," she asserted.

"Then act like it."

Amari began sulking again.

"I'm not trying to come down hard on you, but we've always kept it real with each other. I love you. I wouldn't tell you anything you didn't need to hear. I know it's your life and what you do with it probably shouldn't matter to me, but it does because you matter to me."

"I know I do, and I love you for that, Armand."

"But you're still gonna do what you wanna do right?"

Amari raised her glass to her brother with a sly smile.

"Lord, help her!" he prayed aloud. "And please help poor Mandrel, who has no idea what he's getting himself into."

"Amen," replied Amari.

Armand knew from experience that it was best to drop the issue. Amari was like a lioness clinging to its prey once she got an idea in her head. All he could do was watch her self-destruct and be there to help pick up the pieces.

Chapter 13

Amari was bubbling on the inside with excitement. She and Mandrel were four and a half hours into their first road trip together. If things went according to plan, it would also be the first time they spent the night together.

"This looks like something out of fairy tale," gushed Amari, admiring the orange, crimson, and golden hues blanketing the autumn leaves lining the highway leading to Asheville, North Carolina that early December afternoon. "The foliage here is breathtaking. I thought it would be too late in the season to catch it."

Mandrel peered over the steering wheel to get a better glimpse. "Yeah, it looks like God kept it pretty just for us. I've been to a lot of places, but it's pretty hard to top the beauty of this scene."

Amari checked the GPS. "I think our hotel is up this road. GPS is saying that we should be there in about fifteen minutes."

"It can't come a moment too soon. I'm beat!"

"I offered to help out with driving."

"No, you offered to talk to me and keep me awake while I did all the driving. That's not the same thing."

"Semantics," murmured Amari.

They arrived at the Bear's Den Lodge as scheduled. Light snow began to sprinkle down as they made their way out of the car.

Amari stopped and inhaled, taking it all in. "Could this moment be any more perfect?"

"No, it couldn't." Mandrel kissed her forehead. "Unless, of course, it was about twenty degrees warmer!"

"You wouldn't know romance if it smacked you in the face, Mandrel! Look at this place!" She lifted her hands as if catching snowflakes. "The snow, the mountains . . . us together like this."

Mandrel pulled their luggage from the trunk. "Yeah, it is pretty spectacular. You know there's no one I'd rather be freezing in the snow with than you."

"All right, let's get you inside. Obviously, you can only appreciate the snow from the comfort of a blazing fireplace."

Mandrel dragged in the suitcases as Amari walked ahead to check in. He joined her at the front desk counter.

"Checking in under Amari Christopher. There should be two nonsmoking rooms."

The front desk clerk scrolled through her computer. "I'm sorry, there seems to be some sort of glitch. I see a reservation under Amari Christopher, but there's only one room reserved, not two."

"Don't worry about it. We can just bunk together," resolved Amari.

Mandrel stepped in. "That won't be necessary. I can get my own room." He whipped out his credit card to Amari's chagrin. "One nonsmoking room under Mandrel Ingram please."

The clerk checked for available rooms then broke the news to Mandrel. "I'm sorry, Mr. Ingram, but we're booked to capacity tonight and tomorrow." Amari's spirits lifted again upon her that. "There's a music festival in town. Most hotels around here are pretty full this weekend."

Amari pulled him aside. "Sweetie, it's not a big deal. You can crash with me."

Mandrel was reluctant to accept the offer. "You and me alone in a hotel room? I don't know if that's such a good idea."

"Why not?" she asked innocently.

"Come on, Amari, you know why."

"I asked for the deluxe suite. My room has a big ol' king-sized bed. We can both sleep in it and not so much as graze each other all night. You can even sleep on the couch if it'll make you more comfortable."

Mandrel shrank back. "I don't know. It wouldn't look right."

"To who?" Amari looked around. "Nobody here knows us."

"God does."

"I'm sure God will understand, given the circum-stances."

"No, I'll just call around to see who has a vacancy."

"Didn't you hear the receptionist say almost every hotel in Asheville is booked? Besides, it's freezing outside, and the snow is starting to come down. This isn't a good day to be driving around Asheville trying to find someplace to lay your head. Plus, we're right across the street from the festival. That's why I choose this hotel."

Seeing that he'd run out of excuses, Amari didn't wait for Mandrel to confirm before requesting two keys from the front desk.

"You're awful quiet," observed Amari as they rode the elevator to the fourth floor in silence.

"I don't know how I feel about all this," he admitted.

"Relax, we're not committing a crime. I think you have to do more than spend the night with your girlfriend to gain a one-way entry to hell."

They stepped off the elevator and searched the halls for their room.

"Here it is," said Amari. "Room 426." She slid the key card to unlock the door.

Mandrel pushed open the door and flipped on the light. They were greeted by an expansive hot tub, a luxurious king-sized bed, and a gift basket filled with champagne and chocolates.

"Well, if I didn't know what romance was before, I know now! Is this the honeymoon suite?" wondered Mandrel, setting the luggage down.

"I don't think so," replied Amari, unable to look him in the eye. "I travel for work all the time. This is what most of the hotel rooms I stay in look like. Sometimes hotels go out of their way to make a good impression, hoping that the magazine will give them a mention and some free press."

"They certainly know how to make you feel like a baller, don't they?" He examined the gift basket.

"Hey, I travel first class or I don't travel at all!" declared Amari.

Mandrel flung the box of chocolates aside. "I guess that's why I don't travel at all."

Amari moaned and stretched, ready to divert his attention. "That drive got me feeling all kinds of tired. A hot shower right now would do me a world of good."

"Go ahead." Mandrel yawned and lay down on the bed. "Wake me up when you're ready to go to dinner."

Amari watched in disbelief as Mandrel dozed off. He didn't even seem excited by the prospect of her being naked in the next room. She disrobed in the bathroom, turned on the faucet, and let the scalding water roll down her body. She kept the door unlocked in case Mandrel decided to join her. After ten minutes had gone by, she had to accept that he wouldn't.

Undeterred, she launched the second phase of her seduction: scurry out of the shower dripping wet, clad in only a towel.

"There's more than one way to kill this cat," she muttered and sprang into action.

She painstakingly tousled her hair and adjusted the towel to cover as little of her body as possible. She pinched her cheeks to bring color to them and brushed a thin coat of gloss over her lips.

Under the guise of needing a pair of panties, Amari stepped out of the shower, only to find Mandrel sound asleep and snoring.

She seethed. Nothing was going as planned. She was almost positive she could hear God somewhere laughing.

Chapter 14

"That was unbelievable!" declared Mandrel when they returned to the hotel following dinner. "That restaurant was on point, babe. I'm glad you suggested seeing what downtown had to offer."

She smiled a little. The only "downtown" Amari was interested in could not be found by GPS or map.

"Are you all right?" he asked, alarmed. "You look a little flushed."

"I'm fine, just tired."

Mandrel reached for her hand. "Why don't you take off those walking sticks you call heels?" He peeled off her jacket. "Take off some of these clothes . . ."

At those words, Amari's excitement was reignited.

He led her to the hot tub. "Fill up this tub with warm water and bubbles . . ."

"Ohhh, yes!" purred Amari, already visualizing the two of them making waves in the tub.

"Pour a glass of that expensive-looking champagne. Dip your little sexy self in this Jacuzzi and take a nice, long soak."

"That sounds amazing." Amari started unbuttoning her blouse. She faced him with a seductive grin. "Where will you be?"

"I'll be downstairs. I scoped the gym out on the way up. I figured I could get in about an hour of weights and do a few laps in that indoor pool while you relaxed in the hot tub."

Amari felt as if she had just volunteered to take the Ice Bucket Challenge and was drenched four times with ice water imported straight from the Arctic.

She spoke up. "I have an even better idea."

"What's that?"

She knew her only shot at a happy ending for the night would be to keep him in the room with her. She thought fast. "Let's play a game!" suggested Amari.

"A game?" He frowned. "I'm not really the mood for board games, Amari."

"No, this game is really fun, no boards required."

"What is required?"

"Being naked." She smirked. "The naked truth, that is!"

Mandrel wagged his finger at her. "You're bad, you know that?"

"Oh, baby, I'm mind-blowing, but that's another conversation. For right now, let's focus on the game."

"You still haven't told me what it is."

"It's called Never Have I Ever. The object is to confess to things you've never done."

Mandrel removed his coat. "What's the point if you've never done those things?"

"It's a way to get to know each other without asking a bunch of inane personal questions," explained Amari. "Now let's play. Tell me something you've never done. Start the sentence off by saying, 'Never have I ever.'"

"That's simple. Never have I ever played this game. Boom!" He threw up his hands. "Drops mic, collects trophy, game over!"

Amari laughed. "Don't take that victory lap yet, my friend. Besides, I know you can do better than that. Tell me something else you've never done."

Mandrel plopped down on the sofa. "I have never—"

"You have to say, 'Never have I ever,'" she interjected.

"Okay. Never have I ever . . . peed in a swimming pool."

Amari ogled Mandrel with skepticism before sitting down next to him. "Everybody has peed in the pool before."

"Yeah, everybody who doesn't mind having other folks floating in their urine! That's nasty. Now, the shower is a horse of a different color."

She laughed. "My turn. Never have I ever smoked crack."

"That should go without saying!" exclaimed Mandrel. "Have you ever smoked anything else?"

"The game is Never Have I Ever, not I've Been Known to Occasionally.' Now, it's your turn. You have never, ever what?"

"Um, let's see." He rolled the question over in his mind. "Never have I ever hit a woman."

"I hope not!" bellowed Amari.

"I said 'woman,' not 'girl'! I used to fight with my cousin Fruity all the time, but Fruity wasn't no punk! I can't even say definitively that she's a girl. She could beat me without even breaking a sweat. She's tougher than any guy I know."

Amari winced. "Geesh! I'd hate to run up on her!"

"Nah, she's a sweetheart, just don't tell her I said that."

"Duly noted! Okay, never have I ever been arrested." She paused. "Well, that's not true. It's more accurate to say that I've never been convicted."

Mandrel pushed up the sleeves on his sweatshirt. "Huh?"

Amari waved her hand dismissively. "There was a situation back when I was in college. A brick was thrown through a cheating ex's car window, and there were charges filed but no concrete evidence. The case was thrown out. All right, your turn."

"So you're just gonna gloss over the fact that you busted some guy's window out of his car?" probed Mandrel.

"There no evidence to prove that I did it, but if I did do it, he had it coming," tipped off Amari.

"Is that your excuse?"

"It's not an excuse. It's comeuppance. You break my heart, I break your window, and we're even."

"Is that how that works?"

"Hopefully you never have to find out!"

Mandrel shuddered. "Moving right along. I have never, ever been to Disney World."

She was bowled over. "You've never been to Disney World? How is that possible?"

"We didn't have money like that growing up. Why do you think my parents stopped after three kids and spaced us out light years apart? There wasn't any room in the budget for vacations. I did well to get a bus ticket to go see my grandmother in Tennessee."

"That in itself would've been a treat for me. My grandparents were awesome."

"What about your parents?"

Amari framed her words carefully. "My parents are . . . interesting."

"Do you care to elaborate?"

"Not right now. Maybe some other time."

Mandrel yielded to her decision. "All right, I won't push."

"Thank you. Mark my words, though, Ingram, I will see to it that you get to Disney World if it's the last thing I do, you hear me?"

"I might hold you to that."

"Please do! My turn." She looked up, thinking. "Never have I ever sung karaoke."

"Karaoke?" Mandrel made a wry face. "Get on with the good stuff! If we're gonna play, we need to make it worthwhile. Go deep. What is it that you've never done but always wanted to do?

Her eyes twinkled. "If I go deep, you've got to go deep too."

"Baby, I'm already in the end zone!"

"Okay." Amari sighed and confessed, "Never have I ever been loved the way I want to."

"Come on, Amari. There's no shortage of men who would love to love you. How can you say you've never been loved the way you want to?"

"I've been spoiled the way I want to or pursued the way I want to. Heck, I've even been sexed the way I want to, and I know a lot of women who can't say that! But loved? That's a different ball game."

He delicately touched her face. "How do you want to be loved?"

"Wholly, unconditionally," she stated with certainty.

"That's how God loves you."

"Let me rephrase then. Never have I ever been loved the way I want to by someone I can see!" added Amari.

"I wouldn't be so sure about that. Never say never."

A weighty silence passed between them.

"I guess it's on me again, huh?" asked Mandrel. "Let's see. Never have I ever lied to a woman."

"Of course you haven't," she deadpanned and moved to bed located across from the sofa. "No surprise there, you're one of the good guys."

"I haven't always been so good, Amari. I was just upfront about my dirt instead of lying about it."

"Wait, you've done dirt?" She sat up, stunned. "I guess that's why it's snowing in the South tonight. Hell has started to freeze over!"

He released a hearty laugh. "I never said I was an angel."

"No, I believe the reference you're looking for is saint."

"I guess compared to the person I was a few years ago, I am a saint."

Amari was intrigued. "This game just got a lot more interesting." She leaned in closer to him. "I want to hear about those pre-saint years."

"Like I said, I've done my share of dirt. I've run through women, played the field, but all that stuff gets old after a while. You realize that what you're seeking is not in these streets or under somebody's skirt. The void I was trying to fill could only be filled by the Lord."

Amari groaned. "You sound like my brother. Does the church send you all the same script to memorize?"

He chuckled. "No, it's the truth, but it's one of those things you have to learn for yourself."

"When did you learn it?"

Mandrel stared down at his hands. "After I woke up with some chick who was pregnant."

"Pregnant with your child?"

"No, pregnant with someone else's. I don't even remember her last name. She was just some random person catching a cab one night. We got to talking on my way taking her home. She invited me up, and the rest is history. I got up and threw that skeleton bone right in the closet and never saw her again. I've had one or two one-night stands in my day, but sleeping with a pregnant woman, one clearly showing at that, was a new low for me."

"Well, I think that says more about her than it does about you."

"It said something about both of us, and I didn't like the message. I decided right then and there that I had to start living my life in a different way. That meant I had to start going back to church and getting in the Word. It also meant no more random sex acts, no more just doing whatever the heck I want without thinking about anyone else, and no more dippin' and dodgin' the Lord. I had to face the truth about myself, and I had to face Him."

"I don't know, Manny, it just seems like you have to give up too much of yourself to follow God without getting anything in return. How's that a fair tradeoff?"

"It's not fair. Not because you're getting nothing in return because, in actuality, you're getting everything in return. God is the one receiving the short end of the deal."

Amari listened, curious. "How so?"

"God is perfect, sinless. But He's got to take us with all of our messes and screw-ups and sinful natures. You know what the beauty is in that, though? He takes us just as we are. Once we accept Him into our lives, He sees us the same way He sees His son Jesus. We have access to everything Jesus has access to: health, prosperity, peace, comfort, love. You say you're getting nothing in return when you turn your life over to God, but the truth is He's the reason we have anything at all. He gives us so much more than we could ever give Him."

"Yeah, that sounds good, but some of the brokest, sickest, most miserable people I've ever seen are right there in the church. How do you explain that?"

He shook his head. "I can't really. It's like holding a piece of candy in your hands. If the child wants it, he can take it, but you're not going to knock him down to give it to him. That's how it is with God's promises. The Word is there. His promises are spelled out for you right in the Bible, but if you don't take time out to read it and apply it to your life, you can't be surprised when you don't get results."

Amari leaned back on the bed and propped herself up on her elbows. "Again, you're saying all of the right things, but I work and live around people who have more money than God Himself, who do whatever the heck they want to do when they want to do it. They're not going to church or praying, but their lives are ten times better than the ones buying into all this religion stuff. Why should I stop living my life the way I want to live it and follow Jesus when I can have the kind of life people dream about without Him?"

Mandrel looked up at her. "Having money is good, and we all enjoy a good time, but what happens after that? What happens when the music stops and the money and fake friends are gone? What happens when you get diagnosed a disease that money can't cure? What happens when the world starts getting too crazy?"

"And God is supposed to fix all that?"

"I don't know if 'fix' is the right word, but He'll give you peace while you're in the storm, and He will allow those negative things to work for your good."

"Yeah, but will He *fix it?* If I'm hungry, is He gonna rain down food? If I'm sick, is He going to heal me? If I want a new car, is He gonna send me to the dealership? I mean, what can He actually do?"

"He's not Santa Claus, Amari! Didn't you learn about any of this stuff in Sunday school when you were a kid?"

She looked down. "We didn't go to church or Sunday school, for that matter. After my mom had my brother and me, I don't think she had much reason to hope or to think God could make her life better."

"That's too bad. Accepting God as her Savior and trusting Him could've made all the difference. It still can for you."

"You think so, huh? I believe I'm doing pretty good as it is."

"Yeah, but it can always be better."

Amari watched him in awe. "Last one. Never have I ever met a man like you, Mandrel Ingram." She got up and kissed him on the cheek.

"They can't make too many like me. The world would go crazy," he joked.

"I'm sure it would, especially considering that only one has that effect on me already." She dragged her lips down his neck.

"Amari, what are you doing?"

She continued kissing him. "What does it feel like I'm doing?"

"It feels like you're trying to seduce me."

She pulled away. "Is it working?"

"I thought we talked about this."

"We did, but"—she took off her shirt and tossed it—"talking is overrated."

Mandrel picked up the shirt and shoved it back into her hands. "Come on now, chill out."

She laid it aside and climbed into his lap. "You chill out and let me go to work."

Mandrel pulled back from her, loosening her grip on him. "Amari, I'm for real, okay?"

She stopped. "Is this your way of making me beg for it?"

"Why would I make you do that?"

"I don't know. That's sort of a turn-on for a lot of men."

"Not for me. It has the opposite effect. To tell you the truth, I find it pathetic."

She bolted from his lap. "So I'm pathetic now?"

"Not you, this whole act you're doing. I mean, it wasn't even five minutes ago that we were talking about the Lord, now you're over here ripping your clothes off! I told you I don't want to have sex. Why can't you just respect that? You would expect that from me if it was the other way around."

"I don't understand you. One minute you're all over me and now this."

"I wasn't trying to lead you on. Like I said before, I don't think that we should rush into anything that we might regret."

"Mandrel, we care about each other. How could I ever regret making love to you?"

"Maybe not today, maybe you wouldn't regret it all, but if we wait, I promise you that you'll be glad we did. If we ever get to that place in our relationship, I want it to because we did it right. Not because we got caught up in the moment or felt lonely, but because we've committed ourselves to each other in every way. We're not at that point yet, and I won't take advantage of you like that."

"I guess there's nothing left for me to say except sorry for trying to come on to you. It won't happen again."

"No harm done." He kissed her hand. "It's getting late, and you have a big day tomorrow. I think we should turn in. You can have the bed. I'll take the couch."

Amari acquiesced without protest. She'd suffered enough humiliation for one night. There may not have been any harm done to Mandrel, but there was definitely harm done to her. Rejection for her was never easy, but being rejected by someone she was falling for was a crushing ache unparalleled to anything else.

Chapter 15

Dr. Nelson took a long pause before asking Amari her next question. She clasped her hands together. "Amari, do you equate sex with love?"

"What do you mean?"

"Do you think that if a man sleeps with you, it's because he loves you? If he doesn't have sex with you, the reverse is true?"

"I don't think so. Why do you ask?"

"Because you seemed to take Mandrel's spurning you so personally when it doesn't seem to have been symptomatic of his feelings of you at all. From what I can gather, he appears to be someone serious about his faith. His not wanting to be intimate had nothing to do with you."

"I think I knew that on a surface level, but it still felt like rejection."

"Why do you think you have such a hard time dealing with rejection?"

"Do you know anyone who enjoys being rejected?" she asked with sarcasm.

"No, but I do know people who react to it differently. I think in your case, it goes back to your relationship with your parents."

Amari groaned. "Here we go again."

"You felt that your mother rejected you because of who your father is. Your father wasn't there for you. Your first love, Roland, was unfaithful to you, which is another form of rejection. It's though if a man doesn't have sex with you, regardless of the reason, you feel like he's rejecting you."

"It's not like that," claimed Amari.

"Are you sure?"

"It wasn't just that Mandrel rejected me sexually. I did so much for him. I changed who I was and the way I lived for him. It seems like he owed me something in return."

"Sex?"

"No. Love."

"Which, for you, goes back to sex, doesn't it?"

Amari shook her head. "You don't get it. You just don't understand."

"I don't think the problem is that I don't get it. I think the problem is that you don't want to face the truth."

"If I equated sex with love, how do you explain all of the other guys I've been with? The one-nighters and the flings? I knew they didn't love me."

"But they didn't reject you. They wanted you, and that validated you. At the time, that was enough. The added benefit was that you didn't get close enough to them to care if you never saw them again. You didn't have to experience the pain of loss. The pain that you have carried from losing your father to losing Roland to now fearing that you're going to lose this new relationship if you don't do something differently."

"What does that have to do with Mandrel not wanting to sleep with me?"

"He didn't give you the validation you needed, which for you is accomplished through sex. If you didn't get that validation from him, that means you got it somewhere else, am I right?"

Amari dropped her head. Dr. Nelson was right, and Amari realized that she was far more screwed up than she ever thought possible.

Fifteen Months Earlier

Amari was mentally drafting her next article in her head as she sifted through the clothing racks at Lennox Mall. For her, nothing cured writer's block quite as effectively as retail therapy. She noticed years ago that the more she shopped, the more creative she became, mostly because now there would be the added pressure to earn enough money to pay off her newly acquired purchases. If the new balance on her credit card was any indication, she's be turning out Pulitzer Prize–winning articles in no time. She was eyeing a new one-shoulder jumpsuit when she spotted a familiar face a few feet away.

The long, thin legs and surgically enhanced features were unmistakable. "Toi?"

Toi Timley was one of the few women whose appetite for fun rivaled Amari's, so their paths frequently crossed on the social scene. Toi was pretty, fun, and a constant flurry of excitement who always managed to get invited to the best parties and rarely managed to hold down a steady job.

Toi whipped her head around to see who'd called her. "Amari, is that you?" Toi shrieked and came rushing toward Amari in a low` plunging dress. As soon as Toi reached her, she pulled Amari into a warm embrace. "How have you been?"

"I'm great, staying busy."

"I'll say! I haven't seen you around in forever. I was looking for you at Diddy's party last week."

"I've scaled way back on my club appearances. I just don't have time like I used to. What about you? What's new in your life?"

Toi flipped her blond-streaked extensions over her shoulders. "You know me: shopping, partying, and turnin' up!" she added with a laugh. "I had to pick up some last-minute items before we sail out. I see you're doing the same thing."

"Great minds think alike," quoted Amari, eyeing the designer-labeled shopping bags that Toi was hauling. "I must say, though, your thoughts look a little bigger and more expensive than mine. Did you buy out the store?"

"Well, Julian told me to get whatever I needed for the cruise. I decided that I needed a new Caribbean wardrobe."

Amari was confused. "Who's Julian?"

"He's my new boyfriend."

Amari knew "boyfriend" was most likely a euphemism for "sponsor."

"I thought you were seeing some guy named Thomas."

"Yeah, last month! New month, new man. Most importantly, new bankroll. Julian's a pro ball player." Amari wasn't surprised. Girls like Toi never had a problem finding men gullible enough to subsidize their opulent lifestyles.

Toi squealed. "I can't wait for this trip, can you? I'm so ready to get out of the city and this cold weather and out on a boat to kick back and enjoy life."

"Oh, you're going on vacay for the holidays?"

Toi checked her cell phone. "Yeah, aren't you?"

"Hopefully one day when I have the time. The closest I get to vacation these days is in my dreams. I'll be lucky to have Christmas off."

"No, I'm talking about the birthday bash, but I guess that's still considered as work for you, huh?" She saw the look of bewilderment register on Amari's face. "Amari, don't tell me you're not going with us on the cruise?"

"What cruise?"

"What cruise?" scoffed Toi. "The big birthday cruise for Jamal Warner, of course. His birthday is on the twenty-seventh, so we're spending Christmas and New Year's in the Caribbean."

"Oh, that." Amari didn't have a clue what Toi was talking about. She hadn't heard from Jamal since he left her in the Upper Room. Since she was now spending more time at church and with Mandrel than on the entertainment scene, she was officially out of Atlanta's social loop. It was the equivalent to being the only girl at prom with no date.

"I absolutely cannot wait!" raved Toi. "Seven days on a private yacht, poppin' bottles, frolicking on the beach, bouncing from San Juan to Barbados to St. Lucia and Antigua, St. Maarten, and ending with a huge party in St. Thomas on New Year's Eve before we sail back."

Amari sighed, visualizing herself splashing on the beach with a drink in one hand and a hot guy in the other. "Yeah, I have to admit, it sounds like exactly what I need right now."

"All right, then it's settled. The only thing you have to do is grab your passport and a bikini and get on the boat! I know you're busy, but you have to come, Amari. Jamal is your boy, right? Everybody who's anybody is going to be there. The party boat won't be the same without you."

"I love Jamal, but we have a lot going on at the magazine these days. If it were only a weekend, maybe, but don't think I could squeeze in seven whole days of vacation right now." That much was true, but Amari wasn't about to let on to Toi that the real reason she wasn't going was because she hadn't been invited to the celebration.

"Aw, come on, Amari. You know what they say about all work and no play."

"I work hard, but I do manage to get some play in every now and then."

"I bet you do!" she hedged. "You know I know how you get down, Miss Christopher. Shoot, I've even been down with you a few times. So which of the As are you into these days: athletes, actors, or artists?"

Amari shook her head, feigning modesty. "I don't kiss and tell."

"Please, that's exactly what you do! Most people keep their skeletons in the closet, but you don't mind putting yours right on Front Street! So who is he? Or rather, who are they? I know you like to keep a few riding the bench."

"Yes, I'm seeing someone new," confessed Amari. "He's a very special guy. And for the record, I'm a one-man woman these days."

"Oh." Toi seemed surprised. "Good for you, girl! Is he in the entertainment industry? Oh, wait, is it that rapper Static? I think I've seen the two of you together a couple of times."

"No, the thing with Static was nothing serious. We were just kickin' it, but what I have with the new guy might actually have legs."

Toi's curiosity was piqued. "Really? So who is he? A singer, rapper, music exec?"

"Um, none of those. He's a regular Joe. He isn't a part of the entertainment industry," replied Amari, reluctant to reveal more out of embarrassment. Toi was dating a real game-changer. Amari was dating the man who made sure game-changers had a safe ride home.

Toi was taken aback. "This is new. I've never known you to go for the corporate type, but, hey, if he has a private plane, a few vacay homes, and a well-stocked bank account, who cares if his job calls for a white collar, right? So is he Fortune 500 or entrepreneur?"

"He has his own business," replied Amari, wishing Toi would end the inquisition. There was no way to make cab driving sound glamorous.

"Okay, what does he do?"

"Actually, he's a driver."

Toi's mouth dropped open. "You don't mean like a chauffeur, do you?"

"He's a, um, cab driver."

Toi broke into laughter. "That's funny! You had me going for a second. What does he do for real?"

Toi's laughter, which ordinarily would have resulted in a verbal sparring match, made Amari feel more like a social charity case. "It wasn't a joke. He's a cab driver and owns a couple cabs here in Atlanta."

"Oh. Sorry." Toi composed herself. "At least it's an honest living. Everybody needs a designated driver every now and then. Lord knows I've had to call on a few, but how in the world did you end up dating one?"

"Well, initially, we met at church—"

"You mean the Tabernacle?" she asked, referencing the popular Atlanta venue.

"No, we met at an actual church. I called him for a ride home after a party one night, and we've been seeing each other ever since."

"That's nice, I suppose," said Toi, as lackluster as a pile of dirt. "I'm not trying to be offensive, but a cab driver, honey? I've seen you running around here with ballers of every tax bracket, so what's going on here?"

Amari threw her shoulders back, momentarily regaining her sense of confidence. "Maybe I'm looking for more than just a baller these days. It's called growth."

Toi wasn't quite convinced. "Amari, what are you going to do with some cab driver? You're an It Girl! You know all the power players. You can get any man you want."

Amari challenged her. "What makes you think I don't have the man I want?"

Toi touched Amari on the arm. "The nobility factor is honorable, I'll give you that; but can he provide the kind of lifestyle that you've grown accustomed to? Would he even be comfortable rollin' with your crowd?"

"You know I've never needed a man to pay my way, and the party scene has gotten kind of old for me. It was time to make a change."

Toi lightened the mood again. "The only change you need to be worried about is how many dress changes you're going to make on this cruise! Do you know how long it's been since we hung out? I can't even remember the last time we linked up!" A flash of memory came to her. "Wait, I remember now. It was during All-Star weekend in Miami, you remember that? We had so much fun that weekend!"

"It was a blast," recollected Amari. "I danced the heels off my shoes that night."

"You sure did! But that's how we met Jonathan and Jeremy. I know there's no way you could've forgotten those gorgeous twins we met at the club that night."

Amari couldn't help smiling as she reminisced. "No, I have very fond, vivid memories of that weekend."

"I think we partied for forty-eight hours straight! And when we weren't partying on South Beach, we had our own private party with the twins. Good Lord, they were fine!" exclaimed Toi, lost in her own thoughts. She exhaled. "We live a fabulous life, Amari. People post the kind of stuff on the Internet trying to pretend that they do, but we actually live it! I can't believe you want to give it up."

"I didn't say I wanted to give it up, but I think you can have more than one version of a fabulous life."

"Okay, while you are ordering chicken fingers at Applebee's in your version, we'll be nibbling on fresh lobsters and sipping rosé in ours."

Amari laughed a little. "I'll survive."

Toi was blown away. "Wow, this cab driver of yours must really be special."

Amari nodded. "He is."

"Must be nice," muttered Toi, now the one who was envious.

"It is," confirmed Amari. "Look, I've got to dash, but it was good seeing you again."

"You, too." Toi gave Amari a quick squeeze. "Let's have drinks when I get back."

"Sure. Then you can show me all of your wonderful selfies and tell me about all the fun I missed."

"There's still time, you know. You don't have to miss anything."

"Nah, I think that ship may have sailed for me, literally and figuratively."

"To each his own, I guess. Look, if you and your cab driver are happy, then by all means, go be happy."

As Amari watched Toi traipse down the aisle with bags and excitement in tow, she questioned if carefree days of yachts and decadence were merely a passing image in her life's rearview mirror. Seeing Toi was bittersweet. She was a living relic from her old life and a reminder of both the fun she used to have and how shallow her existence had been. By no means did she desire Toi's life. As best as anyone could tell, Toi was a seasonal stripper who was one baller away from financial ruin, but she was living her life on her own terms and having a blast while doing so. For Amari, that kind of existence was as repelling as it was appealing.

She genuinely cared for Mandrel. He made her want to be a better person, and his presence in her life was the reason she'd been making better choices lately, but there was still part of her who longed to be herself again. It was in those times that she debated whether holding on to Mandrel meant losing a part of Amari, and whether he was worth it.

Chapter 16

Amari still wasn't used to spending Wednesday afternoons in Bible study. It was a mere month ago that her hump days were devoted to dining at her favorite gastropub, where she could get three oysters and a cocktail for ten dollars on Wednesdays. But she knew if she was serious about her relationship with Mandrel, certain concessions had to be made. Giving up "oysters and cocktails" night was one of them.

While she was willing to give up her favorite Wednesday pastime, Amari was not as relenting with her wardrobe. She sauntered into Bible study in a daring draped surplice top and fitted pencil skirt over spiked stilettos that she knew many would take offense to; she just didn't care. With a bit of luck, Mandrel either wouldn't mind or wouldn't notice.

Amari took a seat next to Mandrel, which also meant she had the misfortune of being seated in front of the Melton sisters. The two aging women were every bit as ornery and bitter as their perpetually sour expressions denoted.

"I don't know why you like to get here so early," whined Amari. "Bible study doesn't even start for another fifteen minutes."

"Did you ever consider that I might want to spend a few extra minutes with my favorite girl?" asked Mandrel. "I know that you're a strong supporter of CP time, so I really appreciate you coming early because I asked you to."

She pretended to be peeved. "Yeah, consider yourself lucky!"

Mandrel kissed her hand. "I look at you, and I can't help but consider myself blessed and highly favored."

The oldest of the Melton sisters, Brenda, grunted as she witnessed the tender moment between Amari and Mandrel. "Have you seen what kind of mess has been coming up in here lately? I know the Word says to go into all the world and preach the gospel to every creature, but that doesn't mean we have to go dragging any and everything off the street!"

Amari silently fumed. She knew the comment was directed at her, but she refused to give in to the temptation to turn around and cuss Brenda out.

Her sister Beverly moaned and nodded in agreement. "Well, you know everybody ain't saved. Even for the ones who are, salvation can't buy class."

"God knows that's the truth!" exclaimed Brenda.

Mandrel took note of the fire brewing in Amari's eyes. "You all right, babe?"

Amari tapped her foot and sucked her teeth. "Do you hear those two cows back there yapping? I know they're talking about me. They're too coward to say it to my face though."

Mandrel patted her hand with affection. "Don't worry about them. Focus on why we're here. Focus on the Word."

"I just hate to see loose women coming in the church corrupting good Christian men," replied Brenda, loud enough for Amari to overhear. "Meanwhile, a virtuous woman like my Jasmine can't find a decent man because the tramps got all of 'em!"

"Honey, ain't no use in complaining about it. These men want what they want, even if all they want is the low-hanging fruit. It's too much effort to reach for something higher."

Beverly nodded. "Ain't that the truth! The way some of these women carry themselves and come in here looking, you don't know whether to pray for 'em or pay for 'em!"

Amari turned around caught sight of Brenda's disapproving gaze. "Who is this heifer looking at?" she asked in a raised voice, giving the woman the once-over.

"Shh!" Mandrel pulled her closer to him. "Amari, this isn't the time or the place."

"Oh, but Bible study is the time and place for these old hags to keep talkin' slick behind my back?" Amari faced the two sisters head-on. "If there is something you want to say to me, be a woman about it and say it to my face."

"I beg your pardon?" asked Brenda.

"Lady, you heard me!" spat Amari.

"Brenda, just let it go," pleaded Beverly. "She's probably got a knife or some other concealed weapon."

"You slice and dice people up with your words and little rude comments, but you're worried about me having a weapon?" Amari asked incredulously. "Your tongue is the most lethal thing in this church!"

Mandrel stood up. "Mari, let's just so sit somewhere else."

"Yes, take her on out of here before I lose my religion!"

Amari snatched up her belongings. "You lost that a long time ago."

Mandrel grabbed her hand and began pulling her away.

"Don't start with me, li'l sister!" Brenda called after her. "Don't start nothing you can't finish. I know too much about you."

Amari broke away from him. "Lady, I will drag you all up and down this church. Say something else!" Amari dared her.

"Who in the world let this inbred street trash in here?" shrilled Beverly.

Amari's demeanor immediately morphed; her eyes narrowed into icy slits. "What did you just call me?"

"Baby, let's go!" whispered Mandrel.

"You heard exactly what I called you," Beverly pointed a finger at Amari. "I called you exactly what you are: inbred street trash that's done bedded everything from Duluth to Dodge City!"

"Inbred street trash?" Amari yanked off her earrings and kicked off her heels. Being called a whore didn't bother her, but an attack on her parentage struck a sensitive nerve. "Oh, I'm about to take it to the streets when I snatch you and that dusty wig up out of here!" Amari lunged forward, but was stopped by Mandrel.

The church security team quickly intervened and dragged Amari out.

"Brother Mandrel, I hope you know you can do a lot better than the likes of her!" stated Brenda as Mandrel followed behind Amari. "Look at her, acting just like a wild animal!"

The pastor, overseeing the commotion, stood up and quickly exited. He met with the security team outside.

"Get your hands off of me!" said Amari, slinging away from them.

Mandrel rushed to her side. "Amari, you all right?" he asked, concerned.

"People come here to serve and worship the Lord, not be spectators in an alley fight. We're going to have to ask you to leave, ma'am," instructed one of the security team members.

"Why y'all didn't ask them to leave?" decried Amari. "They started it, talking about me like I wasn't good enough to be in this ol' bougie church. Church is supposed to be for everybody."

"Babe, let's just go," suggested Mandrel.

The pastor stepped forward and extended his hand. "Hello, sister. My name is Joshua Campbell. I'm the senior pastor here at Greater Hope International."

"Dang, I must be in trouble if they sent you to personally escort me off the premises!" Amari slung her Celine bag over her shoulder. "Don't worry. I'm leaving. You don't ever have to worry about seeing me around here ever again."

"Nobody is making you leave, sister. You're very welcome to stay. You seem to be in a lot of pain. Perhaps I'll minister a Word today that'll comfort you and show you the goodness of our Lord and Savior Jesus Christ."

"Yeah, maybe some of that 'goodness' ought to rub off on your church members in there!" charged Amari.

"God is not through with you yet, sister. You're still valuable to God. As long as you have breath, there's still a purpose for you. I'm here as well as the church family to walk with you through this difficult time alone. If you need someone to talk to, let us know and we'll make arrangements for that. He told us there would be trials and tribulations, but through Him, we can overcome all of them."

Mandrel stepped forward. "I'll take care of it from here, Pastor. Thank you."

The pastor was surprised. "Is this your lady friend?"

Mandrel seemed embarrassed. "Yes, she is, sir."

The pastor nodded and placed a hand on Mandrel's shoulder before exiting. "We'll talk, brother."

"Great," grumbled Amari. Mandrel stared at her and shook his head. "What?"

"Why did you have to say anything to those women?" he asked her.

"Me?" yelped Amari. "Who do you think started the whole thing?"

"They didn't say anything to you. You shouldn't have said anything to them."

"Oh, it's my fault that your raggedy church members called me all kinds of whores, hit a low blow about my family, and said I wasn't good enough for you?" she asked with bitter sarcasm.

"I just wish you hadn't caused a scene, that's all. It was embarrassing. You're a grown woman."

"Those women in there are at least twice my age and are so-called Christians. I'm a heathen. I have an excuse. They don't!"

"It was embarrassing for everyone involved, including me." Mandrel released an exasperated sigh. "I don't want to do this here. Let's go."

"No, I'll go. You stay. Stay and find you a nice, quiet Christian girl like Jasmine."

"Please, Jasmine doesn't want me. Jasmine doesn't want any man. Her mother just refuses to admit that her daughter is a lesbian. I told you, you're the one I want. This isn't the end of the world. I just think we should leave."

"I should be the one to leave. This is your church, your home. You belong here, and I think it's become painfully obvious that I don't."

Later that evening, Amari, dressed to the nines in a shimmery black backless hourglass dress and strappy heels, waltzed into Indulgence, garnering all of the attention that she had hoped the revealing outfit would attract. She'd had enough of long skirts and modest dresses, especially after coming to the realization that she would never be the virtuous woman Mandrel wanted, so why bother trying?

She was at the ritzy nightclub to listen and review an artist who was on the verge of being a breakout star on the music scene. Her stamp of approval could be the very thing that could catapult Apollo Rison to being a household name as swiftly as her disapproval could land his album squarely in the recycling bin.

She found her reserved seat in the VIP section. Apollo had already launched into his breakout hit, "Little Things," and was crooning seductively into the microphone:

> *All I want is a little bit of time, so we can last forever*
> *All I want is a little smile, so I can live in absolute bliss*
> *All I want is a little chuckle, so that our lives are filled with laughter*
> *All I want is to love you today, consumed by the memory of your kiss*

The hordes of women in the crowd happily consumed the lines he was feeding him. He tossed his thick locs back for affectation, and the ladies erupted in howls and sophomoric screams. Not Amari, though. She listened intently, noting how he connected with the crowd. She made notes as he altered seamlessly between singing and rapping, doing one as fluently as the other. She was impressed.

He launched into a pitch-perfect rendition of Luther Vandross's "Wait for Love" to the delight of his female audience, who fawned and gushed over every note.

"How many of y'all are going to make me wait for love?" he asked, the words sensuously sliding off his tongue. "How many ladies are ready to make some love tonight? Don't make me wait, baby."

After completing the thirty minutes set with his band, Apollo bid the crowd good night and disappeared backstage.

Amari flashed her press pass to gain access to Apollo in the backstage area. He was enclosed by his media and street teams. As she waited a few feet away for them to clear out, she snared Apollo's attention.

"Hey, excuse me, do I know you from somewhere?" he asked loud enough for Amari to hear. "I know that it sounds like a line, but I'm serious. You look very familiar."

She smiled sheepishly. "We have met before, sort of. I've seen you at a few industry events." She extended her hand to him. "I'm Amari Christopher. I'm an editor for *Rhythm Nation*."

He shook her hand. "*Rhythm Nation,* huh? That's the magazine that goes around scouting the next big thing or revealing the new hot girl, right?"

She nodded. "I take it you've heard of us."

"Yeah, who hasn't?" He took a swig of his bottled water without taking his eyes off of her. "So are you here to give a scathing review or crown me as the new prince of the music world?" he joked.

"I guess you'll have to pick up the next issue to find out, won't you? Do you have a few minutes to spare for a brief interview?"

He turned to his manager. "Do I?"

"For this pretty lady, you better make time!" exclaimed the manager.

Apollo laughed and addressed his entourage. "Give us a few minutes, will ya?"

Within seconds, his team cleared out, leaving Amari alone with Apollo.

Amari sat down across from him and pulled out her iPad for taking notes. "Thank you for agreeing to do the interview. Your name has been buzzing in the streets for a while now. After witnessing that killer performance, I see why."

"Thanks. I'm glad you enjoyed the show."

"Well, you certainly have a way with your female fans. You could have had your pick of the women in the crowd tonight."

"Is that right?" He locked eyes with her. "Any woman I want, huh?"

Amari briefly fell prey to his bedroom eyes before returning to work mode. "I noticed that you rap just as much as you sing. What do you consider yourself to be: a rapper or a singer?"

He chuckled. "I'm an artist, which means I can be anything at any time. I don't like to confine myself to one box or another."

"I'm sure you don't, but I have to describe you as something."

"Describe me as an artist whose music is hip-hop within the subgenre of soul and consciousness with R and B elements."

"I've never gotten a quote like that before." Amari made a note of his description. "Clearly, you're in a class of your own."

"In every way," he confirmed.

"You call yourself Double A, correct?"

"Yes."

"Why? What's the meaning behind the moniker?"

"Literally, it stands for Apollo Anthony Rison. Musically, it stands for Above Average," revealed Apollo. "I want everything I do to exceed expectations."

"I have to admit you defied my expectations here tonight. Like most people, I've heard you on the radio, but I thought you were more of the same: a cookie-cutter studio artist selling sex instead of quality music. I was very pleased to be proven wrong."

"Thank you. I'm glad that you took notice."

"Indeed. They're calling you the South's answer to hip-hip artist Drake. How do you feel about that comparison?"

"We're always waiting for the next big artist who'll change the game," he said, absently scrolling through his cell phone. "No disrespect to my contemporaries, but I like to think that I stand alone in this game. I'm determined to be the change that the music industry has been waiting for. My goal is to inspire and evoke change in music and society."

She raised her brow. "That's a pretty lofty goal."

"To whom much is given, much is required; at least that's what my dad used to preach to us. I want to do more than simply score top-ten singles and make hit albums."

Amari transcribed what he said on to her device. "So what do you think sets you apart from other artists?"

"Well, unlike a lot of my peers, I don't use any profanity or derogatory terms in my lyrics. I create music to be as universal as possible. I want kids and adults to be able to listen to it. I make music everybody can like. I want to bring things that won't turn anybody off. That's why it's important to me to write and produce my own music. It's a process that I don't take lightly. Harmonies and melodies are all important to me. I know the hip-hop genre itself was built upon sampling, but I don't do that. It's not my calling card as an artist. It's another aspect that makes me different and sets me apart."

"That's admirable. I know you said you don't try to emulate anyone in particular, but I'm sure there are some artists who inspire and influence you. Who are they?"

"I guess as a rapper, I'm supposed to say Tupac, Notorious B.I.G., or Jay-Z, but I'm more inspired by artists like John Legend, Michael Jackson, Prince, Alicia Keys, and the soul acts of the 1950s and '70s. The only rapper I make an exception for is Kanye West."

"Why is that?"

"I admire Kanye's approach to his craft," expounded Apollo. "He's not afraid to push the envelope, be innovative, step outside the box, and do things he'll be scrutinized for. He makes the music he wants to make and is an awesome producer and lyricist."

"So then you liken yourself more to being the next Kanye as opposed to Drake?" surmised Amari both verbally and in writing.

"No, I'm going to be the next, the first, and the last Apollo Rison, Double A. I made a commitment to be substantial in music. I don't want to make songs just to make them. Everything should have a purpose. I concentrate on the lyrics and the musicianship that carries the lyrics."

"You don't really seem satisfied with the state of hip-hop and music today. Is that the case?"

"Hip-hop is a genre that's ever changing and always evolving because it's driven by youth. Youth are becoming more liberal and more things are now accepted. I don't like the direction hip-hop is headed, but it's necessary for the genre to grow."

She rolled her eyes as she scribed his quote on her iPad.

Apollo squinted his eyes. "What's that?"

"What's what?" she asked without looking up.

"That look. What's that about?"

"Nothing. You just seem a little arrogant, especially for someone who doesn't have an album out yet."

"Maybe what you think is being arrogant or cocky is really just me being confident in myself and my music."

She cracked a smile. "Is that what it is?"

"Sure. I'm that way when it comes to everything: being a musician, a writer, even being a lover."

Her interest was stirred. "So you're a passionate lover, are you?"

His eyes rode up and down her frame. "Very."

Amari crossed her legs. "I bet you leave a trail of tears and broken hearts wherever you go."

"No. I'm always honest with the women I deal with. I don't make promises or commitments I can't keep, and they respect that."

"On that note, let's talk about your love life."

"Why?" he asked. "What does that have to do with the music?"

"I'm sure your past relationships inspire some of your lyrics, for one. Secondly, a good portion of our reader demographic is female. They're as interested in your personal life as they are your professional one."

"My first and only love is the music. Yes, I have what I like to call 'women of interest,' but women tend to be beautiful, alluring distractions. Relationships require a lot of nurturing and attention, and I can't afford to get distracted right now."

"So all work and no play?"

He reclined back in his chair. "I never said that. I said no relationships."

"Ahhh! You like the relations part and let the ship part sail away," she inferred.

"I don't see the harm in that. No one is bound to the other. No one gets hurts, and everyone walks away with a beautiful experience."

Amari raised her head. "I didn't say anything was wrong with it."

"But not your cup of tea, right?"

"I didn't say that either," she replied with a furtive glance.

Apollo leaned forward. "What are you saying?"

"I thought I was the one asking the questions."

"You were. Times have changed."

She scoffed. "When did that happen?" She wasn't used to dealing with an artist who could match wits with her, especially one so young.

"When I decided to take control of the conversation." He lifted her electronic pad from her hands. "Now tell me about *your* love life."

"Why do you want to know anything about me?"

"Because I think you're exquisite."

She roared with laughter. "Oh, no! I'm not one of those teenage groupies hanging on to your every word. I'm a grown woman. You can't run game on me."

"My publicist told me you might be stopping by tonight. You don't think I did my research before this interview? I know exactly who you are and how you roll."

"Do you now?" She waited before going on, not quite sure what to make of his comment. "Please enlighten me on what you think you know."

He offered an enigmatic simper. "Suffice it to say, I think we're a lot alike. We share the same philosophy on love and relationships."

Amari asked, "How do you figure that?"

"Come on now, Amari. It's a small world, and Atlanta is even smaller. People in this industry talk. You know that."

"And just what are they saying about me?"

"They say you get around."

She rolled her eyes and snatched her iPad back from him. "When you've been in this business a little longer, you'll realize that you can't believe everything you hear."

"You can when you have enough people saying the same thing. Don't worry; I'm not judging you. I think you're living your life on your own terms. That's awesome. Trust me, more people wish they had the nerve to do it."

"I'm not ashamed of anything I've done or who I am," touted Amari.

"What's there to be ashamed of? You're a successful, beautiful woman who isn't afraid to go after what she wants, be it in an exclusive interview or a clandestine rendezvous."

"True, but why bring that up now? What does that have to do with you?"

"I saw the way you were checking me out." He scooted his chair closer to her. "I was checking you out too."

"I scope out everyone before an interview," she replied dismissively. She was determined not to give him the pleasure of thinking that he'd riled any particular interest in her although he had garnered more interest than she was willing to acknowledge.

He shook his head and grinned. "Are we seriously gonna play this game, Amari? Just admit that you're fascinated."

"There's that cockiness again," mumbled Amari.

"I told you; it's confidence," he corrected her.

"Whatever it is, I'm not interested."

He smirked. "You were interested from the moment you saw me up on that stage, admit it. It's cool. We're all grown here."

She smirked, taking stock of his youthful appearance. "Are we?"

"I'm twenty-six, not sixteen."

"And I'm thirty-seven. From where I sit, twenty-six is no different from being sixteen."

"Well, I guess we could debate it, but why do that when I can just show and prove?"

She frowned. "Show me what? And what are you hoping to prove?"

His tongue rolled over his lips. "I have a room at the W. Why don't we start there?"

Amari cackled, both amused and slightly offended. "Boy, you don't know who you're dealing with!"

"Neither do you." He reached into his pocket for his wallet. He pulled out his room card and dangled it in front of her. "So what's up?"

Amari refrained from answering the question and toyed with her iPad. There was no way she was going back to the hotel with him. He represented the life she was trying to get away from. She had Mandrel now; and she couldn't jeopardize that relationship for a quickie. If only Apollo hadn't been so cute or Mandrel so celibate . . .

"You know you want to," he taunted her. "We can go back to my room, and you can show me what's under that sexy dress. I'll make it worth your while. You can believe that!"

"We should not be having this conversation," insisted Amari, more to herself than Apollo.

He braided his hand into hers. "Maybe not, but I haven't heard you say no yet."

"Trust me, I'm thinking it!"

"But you haven't said it," he pointed out, then lightly placed his lips on hers. "Just tell me to stop." He kissed her again.

Amari wondered why her mouth couldn't form that simple word and why, instead, it was kissing another man. It had been so long since she'd felt the weight and the kiss of a man on her, and it was self-affirming to have a man pursue rather than reject her. Amari didn't realize how much she'd missed it until it was right there in front of her.

Apollo stood up and offered his hand. "You coming or nah?"

Amari stared into his open, waiting palm. She was at a precipice. Was she going to side with the woman Mandrel had tried to create or the woman she knew herself to be? Would God be disappointed or was He all-knowing and foresaw this happening anyway? If that was the case, she wondered what would be the point in denying herself this much-needed escape from abstinence. If He was a forgiving God, then she'd be absolved of her sins. If He wasn't, she was bound to screw up eventually if she kept living, so why not let it be now?

Amari rose and enveloped his extended hand. Who would it hurt? Apollo was just as discreet as she was, and he and Mandrel didn't run in the same circles. She could do it, and her boyfriend would never even know. No one would. She theorized that, like lying, it was only relevant if she got caught, and she had no intentions of doing that.

An hour later, she was naked and tangled up in the sheets with Apollo in his hotel room. As Apollo ravished her body, she felt alive and sexy again. This was the Amari she knew herself to be: passionate, carefree, and wild. This was the feeling she'd craved since hooking up with Mandrel, and the one he'd been unwilling or unable to provide. She had no idea how long it would last, but she was bound and determined to drink in every second of it.

Chapter 17

"So why did do you do it?" interrogated Dr. Nelson after hearing about Amari's tryst with Apollo.

"Why did I cheat on Mandrel?" asked Amari. "I mean, there's no real mystery here. The guy was available and I was horny."

"I think we both know that it's not that cut and dried. Go back to the moment when you made the conscious decision to sleep with Apollo. What was going through your head? What were you thinking?"

"I don't know," she replied nonchalantly.

"Yes, you do," Dr. Nelson challenged her. "Think. Concentrate."

Amari tried to weasel out of providing a forthright answer. "I already told you. He was hot, and I just wanted to get laid."

"I think it goes deeper than that. Right before that happened, you had the altercation with the women at church. You said that whole ordeal made you feel like you didn't belong there. You were right back to feeling like you weren't good enough. Do you think that factored into your decision to bed Apollo?"

"I don't think one had anything to do with the other," deduced Amari.

"Are you sure?" Dr. Nelson prodded. "You said at the time you were happy and had started going to church. You were growing spiritually. You also had this wonderful man who adored you and was committed and faithful to you, but he warned you that infidelity wouldn't be tolerated. I don't think you'd simply give all that up for the sake of hormones and a one-night stand."

Amari threw up her hands, riled. "I already told you that I screw up for absolutely no reason. It's what I do, but it's also what I'm trying to stop doing. That's the reason I'm here."

"I hear you, but we need to get to the heart of the matter and break into that layer of subconscious thought and reason. Very few things are done without there being some rationale for it, even if the reason is one you're not consciously aware of."

"I don't think it's that deep, Doc. I think I'm just one of those people who can have a good thing going and just screws it up because I can."

Dr. Nelson backpedaled. "Go back to what you just said; so you knew what you were doing was wrong?"

"Of course I did."

"And you knew Mandrel would be hurt by your actions."

"I knew he would if he found out, but I never intended for him to find out."

"And you also knew it would probably cost you your relationship too, right?"

"It was only a matter of time before that happened. Men like Mandrel don't stay with women like me. I was only speeding up the inevitable."

"Go back to what you just said," instructed Dr. Nelson.

"Which part?"

"You said you were speeding up the inevitable, which would be the demise of your relationship. You expect your relationships to fail. We need to find out why."

"Easy: all of my relationships have been failures. The proof is in the pudding."

"Yes, but do the relationships fail because they're just doomed or do they fail because you consciously or unconsciously sabotage them?"

Amari owned up to her actions. "I guess in this case, it was sabotage."

"Even though Mandrel gave you no reason to feel like the relationship was headed for disaster."

"Every man in my life has turned out to be a huge disappointment. Why would I expect him to be any different?"

"Does that include your father?"

Amari was visibly frustrated. "Why do you keep trying to bring my parents back into this?"

"Because your father, whether he's there or not, teaches you what to expect out of men. He's not emotionally or physically available, or if he consistently lets you down, that's what you come to expect of all men."

Amari disputed her. "My father wanted to be there."

"But he wasn't."

"There were circumstances."

"Tell me, Amari, can you think of any circumstance that would keep you away from your child?"

Amari was quiet, thoughtful.

Dr. Nelson continued. "In my sessions with other people, I often see people making excuses for their fathers but seldom do they make excuses for their mothers' actions. You have to stop making excuses for him. He wasn't there because he chose not to be. The primary role of a father is to provide, nurture, and guide. Your father didn't do that, and it's affected you and the way you deal with men, relationships, and even your spirituality. I think you need to come to grips with that."

"How so?"

Dr. Nelson exhaled. "That's what we're about to discover."

Mandrel showed up at Amari's office with a blushing violet bouquet and an apology, neither of which she was particularly in the mood for a few hours after taking the walk of shame from Apollo's hotel suite during the wee hours of the morning. Too many emotions were infiltrating her psyche. She was still feeling the pangs of guilt for cheating on Mandrel along with the exhilaration that resulted from having great sex.

"This is a surprise," said Amari and invited him into her office.

"You know I don't usually drop by like this, but I didn't want to talk to you on the phone or wait until you got off work."

Amari detected the gravity in his voice. "Sounds serious."

"I wanted to come talk to you about what happened last night."

Her heart raced as she flashed back to her romp with Apollo. "What . . . what about it?" stammered Amari. Was it possible that Mandrel knew? If he did, how in the world would she explain ending up in Apollo's bed?

Mandrel extended the flowers to her. "I'm sorry. I shouldn't have let those women come for you like that at Bible study. I definitely should've stopped you from leaving. I was wrong."

She breathed a sigh of relief. She'd hoped Mandrel wouldn't notice that her hands were still shaking as she accepted the flowers. "Don't apologize; it's fine. I had to leave early anyway to attend a work function."

He sat down in a chair across from her desk. "How did it go?"

Amari pursed her lips together and nodded. "Great. Apollo, AKA Double A, shows a lot of potential as a promising young artist." She sat down at her desk, grateful for the forced space between them. She feared if they sat any closer, he might be able to detect that she'd spent the night with another man.

Mandrel was surprised. "For you to say that, he must be impressive. You always give these young cats a hard time."

"There's always an exception. He was magnificent. The best I've seen in a long time," she added, meaning it in every sense.

"I'm glad you enjoyed yourself. You must've gotten in pretty late last night. I called you on your cell. When I couldn't reach you, I tried the house phone. I think I gave up around midnight."

"You know how these events go. There's the performance and the interview, the after party," rattled off Amari. "Before you know it, it's three o'clock in the morning."

"Wow, you must be pretty tired."

"Worn out, actually."

"I bet I know what will help." Mandrel got up to give her an impromptu massage. "How's that?"

She thought about Apollo's hands caressing her body and stiffened as Mandrel touched her. "You don't have to do that. I'm fine." She wasn't quite ready to have his hands on her yet.

"Everything okay? You seem, I don't know, spaced out or something."

Amari squirmed out of his grasp. "I'm fine," she repeated. "I have a lot on my mind today."

"Oh, yeah? Like what?"

She busied herself with forms and press releases lying on her desk. "Nothing you'd find interesting, just boring work stuff."

Mandrel attempted to show her some affection again by running his hand through her curly mane. "Don't you know that there's absolutely nothing about you that can be defined as boring?"

Amari playfully swatted him away. "Humph! You'd be surprised."

Mandrel returned to his seat. "Hey, that's not another dig at your dull sex life, is it?"

"No, actually I'm okay with the situation now."

"Really?" he asked, pleased.

"Yes. I've accepted things the way they are, and I'm okay with it." She looked at Mandrel, unable to see anything other than Apollo's full lips and dreamy eyes. "I've been finding other ways to cope and contain my raging hormones."

"I'm almost afraid to ask what your coping mechanism is."

"It's nothing to get worked up over," she assured him. "It doesn't involve any of the Ds: no drugs, no drinking, no operating dangerous equipment."

He laughed. "As long as you have the Ps you'll be all right. That's prayer, patience, and perseverance."

She thought of Apollo again. "I'm sure I have all the Ps covered."

"Very good." He kissed her on the cheek. "And now that I know I'm out of the doghouse, I better get on back to work."

"Thanks for stopping by." She moved to walk him out.

"Dinner tonight?" he asked on the way out.

"Sure. Have a good day."

He pecked her on the lips. "You have an even better one, gorgeous."

Amari closed her eyes and pressed her body up against the door, crushed by mixed emotions. Mandrel was such a good man. She questioned how she could betray him the way she had with Apollo. She knew it was wrong.

Then she wondered how something so wrong could feel so good.

***

Armand took one look at his sister the moment she turned up at Mand Cave later that afternoon and announced, "The answer is no."

Amari stomped her foot. "I haven't even asked you anything yet."

He continued inspecting his stock of alcoholic beverages. "You will though. You always do."

"Why must you assume the worst? Did it ever occur to you that maybe I wanted to come by and support my brother's business? How do you know I'm not here to order a drink?" She sat down on a stool across from him.

"We don't open for another hour. Plus, I've known you since the womb, so I'm well aware of who I'm dealing with. Whether you want an alibi, bail money, a kidney, or a cup of sugar, the answer is still no!"

"Obviously, you've been sleeping alone lately," inferred Amari. "That would account for all of the pent-up aggression and general crankiness."

"It looks like I'll be sleeping alone for the foreseeable future too." He handed Amari a letter. "I found out that our final divorce hearing is in a few weeks. I thought we were making some headway, but according to Nia's attorney, I guess she's still hell-bent on getting this divorce."

Amari skimmed over the letter, then reached for her brother's hand to comfort him. "I'm so sorry to hear that. I know how much you wanted to put your family back together."

"It ain't over 'til it's over," said Armand. "Maybe there's still a chance for a miracle. Hey, look at you! You going to church and leading a life of celibacy is a miracle if I've ever seen one!"

Amari looked away and released a nervous laugh. She laid the court order down. "Yeah, who would've believed that?"

Armand picked up on her change in mood. "Okay, what did you do?" he asked with accusation.

She flinched and shrank back from him. "What are you talking about?"

"You looked away when I mentioned going to church and being celibate. You do that whenever you're lying."

"Boy, you're spending too much time by yourself. You're starting to imagine things," she replied, unconsciously avoiding eye contact with him.

"You did it again," observed Armand. "So you can confess now or I can read all about it in the court documents and newspaper when your crimes are made public. Which one will it be?"

She sucked her teeth and mumbled, "There's no crime against having fun."

Armand leaned back against the bar with his arms folded. "That depends on the kind of fun we're talking about."

She occupied herself with a nearby canister of drink stirrers. "The kind of fun that takes place in the Land of Too Much Information."

He groaned. "You finally succeeded in seducing him, huh?" Armand shook his head. "I told you to leave well enough alone. You should never try to come between a man and his relationship with God."

Amari huffed. "Will you relax? God and Mandrel are still down like four flats. I haven't touched him."

"Then what's this about?"

She didn't say anything. Instead, she arranged the stirrers into neat rows on the counter, knowing it was only a matter of time before Armand succeeded in pulling the truth of out her.

Armand looked down at the stirrers. "Is this supposed to be code for something? Mar, we're twins, but that doesn't mean we share the same brain, only DNA. I still need you to communicate in a way I can clearly perceive."

She drew in a deep breath and murmured, "It wasn't Mandrel."

"What?"

"Mandrel wasn't the one who I, you know, touched."

Armand cringed upon hearing that. "Are you kidding me?"

She rolled her eyes and emptied the stirrers from her hand and back into their container. "Give me a break, Armand. It was one night."

"How many nights do you think it took to cost me my marriage?" questioned Armand. "Why would you do something like that?"

"Because this is who I am," she explained calmly. "I'm not some chaste church mouse like Mandrel. I'm alive. I'm sexual. I have needs!"

"What about Mandrel? Did you factor in your relationship with him at all when you decided to explore these needs?"

Amari buckled under Armand's interrogation and her own guilty conscience. "Of course I did, but there's really no reason for him to find out, especially since it's not happening again."

"You can lie to me, but don't lie to yourself," he cautioned her.

Amari raised her voice. "It's not happening anymore! It was a one-time deal. Mandrel doesn't have to know, and nobody gets hurt."

"Surely by now you know that everything done in the dark eventually comes to light."

Amari cut him off. "You're not going to make me the bad guy in the situation," she told him.

"Are you deluded enough to think that you're the victim?"

"I *am* the victim!" she asserted. "I have tried to do everything Mandrel asked me to do. He wanted me to stop drinking and partying so hard, and I did that. He didn't like me wearing makeup; my makeup is gone! He wanted me to dress like I'm auditioning to be an extra on *Little House on the Prairie,* and I did that, too. What more can he ask of me?"

"I didn't think you were doing those things to please a man. I thought it was to please God and to make positive changes in your life."

"At first, I thought so too, but lately it's felt like I'm not being true to myself," she revealed.

"That's your old, sinful nature," rendered Armand, setting out a bowl of nuts and a stack of napkins. "It wants to do what feels good and comfortable. Its allegiance is still to the flesh. Once you accept Christ, you have to ignore the side of you that wants to go back to that way of life."

"But that's what feels right to me!" She considered Armand's assessment. "Maybe we have to accept the possibility that I may not be Christian material."

"Amari, that's nonsense. The Lord will accept you as you are, wherever you are, be it in church or crawling out of some fool's bed."

A scowl washed over her face. "Maybe God does, but Mandrel won't."

"He never told you that you couldn't be yourself around him, did he?"

"No, but when you get enough side-eyes and snide remarks, you get the hint."

"God doesn't want you doing outwardly things to please Him if it's not in your heart. I'm sure Mandrel doesn't either. It's not helping anyone for you to pretend to be someone you're not."

"It's not all pretend. Despite almost coming to blows with those two hags at Bible study last night, I've been enjoying church."

Armand stopped what he was doing to give Amari his full attention. "Yeah, I heard about that. I tried to call last night and ask you about it. Obviously, you were in no position to answer the phone," he cracked.

"I was in many positions, but, no, phone answering wasn't one of them."

Armand shook his head. "Throwing 'bows on two mothers in the sanctuary? What were you thinking?"

"I wasn't. I was reacting. That's what happened with Apollo last night. The opportunity presented itself, and I reacted. I went for it."

"Have you ever heard of a little thing called discipline or self-control?"

"I've heard of it. I just don't always employ it."

"You've made that apparent." Armand continued preparing the bar for customers. "Your actions have consequences, Mar. You probably won't get kicked out of the church for this, but I can't say the same for Mandrel not kicking you to the curb if he finds out about your excursion to the dark side."

"Armand, let's not make this a bigger issue than what it is. It was one night."

"Doesn't even a tiny part of you think you need to tell Mandrel about it?"

She shrugged. "No. Why should I and mess up a good thing? Besides, Valentine's Day is right around the corner. Who wants to be dumped this close to the most romantic day of the year?"

"Amari, the man has a right to know! At least give him the right to choose whether he wants to be with you based on the facts."

"He would choose to walk away if he knew. He's already told me that."

"Can you blame him?"

"Can you blame Nia?" she hurled back.

"No, I can't. I fouled up, and I made it worse by not telling her. She had to find out the worst way possible, which was directly from the sidepiece. You don't want that to happen with Mandrel."

Amari shook her head and tossed back a handful of nuts. "Apollo isn't like that. He wouldn't say anything."

"Secrets usually have a way of coming out when you least expect it. We're living proof of that."

"Don't bring our parentage into this. I got enough of that last night with those biddies. How did those nosey broads even know about that anyway?"

"Again, I say, secrets always have a way of coming out."

Chapter 18

It was around eight o'clock that same evening during dinner with Mandrel that Amari felt compelled to do something big, some sort of gesture, to atone for her night of passion with Apollo.

"I think I'm ready," she told Mandrel as they sat down to her marble-top high bar to eat the Chinese takeout he'd brought to her apartment for dinner.

"Okay, I wanted to say grace first, but you're free to dig in after that."

"You got this from that suspect restaurant down the street, so we're definitely gonna pray first!" insisted Amari. "But I wasn't talking about food."

"Oh?" Mandrel outstretched his arm to grab a napkin from the center of the table. "What's up? What's on your mind?'

Amari exhaled. "I'm ready to take the next step in my spiritual journey," she announced, smiling broadly. "I want to get saved."

He reached over and hugged her. "Amari, that's wonderful! What brought this on?"

"It was just time," she replied. She figured explaining it that way was more appropriate than, "I slept with a twenty-six-year-old behind your back, and I don't want to go to hell for it!"

Mandrel returned to his seated position adjacent from her. "Are you planning to accept the invitation at church Sunday?"

"Actually, I was sort of hoping to do it sooner than that and more low-key."

He was a bit leery. "How soon and how low-key?"

"Right now," she answered. "Can you do it? Can you lead me to salvation?"

Mandrel was caught off-guard, not sure what to make of her request or the timing of it. "Sure, I can if that's what you want."

She nodded. "That's what I want."

"All right. Do you have a Bible around here?"

Amari quickly scanned the dining cove as if expecting a Bible to miraculously surface. "Um, no," she replied, slightly embarrassed. "I used to have one of those little red ones they pass out for free, but it's been a minute since I've seen it."

"That's okay. I can pull it up." Mandrel pulled out his phone from his pocket. "Thank God for technology, right?" He looked Amari in the eyes. "You ready?"

She swallowed hard. "I think so."

"All right, let's do this!" He pushed the takeout boxes aside and began chartering down Roman's Road to salvation. He cleared his throat. "Romans 3:10 tells us that no one is good. 'As it is written, There is none righteous, no not one.' Do you know what that means?"

"Yes. It means nobody's perfect."

"That's right. All have sinned and come short of the glory of God. That can be found in Romans 3:23. See?" He showed the verse to Amari. "Do you know where sin comes from?"

"Satan, I guess."

"Kind of," stated Mandrel and began reading Romans 5:12. "Wherefore, as by one man sin entered into the world, and death by sin, and so death passed upon all men, for that all have sinned."

"The man was Adam in the Garden of Eden," replied Amari, happy to have retained even that bit of knowledge.

"Exactly. Since we all come from Adam, we have all been born into sin, and the wages of sin is death. That means we all have to die and those who aren't saved are destined to go to hell."

She wrinkled her nose. "That sucks."

"Yes, it does, but we don't have to worry about that because the gift of God is eternal life through Jesus Christ our Lord. Jesus died for our sins." He revealed Romans 5:8 to her. "But God commended His love toward us, in that, while we were yet sinners, Christ died for us."

"On the cross," added Amari.

He nodded and smiled. "That's right. His death and resurrection is our ticket into heaven."

"How so?"

Mandrel went to Romans 10:9–11. "That if thou shalt confess with thy mouth the Lord Jesus, and shalt believe in thine heart that God hath raised Him from the dead, thou shall be saved. For with the heart man believeth unto righteousness; and with the mouth confession is made unto salvation. For the scripture saith, whosoever believeth on Him shall not be ashamed." He went on to Romans 10:13. "For whosoever shall call upon the name of the Lord shall be saved."

Amari paused a minute, waiting for him to say more. "Is that it? All I have to do is call on the Lord's name? Do I need to memorize that scripture and recite it onsite when I get to the pearly gates?"

Mandrel laughed. "No, you just need to confess with your mouth and believe in your heart that Jesus died for your sins. Ask Him to be your Savior, to come into your heart and forgive you for your sins."

"I do believe that Jesus died for me," she affirmed, and prayed, "Lord, I need a Savior. Jesus, forgive me for my sins and come into my life and my heart."

Mandrel smiled. "Amen. Now, I'll see you in heaven." He kissed her hand. "Welcome to the Kingdom."

Amari waited for the rest, positive that a laundry list of do's and don'ts was sure to follow. "That's it?"

"That's it."

She was taken aback. "I've had a harder time getting into the club than I did getting into heaven!"

Mandrel slid the food boxes back to the placemats directly in front of them. "It was never meant to be hard. Salvation is easy and free."

"What now? Do I have to make a public announcement on social media or shout it from the rooftops?"

He headed her off. "Keep it simple for now. Join a church and keep reading your Bible. Lead someone else to Christ when you feel ready. I'm sure there are more than a few people in the entertainment industry who need Jesus!"

"I don't think heaven has room for all those hellions!" joked Amari.

"There's always room at the King's table."

Mandrel said a quick prayer to bless the food and to thank God for accepting Amari into the fold. "I'm very proud of you for taking this step tonight. You have no idea what this means to me personally."

"You said you couldn't get serious with a woman who wasn't saved."

He was alarmed. "I don't want that to be the reason why you did it, Amari."

"Oh, no, baby, I did it for me!" She fell into his arms, recalling that it wasn't that long ago that Apollo was holding her the same way. "I did it to save myself."

"Was that true?" asked Dr. Nelson. "Did you receive salvation to save yourself or to save your relationship?"

"It was both. No harm in killing two birds with one stone, right?"

"That was a big step you took," Dr. Nelson commended her. "What led you to make the decision to give your life over to God?"

"You mean aside from guilt over sleeping with Apollo? It was time, you know."

"Time?"

"Time for me to get serious and stop playing and treating life like it was some kind of game. I realized that my clock could get punched out without a moment's notice like Roland. Eternity is too long not to have a destination plan."

"How did it make you feel?"

"It made me feel like I wasn't alone, and it made me feel like I had something to look forward to after death."

"How did salvation change your relationship with God?"

"I started talking to Him more and wanted to know more about Him. My brother likes to go on about the promises God has made to His children. I wanted to know what those promises were and how I could get a hold of them. It was almost like being a part of a new world."

"Yes, but there were still unresolved issues in your old world."

She nodded. "Yes, accepting Christ into my life secured my future, but I still had a lot of present drama to sort through. It was like I was torn between two worlds. There was my old life, which was comfortable and familiar. It was the world that had Apollo in it. To be honest with you, that world wasn't all that bad."

"It wasn't all that great either."

Amari shook her head. "No, it wasn't."

"You seem to have struggled with being the person you used to be and being the one God wanted you to be. In the same vein, you were one person with Mandrel and another one with Apollo. Which of these women did you really want to be?"

Amari mulled it over. "Neither and both at the same time."

"Why is that?"

"The Christian and Mandrel thing seemed like the right thing to do on paper, but being with Apollo is what felt right. It felt more like me."

"How so?" Dr. Nelson crossed her legs and leaned in. "Is it because he'd have sex with you and Mandrel wouldn't, giving you a sense of validation you didn't get from Mandrel?"

"It was like I knew Apollo was real, you know? I knew his type. I could touch him; I could feel him. I knew how he felt, that he wanted and accepted me. With Mandrel, it was all these stipulations and not being good enough. I couldn't touch him. It was like I couldn't really know how he felt about me since he didn't want all of me."

"Humph." Dr. Nelson sat up. "So if a man isn't physically present in every way, you have a hard time believing that it's real."

"I already know what you're going to say," Amari cut in. "That it's just like my relationship with my father."

Dr. Nelson shook her head. "Actually, I was thinking that it's more like your relationship with God."

Chapter 19

As Amari adjourned a midmorning meeting with her writing staff and the writers began to scatter to their perspective cubicles, Amari was approached by her administrative assistant.

She handed Amari some handwritten messages. "These are for you. Daniel has been calling about that album review you were supposed to submit yesterday. Don't forget about your lunch with Mandrel at one. Also, you have a visitor waiting for you in your office."

Amari frowned. "I didn't have any interviews scheduled for this morning. Who is it?"

"Apollo Rison, AKA Double A. He didn't have an appointment, but he said you wouldn't mind seeing him."

Amari was taken aback. "Did he now?"

"I can send him away and tell him to schedule something with you if that's what you want."

"No, it's fine. Thank you, Jess."

Amari moved at a slow gait to her office. She wondered what Apollo wanted and why the thought of seeing him again gave her butterflies.

When she walked in, she found Apollo sprawled across her desk chair idly reading a back issue of *Rhythm Nation*. She was both repulsed and turned on by the nerve of him to do that. "Make yourself at home, why don't you?"

"Don't mind if I do," replied Apollo and flipped a page of the magazine.

"They have those down in the lobby, you know." Amari closed the door behind her. "You didn't have to show up in my office unannounced if all you wanted was some old copies of the magazine. You could've helped yourself to our recycling bin."

He tossed the magazine on her desk. "What I want just walked in."

She rolled her eyes, unmoved by his grandstanding. "What do you want, Apollo?"

He stood up and walked around the desk to face her. "Maybe I want some of what you gave me the other night."

Amari shook her head. "Sorry, the candy shop is closed."

"Really?" Apollo circled his arms around her waist. "I thought it stayed open all night. It has before."

She disengaged herself from him. "Look, Apollo, I hope you didn't come all the way up here for a booty call because it's not happening!"

"It's too early for a booty call." He kissed her neck. "It's the perfect time for a nooner, though."

"I'm working," she said firmly, then loosed herself from his grip.

"What about tonight at your place then?"

"Boy, the only sheets of mine that you'll be getting in between come with a glossy cover with *Rhythm Nation* stamped across the front."

Apollo stepped back, offended. "Oh, it's like that?"

"What did you expect?" she asked him. "You knew this wasn't a relationship, just sex."

His lips curled into a smile. "Good sex, though."

Amari turned away from him and started sifting through her mail. "It was okay."

"That's not what you were saying the other night, now was it?" Apollo pulled her closer to him. "Plus, the scratches you left on my back let me know that it was more than just okay."

She exhaled. The younger ones were always needlessly cocky regarding their sexual prowess. Apollo was no exception. "That was a one-time hit it and quit it, and it's never happening again."

He snickered. "Never? You sure about that?"

"I'm very sure. It shouldn't have happened then. I have a boyfriend."

Apollo shrugged. "What's your man got to do with me?"

"He has absolutely nothing to do with you, but he has everything to do with me!"

"Couldn't be everything. Otherwise, you wouldn't have ended up in my bed," bragged Apollo.

His arrogance bordered somewhere between amusing and annoying. Amari could tell she'd have to put this young buck in his place. She cleared her throat and looked him squarely in the eyes. "Apollo, you're young and new to the business, so you may not know how these things work yet. The other night was fun, but I'm a grown woman."

"I know. I like older women."

"And I like older men. There's only one thing you can do for me, and you've already done it. I think you'd fare much better with those wide-eyed teeny-boppers who follow your every tweet and throw their panties at you. Now is our business done here? If so, please see yourself out; and, next time, schedule an appointment if you want to see me."

Apollo stared at her a few seconds.

Amari was nettled. "What? Is there anything else I can help you with?" She expected him to make one last imploration before sulking out with his tail between his legs. She didn't like being harsh with him, but she had to be sure that he got the message.

Apollo lingered a few seconds longer before he strolled over to the door. Instead of opening it like she expected him to, he locked it.

She crossed her arms in front of her chest. "I thought you were leaving."

"I never said that." He grabbed her and penned her against the wall.

Shocked, Amari pushed him off of her. "What are you doing?" she shrieked. "Are you crazy?"

He chuckled. "Are you going to play this game again?"

"There is no game, Apollo. These antics may work on girls your age but—"

"Will you get off the age thing?" demanded Apollo, irritated. "You ain't dealing with some little boy. You think you're the first older woman I've been with or even the oldest one I've been with? I turned them out like I turned you out." She glared at him. "What, you don't think I know how much you enjoyed being with me?" he asked her. "I could get it right now in this office if I wanted to."

Amari blew him off. "You could try, and you'd fail. Like I said, I'm not one of your groupies."

"No, but you're a woman, and I know women, especially ones like you. You like to be chased. You like to make a man beg for it first, right?" Apollo stroked the side of her face with his finger, goading her. "Isn't this what you want?" He set his lips on hers.

Her resolve was disappearing by the second. Apollo's sex appeal could not be denied; neither could her attraction to him. Amari was caught between being good and doing what felt good.

As he was kissing her, Amari had a moment of clarity. She couldn't make a potentially detrimental decision based on hormones and temporary feelings. Her relationship with Mandrel was at stake, so was her newfound spirituality.

"Apollo, I told you I have a man," she explained again in between kisses. "We can't do this."

"Yes, we can," he whispered, gliding his hand over her curves. "He won't know unless you tell him."

"God might tell him. I'm a Christian. I'm saved now."

His hand crept beneath her skirt. "That's all I want to do, baby: save you from a dull sex life. Whoever that dude is you're with ain't puttin' it down like I am."

There was magic in his hands. His touch turned her into mush. She swooned, wanting to indulge but trying to stop herself from giving in. "I can't do this here, not at work."

Apollo swept her over to the desk. "Why do you think I locked the door?"

Amari knew that it was wrong. The act was wrong. Her feelings were wrong. She should've been strong enough to resist him. She should've been able to stick to her guns and her principles. She was now a new creature in Christ. She should've cried out to the Lord and allowed Him to help her.

Instead, she reverted to her old nature and hoped that there were no hidden cameras in the building and that the walls were soundproof.

"I think I worked up an appetite," concluded Apollo thirty minutes later, zipping his pants.

Amari smoothed out her skirt. "I think we both did."

"Unfortunately, as delicious as you are, I need some tangible sustenance." He pecked her on the lips. "You wanna grab some lunch?"

Amari was about to take him up on his offer, figuring the least he could do was feed her after all the work she'd just put in, when she remembered that she'd already made plans. "Oh my God. Lunch!" Amari checked the time on her cell phone. It was already half past one and she was facing a twenty-minute trek across downtown. She grabbed her purse. "I was supposed to meet Mandrel at one!"

"Who?"

"My boyfriend." She scurried through her missed messages and phone calls. "It's after one-thirty." Unbeknownst to Amari, because her phone was on silent, Mandrel had already called three times and sent four text messages.

Amari scooped up her keys and slipped her heels over her feet. "I've got to go. So do you."

"Hold up," said Apollo, tucking his shirt into his pants.

Amari flung open her office door only to find Mandrel on the other side with his fist raised, ready to knock.

She gasped. Her heart sped up. "Baby, what . . . what are you doing here? I was just coming to meet you."

"I waited on you for about twenty minutes," said Mandrel. "I tried to call a bunch of times, left you text messages."

"I'm sorry, my phone was off. I was . . ." She looked back at Apollo. "I had an interview. Mandrel, this is Double A. He's an up-and-coming artist. I told you about him, remember? I went to a listening party for him the other day," she rambled nervously, and let Mandrel into the office.

Apollo extended his hand to Mandrel. "What's up, man?"

A jittery Amari watched on, remembering how just minutes ago, the same hand that was now shaking Mandrel's hand was gripping her in private places.

"Hey." Mandrel received his hand. "I've heard a lot of good things about you. My girl here is a huge fan of yours."

Apollo smirked and looked over at Amari. "Is that right?"

"I'm a fan of good music," explained Amari, uneasy with the conversation and anxious to get rid of Apollo. "Well, thank you for coming in, Apollo. I think I have enough information for the article. I'll call you if I need anything else." She ushered him out.

"You don't have to kick the man out," said Mandrel. "I'm only here for a second. I just came to drop you off some lunch." He dropped a bag on her desk from the restaurant where they were supposed to meet. "I brought you something back. I figured you were too busy to get away."

Apollo placed his hand on Amari's shoulder. "Our girl here is a busy woman."

Amari shirked away from him and glared at him for the "our girl" reference. She stood next to Mandrel. "I'm never too busy for you, baby. Thank you for bringing lunch by. That was so sweet of you."

"Well, I'll let you lovebirds do your thang," said Apollo. "I'm sorry I had her all tied up for lunch, but it was gettin' good and she didn't want to stop."

"He means the interview," clarified Amari. "I didn't want to stop the interview."

Apollo looked puzzled. "What else would I mean?"

Amari didn't say anything. She couldn't decipher whether Apollo was needling her or the guilt from having Mandrel in the same room where she and Apollo had just had sex was making her hear things.

"I've got to hit the studio, so I'll talk to you later, Amari." Apollo faced Mandrel again before walking out. "It was good meeting you. Take care."

"You do the same," said Mandrel. "And good luck with everything."

"Thanks. I'm out."

"He seems cool," noted Mandrel after Apollo left.

"He's all right," said Amari, trying to downplay it. "A little arrogant if you ask me."

"He's young; he can't help it. Besides, I thought ladies liked that."

"Some women maybe." She wrapped her arms around his neck. "But I like my men sweet, kind, and God-fearing like you."

"Is that right?" Mandrel hugged her and buried his face in her neck. "You smell good."

"Thank you," replied Amari, praying that what he smelled was her perfume and not Apollo's cologne.

Chapter 20

Mandrel had to work that following Monday, so Amari, bored and feeling frisky, decided to take advantage of the rare opportunity to surprise Apollo at his hotel suite.

As she swerved down the highway with the Atlanta skyline and sun setting in her rearview mirror, she felt herself bubbling over with excitement. It wasn't just the thrill of being with him again. It was the solace she found in heading back to comfort and familiarity, a place where she could still find remnants of her old self without unearthing judgment or condemnation.

After leaving her car with the valet, Amari zoomed up the elevator to Apollo's floor and met him at the door wearing a seductive smile and a full-length coat.

He appeared at the door carrying sheets of music that he'd been working on. He wasn't smiling, but he didn't seem annoyed by her impromptu presence either. "Well, this is an unexpected visit."

"Is it a welcomed one?" ventured Amari, braced for the possibility of being unceremoniously sent away.

Apollo looked her up and down and sighed. "I don't know yet."

Amari shifted her weight from one stiletto to the next. "Well, do you have plans tonight?"

"Yes."

She nodded; so much for surprising him. "My apologies. I shouldn't have just come by like this. Enjoy the rest of your night." Amari turned to leave.

"Hey, wait a minute." Apollo reached out for her arm. "I have plans, but plans can always be altered. What did you have in mind?"

She turned around and faced him. "Nothing. And by 'nothing,' I mean *nothing*." She opened her coat just enough for him to glimpse the negligee she was wearing underneath.

Apollo's mouth fell open.

With that, she knew she had him. "So how are those plans looking now?"

He cracked a smile and grabbed her by the waist, pulling her into his hotel suite. "I think my plans just changed."

Amari fell into a passionate kiss with Apollo. He closed the door and peeled back her coat. "Dang, baby, is all this for me?"

"For a little while it is."

Amari soaked in all of his admiration and lust. Having him want her was intoxicating. For once, the voice that usually convicted her when she wanted to see Apollo was silenced. Perhaps it was because the Lord did not dwell in Apollo's hotel suite, and that was fine with her, preferable even. It didn't matter to Amari that the hotel room reeked of stale beer and cheap takeout. That was to be expected. At twenty-six, he probably lived on hot wings and boxed food. All that mattered at that moment was that she was a woman to be desired and touched. She knew the moment would pass soon enough, but she could still cling to the memories long after Apollo vanished.

"You want something to drink?" asked Apollo. Multiple rounds of sweating it out between his Egyptian sheets had left both of them exhausted and parched.

Amari's chest heaved up and down as she tried to catch her breath. "A beer would be great right now. Can you make that happen?"

He planted a soft kiss on her lips. "Baby, I can make anything happen."

Amari followed Apollo with her eyes as he made his way across the suite to the refrigerator in the kitchenette. "You want something to eat? I got some eggrolls and Kung Pao chicken in here."

"The beer will suffice, thank you."

Apollo walked back over to the bed after procuring a Corona from the refrigerator. "Yeah, I guess you're already full and satisfied, ain't you?" He handed her the chilled bottle. "So how does it feel to be making love to a future Grammy winner and multi-platinum artist?"

Amari unscrewed the top. "First of all, do you honestly think you're the most famous person I've ever been with? I've slept with actual Grammy winners, not just wannabe nominees." She took a swig from the bottle. "Second, this isn't making love. It's sex."

Apollo slid into bed next to her. "So I guess you save all the lovemaking for your boyfriend."

Amari shook her head. "Actually, I don't. He's a devout Christian. He doesn't believe in premarital sex."

Apollo was dumbfounded. "You mean ol' boy ain't hittin' that?" He leaned over and grabbed a handful of her thigh. He shook his head. "That fool doesn't know what he's missing!"

She moved his hand. Thinking of Mandrel made Apollo's touch feel sullied. "You can't miss what you've never had. Anyway, I think he's more concerned about what he's gaining."

Apollo leaned back on the bed with his hands pinned behind his head. "You mean other than sexual frustration and vasocongestion?"

Amari frowned. "Don't minimize what he's doing. He feels like celibacy is drawing him closer to the Lord. You do believe in God, don't you?"

"Yeah, I believe in God." He looked over her naked body. "I don't believe in letting all this goodness pass me by, though."

Amari sat up. "So what I've got between my legs means more to you than your relationship with God?"

"Apparently, what *I've* got between *my* legs means more to you than your relationship with God and that choir boy you're dating," retorted Apollo.

She rolled her eyes. "Don't flatter yourself."

"Well, you're here, ain't you?"

"I'm what they call a new convert. I'm on a probationary period. I'm still allowed to sin," she reasoned.

Apollo sneered. "What kind of church is telling y'all that? Shoot, that's where I need to be!"

"Do you even go to church, Apollo?" She tossed back the beer.

He hurled the question back to her. "Do you?"

"Yes." She set the bottle on the nightstand and lay back down. "At least I do now. Most Sundays."

"But not every Sunday?" inferred Apollo.

"More Sundays that I was going a year ago, I can tell you that! And that's saying a lot, especially to keep going after almost duking it out with two deaconesses! Then again, I doubt that there's a pew with your behind in the seat every Sunday either."

He shrugged. "There used to be. First pew on the left. I grew up in the church: Sunday school, Bible study, youth ministry, all that. I pretty much got my start singing in the choir."

"What happened to make you stop going?"

He sighed heavily. "Life, I guess. It started when I was in college. I only went to church on the weekends I came home, but that was only once every couple of months. Then I started recording and doing shows on the weekend. After a while, I got to where I couldn't really fit it into my schedule, you know?"

Amari raised a brow. "Couldn't fit God into your schedule?"

"I could fit God in it, just not church. I still pray, and I read the Bible, when I can remember to. I kinda found spirituality in my music. That's my religion now."

"Isn't that blasphemous?"

There was a brief pause, as if he were contemplating his response. "No, I don't think so," answered Apollo. "I mean, God is the one who gave me this gift, right? I'm only doing what He's blessed me to do."

Amari bolstered her elbow on the bed and rested her head on her hand. "Maybe. It sounds to me like you're worshiping your career more than you are Him. I'm not judging. I'm no better than you are. It just seems like . . ." Amari struggled to find the words for what she wanted to say. "I don't know, maybe we should be doing more."

He picked up the discarded beer bottle. "Like what?"

"I'll let you know when I have the answer."

"I sent a big ol' check to my mama's church about a month ago to help pay for their new parking lot," trumpeted Apollo before taking a gulp from the bottle. "That ought to hold my place in the 'good boy' line for a minute."

She laughed. "Maybe we have more in common that I thought."

"Oh, you gave the church some money too?"

"I have, but that's not what I meant. Like you, I tend to throw money at the problem and hope it goes away or earn me some brownie points with the Man upstairs, not to mention the man in my life." She looked down at the satiny stripes woven into the gray sheets. "Right before I came over, I went online and bought my boyfriend and his son some tickets to Disney World."

"Why?" He brought the bottle to his lips again.

"Because I knew I was coming to see you, and I knew what we were going to do. I thought it might lessen some of the guilt for stepping out on Mandrel, not to mention all the lying and sneaking behind his back."

"Heck, it ought to count for something, right? Those passes don't come cheap."

"No, they don't, but it still doesn't feel like it's enough to make up for being a horrible girlfriend."

"If you feel that bad about it, why did you come?" he asked with bold indifference.

She reached over and held his face in her hands. "Because being with you is of the few times I get to feel like I'm me."

He groped her with his free hand. "Yeah, I like to feel you too."

"Very funny." She allowed him to kiss her until she felt him exerting himself for another round of copulation. She stonewalled him. "Down, boy. That's enough!"

He fell away from her. "I thought you were ready for phase two."

"Is that the phase where I get dressed and go home? Because you've had all of the goodies you're getting tonight," declared Amari.

"I know how to make you change your mind."

She fiddled with the gold chain dangling from his neck. "What's in it for you? Tell me why you're doing this."

He finished off the beer and flung it into the wastebasket across the room. "Doing what?"

"Me."

He towered over her in the bed. "Are you for real? Look at you." He rubbed his hand over her bare torso. "All this soft skin and you come over here smelling so good, looking good." He leaned down to kiss her again. "Tasting good."

She thwarted his advances again. "I've been to your shows, Apollo. You can have your pick of groupies and cougars, so why me?"

He traced the profile of her body with a finger. "Aside from you having a body out of this world and that thing you do with your tongue, I like your vibe. You don't sweat me; you let me do me. You ain't tryin' to turn this into no relationship type of thing."

"So you like that I'm easy?" inquired Amari.

"I like that you don't stress me out. All the other chicks out here all want something from me, be it the limelight, some money, a baby, or whatever. You ain't like that."

"How can you be so sure?"

"You got your own. You don't need me. Plus, you said it yourself; we're a lot alike. We're creative. We like to live in the moment. We go for ours, make our own rules. We don't take life or sex too seriously. We don't let anyone or anything hold us back."

"What do you think I want from you then?"

"What I just gave you and what I'm trying to give you again if you'll let me." He burrowed his face into her bosom.

She fumed and lifted up his head. "Apollo, are you even listening to me?"

He yielded. "I guess I don't have a choice."

"No, you don't, not if you ever want to get to phase two."

Apollo weaved his fingers in and out of hers. "I don't think you want anything from me except to have your back blown out every now and then. Maybe I should be asking you that 'why me' question."

She smiled up at him. "You're cute and sexy. I like your aura."

Apollo puffed out his chest a little. "So you're feelin' me, huh?"

"I didn't say that. I just said I liked your energy."

"Yeah, you're feelin' me," he bragged.

She eased her fingers away from his. "I have a boyfriend, Apollo, and one whom I care about a great deal."

He swatted his hand as if dismissing Mandrel entirely. "Later for that dude. You can't be yourself with no choir boy like that. I saw him; he ain't the man for you."

"And I suppose you are?"

"I ain't saying all that! I'm just saying you ought to at least be with someone of your level. I bet he doesn't even know who he's dealing with."

"Yes, he does. He's seen me at my worst, and he still saw the good in me."

Apollo sucked his teeth. "He doesn't know the real you, not the chick who likes to drink and talk dirty or who loves it when I smack that."

"No, he doesn't know that side of me, but he brings out something better in me. He makes me actually want to be a decent human being."

"Yeah, but does that mean you can't be yourself?"

"It means I can learn to be a better version of myself, somebody I like and don't mind looking at in the mirror in the morning."

He lifted up her chin. "The person I'm looking at right now looks pretty good to me."

"You're young. I don't expect you to understand."

He tossed up his hands, disheartened. "Why are you back on this young thing? Age ain't nothing but a number."

"It's usually young people who say that," mused Amari.

"I'm serious. What does age have to do with what we do or how I make you feel?"

Amari shook her head. "It's not that. I'm nearly forty. No offense to you, but I can't afford to get caught up with someone who's barely out of puberty."

"I keep telling and showing you that I'm a grown man." He pointed to himself as he spoke. "I've lived more in these twenty-something years than most folks do in a lifetime."

"I'm sure you have. You've got a record deal, a hit single on the charts, thousands of fans. You're living out your dreams. How many people can say that?"

"And I've lived enough to know that a man who doesn't think you're good enough for him probably isn't good enough for you."

"Mandrel isn't like that. He just wants me to be the person God created me to be. He wants me to live up to my full potential."

"Well, if it counts for anything, I think you're pretty awesome the way you are."

Amari shook her head and sat up again, reaching for her clothes at the foot of the bed. "Don't do that."

"Don't do what?"

She rolled one leg of the lace-top thigh-high pantyhose over her foot and pulled it up her leg. "Don't start getting any ideas about us. Don't start catching feelings, Apollo. I mean it!"

Apollo pushed the blankets off and stood up. "You're cool folk and all, but that's the last thing you have to worry about. Don't no strings come attached to this." He moved his hand to his groin region. "Or this." He placed his hand over his heart.

"That's good. No matter what happens, I wouldn't want you to get hurt in all this."

"Nah, I never let myself get jammed up like that. I'm a free spirit, remember, just like you."

Amari continued dressing. "And I don't want you to feel like you can't date other women. You can see whomever you want."

Apollo wriggled into his boxer shorts. "I know that—with or without your permission."

"Fine, all I ask for is your discretion. That means no cheap shots on social media or uploading pictures or any of that." Amari stood up and drove her arms into the sleeves of her coat. "Just let this be our little secret."

Apollo straightened out her collar as she buttoned her coat. "I won't tell a soul. I don't put my business out there like that, especially now that people are starting to take notice of me."

"All right." She tightened her belt. "The last thing I want is for my boyfriend to get hurt."

"You mean the last thing you want is for him to find out."

Amari paused, annoyed by his miscomprehension. "That's what I said."

"Not really. If you cared about him getting hurt, you wouldn't be here. You only care about him finding out."

Amari snared her purse, which was sitting on his nightstand. "That's not true! I don't want him finding out because I don't want him getting hurt. Mandrel hasn't done anything to deserve that."

"What have you done to deserve having to pretend to be somebody you're not?"

"I'm not pretending. The person who Mandrel thinks I am is the person I actually want to be."

Apollo looked away and picked up the pillows that had fallen to the floor. "Yeah, okay."

"What?" She stopped him. "Why are you looking like that, like you don't believe me?"

"I'll believe it when you believe it." He slung the pillows onto the bed. "Look, Amari, I'm not trying to get in you and your man's business, but it seems to me that you're trying too hard. Stop trying to be this person you're not. If you're going to try to do anything, try being yourself. If he doesn't like it, he ain't the one."

Chapter 21

Armand caught up with his sister for an early morning run at the park the next day. She was dragging about with an oversized cup of coffee and shades covering her eyes, which were bloodshot from too many drinks and not enough sleep.

"You know it's too cold to be out here," whined Amari, shivering.

Armand twisted his face a little. "It's just a little nip in the air, that's all."

"A nip?" she scoffed. "I can see my breath, Armand! That's more than a nip. Need more proof? Look around." She slung her head left to right. "How many other black people do you see out here besides us?"

Armand blew into his hands to warm them in the forty-degree temperature. "You'll heat up once we get moving."

"Or I could walk back to my heated car and drive to my heated apartment and slip into my warm bed."

"What's up with the attitude?" asked Armand and took a good look at her. "Wait a minute. I recognize that look," noted Armand.

"What look is that?" grumbled Amari before bringing the steaming cup to her lips.

"The 'fresh from outta somebody else's bed' face."

She was astonished by how perceptive he was. "It's that obvious, huh? How can you tell?"

"I work in a bar. I see it all the time. Shoot, I've had that look a few times myself. You have all the classic symptoms." He gently tousled her messy bun. "Hair out of place." He looked down at her outfit. "Clothes that look like they've been slept in or stepped on, the guilt practically seeping out of your pores."

Amari summed it all up. "Then you already know that waking up in the wrong bed is like a night of hard partying. Yeah, it's awesome in the moment, but the next day, you're like Beyoncé, waking up in the kitchen and wondering, 'How the heck did this happen?'"

Armand began stretching to prepare to run. "So why did you do it? What happened to it being a one-time thing?"

"That's all it was supposed to be!"

"Obviously, that plan was tossed aside, along with your panties and your morals. I can only hope your birth control wasn't tossed out with it."

Amari sucked her teeth in response. "It wasn't like that. Armand, I know it sounds cliché, but neither one of us planned things to get so out of hand. It really did just happen."

Armand stopped stretching and shook his head. "It never just happens, Mar."

"You said that's what happened with Kim."

"That's because I was trying to save my marriage. I would've said anything to keep Nia from leaving, but I knew I was lying. So did my wife." He bent over to tighten his laces. "The fact is I watched Kim come into the bar every day after work for two weeks. I noticed when her skirts started getting shorter and when our conversations at the bar started to get longer and more personal. I knew she was flirting, and I knew if we kept heading down that road, we would eventually end up in bed together. Nothing that happened was a surprise to me. I doubt that whatever went down between you and ol' boy last night was a surprise to you either."

Amari slurped her coffee. "Okay, you may have a point," she conceded. "There's no point in frontin.' Nothing happened that I didn't want to happen."

"You're an adult, so I can't tell you what to do. I will say that you're playing with fire. What's even more messed up is that you've watched the hell I've gone through for months, yet that wasn't enough to keep you out of some dude's bed."

"The situation with Apollo and me is totally different from you and Kim."

"How?"

"First of all . . ." Amari exhaled, trying to stall long enough to think of a logical argument. "Apollo isn't going to call and blab everything to Mandrel like Kim. He's not trying to ruin my relationship or interfere with my life. We meet up, do our thing, and go back to our regularly scheduled lives."

Armand launched into a light jog. "You think it's that simple, huh?"

"I think it can be." She sighed and picked up her pace. "I guess this puts me right back at the end of the line."

Armand was confused. "End of what line?"

"The 'getting right with Jesus' line. I feel like all that salvation I got is for nothing now."

He slowed down to let her catch up. "Why?"

"Because I messed up," admitted Amari, spiritually defeated.

"Pick up your feet, will you?" urged Armand, quickening his stride. "You didn't do anything to earn your salvation, so what makes you think you can do something to lose it? You can't. That's why it's a gift."

Amari jogged alongside him, careful not to waste any coffee. "That's nice of you to say, but I'm not that naive. If I've learned anything in almost forty years, it's that no one gives away anything without expecting a return on the investment."

"All God wants in return is for you to believe in Him, trust Him to supply your needs, and love His people."

"That sounds good but—"

"But nothing. That's it! Mandrel isn't much different. He didn't ask you for anything. He just wants your love and loyalty."

"He has that!"

Armand side-eyed her. "He has half of that."

Amari stopped to catch her breath. "I'm trying, Armand, but all of this is new to me. I'm not perfect."

Armand halted. "No one expects you to be, but at least be honest with the man or let him go. It's the right thing to do."

"I'm afraid if I'll lose Mandrel if I tell him about Apollo."

Armand raised his hand to shield his eyes from the glaring sunlight. "I won't lie to you. You may lose him, but it won't be because you're not perfect or good enough. It'll be because you lied and cheated on him."

Amari didn't want to face that it was her own actions, not Mandrel's impossible standards, that would cause him to turn away from her.

"Shouldn't all of my good deeds and intentions count for something?" asked Amari, attempting to barter her way out the situation.

"Not when you have wrong motives, which you obviously do." Armand had another idea. "I think I know what you should do."

"What?" Amari grilled him. "Tell me how to get myself out of this mess!"

"There's this therapist I know," began Armand.

"Therapist?" spat Amari, frowning. "I'm not talking about this with some quack-job therapist!" She huffed and crammed her cold hands into her pocket. "I thought you were going to suggest something I could actually do to resolve this without having it blow up in my pretty face."

"Don't underestimate the power of having someone there to talk it out with."

"That's why I have you, silly," replied Amari. "I can talk to you without worrying about billable hours."

"All I can tell you is that talking to the therapist really helps put things in perspective. She's a Christian and powerful woman of God. I can confide in her about anything."

Amari shook her head. "Having women all up in your business is how you got into trouble in the first place, Armand." Amari thought for a moment, silently weighing her options. "I don't know what to do. If I come clean, I'll probably lose Mandrel. If I get caught, I'll definitely lose him. At the same time, I'm not ready to walk away from Apollo either. It's like I'm doomed no matter what I choose."

Armand started jogging again. Amari reluctantly joined him. "In a way, you are doomed if you stay on the path you're on," he told her. "You can't have one foot on holy ground and one foot in the world. The same holds true for your relationship. You can have Apollo or you can have Mandrel, but you can't have both."

Dr. Nelson listened intently as Amari continued to purge herself of everything that had transpired over the past year and a half. "Did you really want both men or was there something else you were after?"

"I wanted the security of knowing I belonged somewhere," recounted Amari.

"Explain."

"I wasn't sure if I really fit in Mandrel's world, and I wasn't one hundred percent ready to give up the world I was accustomed to with Apollo."

"So you tried to live in both?"

Amari nodded. "I tried, but I learned that you have to make a choice. You can't straddle the fence, be it choosing man or the other. God's way or man's way."

"What did you decide?"

Amari shook her head. "For a while, nothing."

"Nothing?" asked Dr. Nelson, surprised.

"That's something else I discovered. Even indecision is still a decision. When you wait too long to make a move, your fate is decided for you. It's a lesson I've learned the hard way."

Chapter 22

Thirteen Months Earlier

Amari's sound sleep was interrupted by someone buzzing for her at her complex's entrance gate early that Saturday morning.

"Who is it?" growled a still groggy Amari into the telephone.

"Delivery for Miss Amari Christopher," replied the voice on the other end.

"Oh?" Hearing that perked her up instantly. "Come on up."

Amari threw a robe over her nightie and met the delivery person at the door.

"These are for you," said the deliveryman and handed her a bouquet of radiant red roses and spray roses along with pink Asiatic lilies beautifully arranged in a glass vase.

She happily received them. "They're lovely. Thank you."

"You're welcome." He tipped his hat to Amari. "Happy Valentine's Day, ma'am."

"Same to you." Amari closed the door behind him and read the card tucked down in the bouquet:

> *Big things planned tonight, can't wait see you.*
> *Mandrel*

She sighed, smiling. Was there anything Mandrel wouldn't do to keep a smile on her face?

"Well, other than that," she thought aloud, answering her own question. Amari's smile faded almost as quickly as it appeared. There was the one thing he wouldn't do, which, unfortunately for Mandrel, Apollo did exceptionally well. She wondered why she couldn't have the great relationship and great sex in one man.

She found a suitable place for the roses in the center of her coffee table and stood back to admire them, determined that today would be all about Mandrel. It would be as if Apollo didn't exist. Her plan worked for all of five minutes before Apollo called.

"What you up to?" asked Apollo after Amari answered the phone.

She turned the vase to the left a little. "Looking at the gorgeous roses that were just delivered to me."

"I guess that means your heart is already spoken for today," assumed Apollo. "So who are you huggin' up on for Valentine's Day?"

"My boyfriend. Who else?"

Apollo grunted. "How long is that gon' take?"

"I don't know. He's planning some big surprise for me tonight."

"How do you know I wasn't planning one for you too?"

Amari rolled her eyes. "I know exactly what your idea of a surprise consists of." She hesitated. "Wait, don't you have a date tonight of all nights?"

"Yeah, I've got a date with my favorite lady."

"Really?" Amari tensed a little upon hearing that. "I didn't know you were seeing someone. It's not serious, is it?"

"It's been pretty serious for about ten years now." Apollo laughed. "I'm talking about my music. I'm performing tonight."

She giggled, relieved. "Oh."

"You sounded kind of jeally there for a second," he remarked, smug.

"Jealous of who?" retorted Amari.

"Jealous of whoever you thought my favorite lady was."

"No, I have many traits. Jealousy is not one of them. You're free to see whomever whenever you'd like. We're just"—she scrambled to find the right word—"friends."

"Just friends, huh?"

"That's all you want it to be, right?" she asked, as much to him as it was to herself.

"Yeah, as long as the benefits package comes along with that."

She played coy. "I'm sure that can be arranged."

"Can it be arranged after my set tonight?"

"Apollo, I told you. I have a date."

He continued to pursue her. "What you doing after that?"

"I can't answer that with any kind of certainty. I don't know how long the date is going to be."

"Dip out on him early," suggested Apollo.

Amari was tempted but ultimately decided against it. "I'm sorry, Apollo. I can't."

"Why not?"

She didn't have an answer.

"Look, I should be done by eleven. Come through any time after that. I can't move into my new place for another month, so I'm still at the hotel. You know the room number."

"Apollo, I—"

"No excuses. I'll see you later. Wear something red and sexy." He hung up without another word.

"Apollo, wait! Apollo? Hello?" Amari tossed the phone and fell back on her bed frustrated. "Ugh!"

It was all becoming too much. Loving Mandrel and sleeping with Apollo was starting to take its toll mentally, spiritually, and physically, but walking away from either one of them seemed as impossible as making it work with both of them.

Later that evening, Mandrel showed up to pick up Amari looking dapper in a black wool blazer, a white button-down shirt, and dark slacks.

Amari opened her front door and whistled. "He cleans up nicely," she boasted.

He grinned and walked in. "Thank you. It's a special occasion."

"Yes, it is. It's also a mysterious one. Are you finally going to tell me where we're going? I don't even know if I'm dressed appropriately."

Mandrel looked over her scarlet fringe-hemmed cocktail dress. "You look beautiful and absolutely appropriate. I can't wait 'til everyone sees me with the most attractive woman in Atlanta on my arm."

"Thank you. I can only hope to be half as beautiful as those roses you sent to me."

"I'm glad you liked them."

"I loved them." She kissed him on the cheek.

"Consider them to be the appetizer for a night you won't soon forget," he promised.

"Is that right?" Amari began pondering the possibilities. "I can't wait. I also can't wait to give you a surprise from me! Wait here." Amari disappeared into her bedroom and returned with a red gift bag.

"Somebody is in the Valentine's spirit, I see."

"Yes, I am! Open it." She held out the bag to him.

"Amari, you didn't have to get me anything. Having you in my life is more than I could ask for."

His kind words only magnified her feelings of remorse for being unfaithful to him. "I wanted to do this for you. Just open it."

Mandrel pulled out the white tissue paper and found Mickey Mouse ears and a Disney World brochure at the bottom of the bag. "What's all this?"

"Open the brochure."

Mandrel opened the brochure. Inside were two passes to the parks at Disney World. He was stunned. "Amari, is this . . ."

"You said you've never been. Now you and your son can go. My treat."

"Baby, this is nice, but it's too much!" He handed the gift back to her.

Amari refused to accept it. "Considering everything you've done for me, it's nothing." She thought, *And it's the least I could do considering everything I've done to you.*

"This is such an extravagant gift. I don't feel worthy."

"Will you stop? What's the point in having all this money if I don't spend it on the people I care about?"

Mandrel looked down at the passes again. "Are you absolutely sure about this?"

"Yes, baby, more sure than I've been about anything in a long time."

Mandrel pulled her into a hug. "Thank you so much. You have no idea what this means to me."

"I'm just happy I could do it for you. Seeing that look on your face made it worth every penny."

"I don't know how I got blessed with such an amazing woman."

Amari pulled away from him. She didn't deserve that title. There was nothing amazing about a woman who cheated, especially one who tried to absolve herself with expensive gifts. "All right, let's get this party started! You ready?" Amari grabbed her purse from the sofa.

Mandrel held out his arm for her to go ahead of him. "After you, my lady."

Amari walked out with Mandrel behind her. As she turned to lock her apartment door, her cell phone rang.

"You want me to grab the phone for you?" offered Mandrel, seeing that her hands were occupied.

"Yeah, thanks." Immediately, she moved her purse out of his reach, thinking that it could be Apollo on the other end. "I mean, no. No phones tonight. It's just me and you."

Mandrel slipped his hand into hers. "I like the sound of that."

After they'd been driving for nearly thirty minutes, Amari couldn't stand the suspense a moment longer. "Mandrel, if you don't tell me where we're going, I swear I'm going to tickle it out of you!"

He laughed. "All right, all right, you win. Open the glove compartment."

Amari obeyed and found a long white envelope inside. "Is this for me?"

Mandrel nodded. "Happy Valentine's Day, baby."

Amari squealed with delight and ripped open the envelope and pulled out two tickets. She was still giddy until she read one of the tickets. Her heart sank. "Is this where we're going?"

"Yeah. You excited?"

Amari gulped. Her hands began trembling. "I'm, uh . . ."

Mandrel grinned, proud of himself. "Speechless, right?"

She nodded. Speechless wasn't even the word for it. Amari read the tickets again to make sure she'd seen them correctly. She couldn't believe this was happening, but there was no mistake about it. Mandrel had purchased front-row tickets to see Apollo in concert that night.

"Why?" she managed to eke out.

"You're crazy about the guy, aren't you? I asked myself, 'What could be more romantic than taking my girl to see the one man she loves more than anybody?'"

"I don't love him all that much. I hardly know him," she added quickly and put the tickets back in the envelope.

Mandrel glanced over at her while keeping his hand on the steering wheel. "You sure about that?"

She panicked. "What do you mean?"

"I listened to the way you went on and on about him after you saw him perform. You're playing his songs whenever we're riding in the car together."

"I don't play anything. It's what's on the radio."

"Plus, I know that ladies love him."

"Not me!" she objected. "I mean, he's okay, but the only man who has my heart is you."

"I know you don't love him like that, but I bet if I gave you a hall pass . . ."

"What?"

"Suffice it to say, I don't think you'd turn down the opportunity."

She vigorously shook her head. "I like him all right as a musician but he's not my type."

"She doth protest too much," taunted Mandrel.

"What's that supposed to mean?"

Mandrel turned into the parking lot of the venue. "Dang, baby, calm down! It's okay to have a celebrity crush. Everybody's got one, including me. Don't you think I'd take a second and third look if Sanaa Lathan or Rihanna walked by?"

"I just don't want you to think any other man has my affection or my attention. It's all for you."

"I know that, and I'm not the least bit threatened by some kid with a guitar and a record deal."

"Nor should you be. I only have eyes for you," insisted Amari. The rest of her body couldn't be accounted for.

After leaving the car with the valet, Mandrel and Amari walked hand in hand into the hotel ballroom where Apollo was scheduled to perform.

"You all right?" asked Mandrel, leading her to their designated table near the front of the stage. "Your hands are all sweaty."

"I'm fine, just excited." Nothing could have been further from the truth.

"I promised you a night you wouldn't forget." Mandrel pulled out a chair for her to sit down.

"This is definitely living up to that promise," said Amari, wishing for a quiet, drama-free night at home for once. She would've gladly chosen to spend Valentine's night alone in her apartment over spending it with her boyfriend and her lover.

"The performance isn't all that's included in this romantic package. There's a four-course meal, a meet-and-greet after the show, and look." He pointed to an ice bucket on the table. "Complimentary champagne."

"Right on time," muttered Amari and reached for a glass.

Amari tried to forget that the inevitable would occur as they dined on bacon-wrapped scallops, filet mignon, asparagus spears, and crème brûlée by candlelight. Once Apollo's band began setting up, she knew that it was only a matter a time before she had to face him. When the emcee took the microphone to announce his arrival, Amari's nerves began to rage again. She couldn't have him and Mandrel in such close proximity to her without suffering self-reproach.

"To cap off what is officially the most romantic night of the year, we have for you Top Notch Records' newest recording artist, Double A, bringing you his hit singles and delivering the romance and sexiness to all the ladies tonight," broadcasted the emcee. "Who's ready for that?"

The crowded cheered and applauded. All except Amari, who was praying that there would be a power outage or catastrophe that would cause the show to be canceled.

"Without further ado, performing live, Atlanta's own, Double A!"

The spotlight zoomed in on the stage as the lights dimmed and the band revved up. Apollo, dressed in a black leather jacket and T-shirt, fitted jeans, a gold chain, and expensive tennis shoes, stepped onto the stage to the frenzy of the women in the audience.

Amari looked up at him. Their eyes locked on one another. He was hot; there was no doubt about it.

Apollo approached the microphone. "How's everybody out there tonight? Thank you for coming out, supporting me, supporting real music, supporting real love. Right now, I want to do something for all of the lovers in the house. Where are all of my people in love?" The crowd responded with cheers and screams. "Yeah, I see you! Love is a beautiful thing when you find the right one. I don't know about y'all, but I'm still looking for the right one. I wonder if she's out here tonight."

The single women in the crowd howled and offered up themselves.

Apollo wrapped his hand around the microphone stand and spoke closely into it, keeping his eyes on Amari. "I think I may have found her. You know it's kinda funny because I've never felt this feeling before."

Amari squirmed nervously in her seat. She could feel beads of sweat crawling over her skin. She looked over at Mandrel and tacked on a smile. The last thing she needed was for him to sense how uncomfortable she was or to ask why.

Apollo went on. "Let me tell you about this girl. You see, she keeps me alive with a single glance 'cause the color of her eyes put me in a trance. If you feel the drums behind me, it's really my heart beating. She keeps it beating slow; she keeps my blood pumpin'. And for somebody so ill, that's really saying something. I just imagine her face; her beauty's so sublime. It makes her take over my thoughts and dominate my mind."

Mandrel reached over and laid his hand on top of Amari's. "You enjoying yourself, babe?"

She pursed her lips into a taut smile. "It's like something out of a dream," she said, meaning that it was like living out a nightmare. There was a man beside her who wanted to love her, and a man in front of her who plain wanted her. It should've been every woman's fantasy, but it was the source of her emotional torment.

Apollo lifted the microphone and made his way into the crowd. "This next song is called 'Feelin' You.' Listen to the words and get close to the one who makes you feel like this."

Mandrel scooted his chair even closer to Amari's and draped his arm around her. She was hoping he couldn't feel her body tensing up or feel the reverberation from knee shaking and her foot incessantly tapping the floor.

"Are you cold?" asked Mandrel. She was visibly trembling.

"A little," replied Amari, thankful for Mandrel providing an explanation for her anxiety.

Mandrel removed his jacket and swathed it around her. "Better?"

Amari nodded. It didn't do much to quell her nerves, but it did put a barrier between her and Mandrel. Maybe now he wouldn't feel her shaking.

Apollo approached Amari and Mandrel's table as he began to sing:

> *You are my every atom, you are my molecule*
> *You are my science teacher, and I can't wait for school*
> *See I just want you to know, I'm really feelin' you*
> *If you could be my Cinderella, girl, I'll be your glass shoe*

He stopped and rapped directly to Amari.

> *Excuse me, madam, I meant your glass slipper*
> *And you can be my missus, just as long as I'm*
> *your mister*
> *And you are so divine, just like the archangel*
> *And you're almost as precious as the baby in the*
> *manger*

Once Apollo finished the song, Mandrel clapped as Amari mentally sank through the floor. She felt as if everyone in the room knew that she was sleeping with Apollo, and like her lies and secrets were closing in on her.

After the set was over, Mandrel insisted on dragging Amari over to take pictures and speak to Apollo. Not wanting to raise his suspicions, she acquiesced without much protest.

"Look, it's the lovebirds," said Apollo when the two of them advanced toward him.

"Awesome show, man," commended Mandrel, shaking his hand. "You've made it easy for a lot of men to get lucky tonight!"

Apollo laughed. "That's what I get paid to do, ain't that right, Amari?"

She held tightly to Mandrel. "The show was nice."

"You came back, so you must've really enjoyed the show last time."

She deflected. "It was all Mandrel's doing. I had no idea we were coming here tonight."

"I wanted to surprise her," added Mandrel. "I knew she'd get a kick out of hearing you perform again."

"That's how it usually is. Women come once"—his gaze sent an electric charge throughout Amari's entire body—"and they keep coming over and over again. So was it as good as it was last time?"

Amari bit her lip, trying to give the politically correct answer. "It was good, but you're a great performer. I wouldn't expect anything less."

"Yeah, but I bet what you really enjoyed after the first show was the after party," hedged Apollo.

"Oh, so she had a good time, huh?" asked Mandrel and turned to Amari. "You know, you never did go into any details about that."

Amari glared at Apollo as she replied to Mandrel. "That's because it wasn't worth mentioning."

Apollo flashed a smile. "I thought the after party was off the chain. You looked like you were enjoying yourself."

"I'm sure she did. She got in pretty late that night," recalled Mandrel. His cell phone rang.

Apollo smirked. "I don't think any of us got much sleep that night."

Amari shot daggers into Apollo with her eyes.

Mandrel looked at the phone. "It's one of my drivers. I've got to take this. Excuse me." He stepped off away from them.

Amari laid into Apollo once Mandrel was out of earshot. "I know what you're doing. It's stupid and childish and it stops right now!"

"What am I doing?"

"Antagonizing Mandrel!"

"Are you talking about that?" He brushed it off like it was nothing. "I was just having some fun. You know I wasn't gonna tell him anything."

"No, I don't know that, Apollo. Besides, he's not an idiot. You don't think he'll be able to figure out all the innuendos you keep dropping?"

"If he's keeping his woman happy, what does he have to worry about li'l ol' me for?" Amari was quiet. "Did I hit a nerve?"

"Shut up," hissed Amari.

"Yeah, I think I hit a nerve or something," deduced Apollo, pleased. "So he can't keep his woman happy and satisfied the way I can, huh?"

Amari rolled her eyes. "It's not what you think."

"Oh, it's exactly what I think!" Apollo chuckled. "It's cool. Don't worry, princess, you're welcome in my bed anytime."

Amari fumed and stormed off.

Mandrel caught up with her. "Hey, babe, you okay? Did somebody say something to upset you?"

"No, I'm not feeling well. Can we go now?"

"Sure, let me get our coats."

As Mandrel left to retrieve their jackets, Amari looked back at Apollo, who was flirting with a group of women who'd come up to meet him. She'd escaped disaster yet again, but she knew it wouldn't be long before her luck ran out.

Chapter 23

Twelve Months Earlier

"What's going on around here?" asked Amari, seeing boxes and clothes scattered all over her brother's apartment. "Are you moving?"

Armand tossed a pair of pants into an empty box. "I guess you can call it that."

"Is your lease up already?"

"No, my time is up . . . for the bachelor life, that is." He broke into a beaming grin. "I'm going back home to Nia and the kids."

"Oh, Armand, that's awesome!" exclaimed Amari, leaping into his arms. "I'm so happy for you! When? How did this happen?"

He released her. "We've been spending a lot of time together lately. It started out with the two of us dealing with the kids and trying to do stuff with them as a family. Then we started talking more and laughing more, which is something we hadn't done in a long time. We've had a lot of conversations about what went wrong and what we'd do differently. You know we never really went to church during our marriage, but I told her how much having the presence of God in my life has made a difference. She started reading the Bible with the kids and me, and we've started praying together. I started dating my wife again.

"Yesterday was supposed to be our final divorce hearing, but she went to the lawyer and called it off, saying she wants to give us another chance. Then she asked me to come back home."

"So things have been good between the two of you?"

"Mar, it's better now than it ever was before. We listen to each other more, and we've stopped being so selfish and worrying what this person ain't doing or what that person ain't doing. There's not all that arguing anymore. We try to follow what the Word says, and we put our marriage first. I can't tell you how good it's been between us."

"Welp, you said it was going to happen. You said you were praying for a miracle. God must've heard you. Either way, this is the best news I've gotten all day!"

"I'm glad to hear it, but it took a lot more than praying to get us back on track. We had to put in the work. We had to be honest with ourselves and each other, and that was hard. There were many times when I was like, 'Screw it, let's get the divorce and be done with it,' but I would've ended up carrying this baggage to my next relationship. Not to mention that I was still very much in love with my wife. I realized that I always will be."

"How did you come to that conclusion?"

"Talking it out with my therapist Dr. Nelson and by just being brutally honest with myself."

"So honesty really is the best policy then?"

"I can't speak for anybody else, but it is for us."

Amari leaned against the wall and exhaled. "I wonder if I should tell him."

"Tell who what?"

"Tell Mandrel about the thing with Apollo."

"You want to tell the man who's been celibate waiting for you that you've been sleeping with someone else? I thought you said cheating was a deal-breaker for him."

"It is, but look at you and Nia. You cheated and she forgave you."

"But do you have any idea how much Keith Sweat begging I had to do to get her to even talk to me?"

"What happened to honesty being the best policy?"

"I said it was the best policy for us. Plus, we're married with two kids. We had a lot more to lose than you and Mandrel. There's nothing to stop him from walking away from you."

"What if I pray about it?" proposed Amari. "God might tell him to forgive me."

"He might and He might not. Mar, there are natural laws and there are supernatural laws. Just because a person is forgiven in the supernatural doesn't mean there won't be consequences in the natural world. I could take a gun and shoot you right now. God will forgive me, but I'll still have to go to jail. That's the way it is."

"It worked for you."

"Saving my marriage was part of God's divine plan. If Nia and I didn't need each other to carry out God's purpose, it probably wouldn't have happened."

"Okay, well, can't the same be said about my affair with Apollo?" she reasoned.

"My reconciliation is God's divine will. Your sexcapade with Apollo was permissive will."

"What's the difference? They both represent God's will."

"Please don't try to use that logic on Mandrel, not if you want to have a shot in hell of keeping him."

"Are you saying I shouldn't tell him about Apollo?"

"I'm saying you shouldn't have cheated in the first place. Whatever happens next is out of your hands."

"I'm just going to have to trust him and believe that what we have is strong enough to withstand this."

"I hope you know what you're doing. I still wish you consider going to see Dr. Nelson. The last thing I want is to see my sister get hurt, but at least she can give you coping mechanisms for when it happens."

"And you think that's what's going to happen? You think I'm going to get hurt?"

"Honestly, I don't see how it can be avoided."

"It sounds like you were in pretty deep," assessed Dr. Nelson.

"Pretty deep? More like in over my head!" declared Amari.

"Amari, what do you think the root cause of all this was? I think we both know that this wasn't just about sex."

Amari shook her head. "No, it wasn't. It was about being accepted."

"Can you explain what you mean by that?"

"I think all my life, I've been looking to be accepted. First by my parents. When that didn't work out, by Roland, but then he cheated on me, so then it became being accepted by my colleagues and people in the industry. It soon went from that to being accepted by random men, then one man: Mandrel. When I felt rejected by him too, I sought acceptance with Apollo and, eventually, from God."

"So you wanted acceptance from everyone but why is that?"

"Because I couldn't accept myself," she replied softly.

"Which takes us back to not being accepted by your family and your parents."

Amari nodded her head. "Maybe my parents are to blame for me being screwed up after all."

"This isn't about who's to blame for what's happened in the past. It's about coming to terms with what happened and making better choices in the future."

"How do I do that?"

"By facing the truth."

Chapter 24

Twelve Months Earlier

It was as if Mandrel knew she had a confession to make, and he decided to make it as difficult as possible for her to go through with it.

He'd taken her to Aria, where they feasted on pan-roasted Nantucket Bay shrimp and Blue Ridge Mountain trout. Before that, it was listening to jazz on a blanket in the park and calorie-splurging on lemon custard ice cream. It was one of the most romantic dates she'd ever experienced, which only made the timing of her confession worse. However, she knew she couldn't go another day keeping this secret. For once in her life, her conscience wouldn't let her.

"I believe you've given every other woman in this room a complex," observed Mandrel. "I don't think they're used to seeing someone as radiant as you look tonight."

She blushed. "Thank you. You've made this one of the most special nights of my life."

"Consider it payback for making these the most special months of my life." He kissed her hand. "While I'd like to pretend that I'm just a romantic guy, I do have an ulterior motive for putting all of this together tonight."

"What's that?"

Mandrel sat up straight and cleared his throat. "First, let me say how proud of you I've been these last months. I've watched you grow from being a woman of the world to someone who has dedicated her life to Christ. It's been a beautiful transformation to watch."

"I can't take all the credit for that, Mandrel. You were the one who kept pushing me to be a better Christian and a better person. I don't think it would've happened if it weren't for you."

"Nah, God just used me as His instrument, but you made the commitment to turn your life around, and you followed through on it. Not a lot of people can say they've done that. You're to be commended."

"Thank you."

"You're welcome. Now, on a more personal note, I've watched you for other reasons. I knew from the moment I saw you at church that you were different. Not only were you drop-dead gorgeous, but you had this fire and light about you that's magnetic. To be honest with you, I wasn't sure if I could handle a woman as passionate and wild as you are. But beneath all that lies a heart that's so full of love and compassion, and it's that part of you that I fell in love with. The list I made when we met about all the things I like about you has doubled and has gone from all the things I like to all the things I love."

She looked up at him, floored. "Love? You don't mean like the church kinda brother-sister love, do you? You're talking about the real thing."

"Yes, Amari, I love you," he replied in sincerity. "I know it's taken a minute for me to get there. I've been feeling it for a couple of weeks, but I didn't want to say it until I was absolutely sure I love you. I really do. You're the woman I see being my wife one day, preferably sooner rather than later."

She was still in shock. "Where is all this coming from? Why now?"

"It's always been there. I know that it hasn't been easy to be in this relationship with me, but you've been patient with me. You honored my beliefs even when you didn't want to. You've been honest and faithful, and you've made me happier than I've been in a very long time. " He reached into his pocket and pulled out a small velvet box.

She gasped. "Oh my God, Mandrel, is that . . ."

"No, it's not a ring, not yet at least. It's a necklace, but it's a token of my love and appreciation."

He opened the box to reveal a heart-shaped natural morganite stone, complemented by a single twinkling diamond, set on a rose gold chain.

She reached for the box. "This is so beautiful! Mandrel, no man has ever meant to me what you do. You've brought so much into my life. You've saved me literally and spiritually. I can't thank you enough for that."

"You don't have to, baby. God did it all. He's the one who led me to you in the first place."

Amari was deeply affected by the loving gesture, but she was also met with the resurgence of guilt that she'd fought to deny. Her heart felt like it was both melting and breaking. These were the words she'd longed to hear from the kind of man she'd always wanted to hear them from, but she knew that the woman who Mandrel had just described didn't exist, at least not in her. It would be wrong to continue to let him think she was that woman.

"Before we go any further in this conversation, there is something I need to tell you," she began.

"What is it?"

"I . . . I love you too, Mandrel. I think that you're the most caring, spiritual, trustworthy man I've ever met. I feel so honored to have your love and your respect."

"You'll always have that."

She looked down at the necklace. "I'm not so sure about that. Mandrel, I'm not the woman you think I am, at least not the one that you want me to be. I'm not perfect, not by a long shot."

"Amari, I know you have a past. We all do, but that's not the woman you are now. The woman you are today is the one I fell in love with. All that other stuff doesn't even matter to me." He smirked. "Who wants a perfect love story anyway?"

She laughed a little and added, "Cliché, cliché." Amari shook her head, tearing up. She looked down at the necklace. "I don't deserve this. I don't deserve you."

"Of course you do, Amari." He cupped her face in his hands and wiped away a tear. "The devil has got you convinced that you don't deserve to be happy, but I'm going to spend every day of our lives proving him wrong. It'll be my privilege and honor to put a smile on that gorgeous face every day until the Lord calls us home."

"It's not that. It's . . ." She dropped her head, unable to go on.

"It's what?" pressed Mandrel, now concerned. "Talk to me, baby. What's going on?"

She raised her eyes to meet his. Seeing him gaze upon her with such love and concern was almost too much to bear. He looked at her the way she'd waited her whole life to see a man look at her. She wondered if he would look at her the same way if he knew the truth.

She prefaced her confession by saying, "I want you to know that I tried—I really tried to be the woman you wanted me to be. The woman that God wants me to be."

"I know you have," he reassured her. "And I love you for that."

"Trying to become a person you've never been before is sometimes easier said than done." She paused to gather her thoughts. "You see, Mandrel, I've spent the last thirty-eight years doing things my way. I didn't think too much about what the Bible said or trying to live according to God's Word. Life was mostly about having a good time, making money, and living every day like there are no consequences, because for a long time, there weren't any."

"There are always consequences, babe. How you live your life, whether good or bad, catches up to you in the end."

She became pensive. "I understand that now. That's what I'm afraid of."

"Amari, God has forgiven you for everything you've done. That's the beauty of accepting Christ into your life. When He died on that cross, it was for all sin: past, present, and future. You only have to accept His forgiveness and try to do better next time."

"Yes, God can forgive me, but I don't know if you can."

"Of course I can. Is that what you're worried about? I told you that your past means nothing to me. I meant that."

"What about the present?"

He shrugged. "What about it?"

"I haven't been honest with you, Mandrel," she confessed. "Truth be told, I've been lying to you for weeks."

Mandrel wrinkled his brow, not sure if Amari was exaggerating or simply confused. "Lying about what?"

"I've . . . I've been seeing someone. I've been sleeping with someone else." Her courage started to falter when she gauged his straight-faced reaction. "It didn't mean anything. It was just sex, but it happened . . . more than once."

He was dumbfounded. "How can sex not mean anything to you?"

"It meant something, but not the way you mean. Mandrel, I love you. Apollo was just—"

He butt in. "*Apollo?* Are you talking about the artist you were so excited about?" She nodded. "I guess this explains your excitement, doesn't it?" he asked flippantly.

She shook her head. "It's over. It never should've started, but I was lonely, I guess."

"When were you lonely, Amari? I spend practically every day with you. In fact, you've canceled dates with me for work or to go hang out with your friends."

"I was tired of sleeping alone. Apollo could give me the one thing you wouldn't."

He looked at her somberly, taking a moment to process what she'd just said to him.

"Are you mad? Do you hate me? Say something."

He sat quietly for a few more seconds. "No, I'm not mad."

She was stunned. Her mouth gaped open. "Really?"

"Yes, really. We're all human; we all make mistakes. You'll be fine. I'm glad you told me. I know that couldn't have been easy for you to do."

She shook her head. "No, it wasn't, but I couldn't go on carrying this secret. It was killing me a little more each day. I've wanted to tell you for weeks. I didn't know how to, and I was afraid of how you were going to react."

He reached for her hand. "Well, the truth is out now. You can stop torturing yourself."

She clasped her hands over his. "So you forgive me?"

"Yes, I forgive you."

"And you're not mad? I mean, you understand why I did it, right?"

"I'm not mad, Amari. I told you that, and I meant it."

She leaned across the table and kissed him. "Thank you! Thank you for loving me enough to forgive me. I love you so much!"

"I love you too."

"And I can't wait to spend the rest of our lives together. More than anything, I want to be your wife and to show you that I am worthy of your trust and your love." She reached for the necklace box and gazed down at it once more. "It's the most gorgeous necklace I've ever seen. I'm never going to take it off."

"I know you wouldn't." He closed the box and slipped it back into his pocket. "But that's something you will never have to worry about."

She was rendered speechless. "Wait, what?"

"I can't give you this necklace, Amari."

"Why not?"

"Do you know what this represents to me? It's a symbol of my love and our commitment to building a future together."

"I'm committed to that. I'm committed to you," swore Amari. "That's why I told you about it. I didn't want there to be anything that the devil could use to rip us apart."

"I appreciate your honesty more than you know, but it doesn't change the facts."

"No, it doesn't. The fact is that you love me. That has not changed in the last five minutes."

"The fact that I was referring to is the fact that you had another man's penis inside of you. That's an image I don't think I could ever get out of my head."

"But you said you forgave me," she wailed.

"I do, and I still love you, Amari; forgiveness and acceptance are two different choices. I told you that infidelity was the one thing I couldn't let ride. You knew that."

"So that's it? We're over like that?"

"Just like that," he confirmed and stood up. "But I wish you all the best. I pray that God will send someone who can give you what you're looking for. In the meantime, I hope you continue to walk in love and continue your walk with the Lord, but as far as the two of us are concerned, that's over."

"But I don't understand, Mandrel," she wailed. She didn't care that people around them were starting to look on. "I was honest with you about everything. I trusted you, and you said you forgave me."

"It just wouldn't work. I'd always wonder if you were stepping out on me, and I wouldn't be able to trust you. That's not fair to either of us." He left enough money on the table to cover dinner and kissed Amari on the forehead. "I love you, but this isn't meant to be."

"I gave up a good relationship, maybe even my best relationship, for sex," concluded Amari, remorseful. "Looking back on it, it all seems so stupid."

"What does?" asked her therapist.

"Getting involved with Apollo in the first place. I didn't think that whole thing through or look at the bigger picture."

"You were the proverbial bird who sees the bait but ignores the trap," gleaned Dr. Nelson.

Amari agreed wholeheartedly. "Definitely."

"How did losing Mandrel make you feel?"

Amari shifted in her seat. "At first, it was confirmation that, whether I do something to screw up or not, every man in my life leaves eventually."

Dr. Nelson looked down at her notes. "So you were back to feeling that sense of loss and rejection."

"Yes, but then something else happened that made me realize that everything happens for a reason. No matter how badly we mess up or how far we get off course, God really is in control."

"What happened to bring you to that conclusion?"

Amari smiled. "Eric happened."

Chapter 25

Twelve Months Earlier

Amari spent the next day in bed sick to her stomach. She didn't know if it was the dinner, getting dumped, or depression that had made her so ill. All she knew was that she had no desire to move any farther than the corners of her bed.

It was in the silence of solitude that her empty apartment provided that she could fully comprehend what she'd done. Twenty-four hours ago, she had a good man, probably the best man she'd ever known, and she'd blown any chance of lasting happiness with him. And for what? Apollo, who was way too young, too feckless, and too ambitious for her to ever take seriously.

She'd tried calling Mandrel to make amends, only to be met with a terse, "This isn't a good time." When she asked when it would be a good time, he informed her that it wouldn't be anytime soon and told her to have a blessed day.

She thought back to the night she had dinner with Mandrel, when she had given her life to God. She assumed by doing so, her life would start making sense, but it seemed that the moment she began going to church was when it all started to unravel. At least before when things got out control, she could pour a drink or fire up a blunt to numb the pain. She could call up one of her many paramours and allow him to whisk her away for a weekend of wild partying and wilder sex. Her problems always seemed less daunting when she returned from those jaunts.

For the first time, she was made to face real life and the consequences of her decisions, without the benefit of a chaser. She had to deal with them head-on, just as God seemed to be dealing with her. Was it His plan all along to leave her bereft of her crutches to force her to rely solely on Him?

She reached in her nightstand and pulled out the Bible Mandrel had given her. She wasn't able to crack its mysteries before. Perhaps the sting of rejection would help elucidate some of its meaning.

She flipped over to Ephesians 5. Her eyes zoomed in on verse three. She read aloud, "But fornication and all uncleanness or covetousness, let it not even be named among you, as is fitting for saints; neither filthiness, nor foolish talking, nor coarse jesting, which are not fitting, but rather giving of thanks. For this you know, that no fornicator, unclean person, nor covetous man, who is an idolater, has any inheritance in the kingdom of Christ and God."

She frowned at the notion that she could very well fit that description. "Well, that's depressing! Where are all of those happy, encouraging scriptures Mandrel is always talking about?"

She scoured the Bible and found more comfort in the book of Isaiah. "Fear not, for I have redeemed you," she read. "I have called you by your name; You are Mine. When you pass through the waters, I will be with you; And through the rivers, they shall not overflow you. When you walk through the fire, you shall not be burned, nor shall the flame scorch you. For I am the Lord your God, The Holy One of Israel, your Savior; I gave Egypt for your ransom, Ethiopia and Seba in your place. Since you were precious in My sight, you have been honored, and I have loved you; Therefore I will give men for you, and people for your life. Fear not, for I am with you."

Upon the reading of God's promises, Amari felt an inexplicable sense of peace. She knew that no matter how many times she messed up or who turned against her, she would also be valued in God's sight and would also be under the umbrella of His love and protection. He would be with her when no one else was, and she could take comfort in that.

It was in the midst of that epiphany that Amari started feeling queasy again. Whatever kind of bug she had, it was doing a good job of getting the best of her. She tore herself away from the bed and ransacked her refrigerator for some ginger root. It was one of her go-to remedies for alcohol-induced nausea. She started keeping it on hand after seeing how ginger tea quelled Nia's incessant morning sickness when she was pregnant with Trey.

Right then, Amari had a conviction that nearly made her heart stop. She dropped the mug she was holding. She didn't even hear it crashing to the floor.

She swallowed hard. She had considered every rationale for her sudden bout of nausea except one.

Panic began to set in. Her hands were shaking. "My calendar. Where's my calendar?" she muttered to herself and began frantically searching for her cell phone.

She found it at the bottom of her purse, and she immediately began scrolling through her calendar trying to remember the last time she purchased tampons. More importantly, the last time she had to actually use them.

She winced. It was over a month ago, right around the time she began sleeping with Apollo. How had she not noticed that her period was at least two weeks late?

Amari took a deep breath and consoled herself saying, "This could be a false alarm. You've had those before."

Being a woman who was no stranger to the occasional pregnancy scare, she kept a supply of pregnancy tests in stock for such times as this. She flung open her medicine cabinet and snatched down the box labeled EARLY PREGNANCY TEST. She swiftly undressed and urinated on the stick.

"I can't be pregnant," she told herself while waiting for her test results. "There is absolutely nothing maternal about me." She laughed to herself. "There is no way I could be pregnant!"

She thought back. Hadn't she and Apollo been careful?

"There was that one time," she recalled then put it out of her mind. Even then, they'd taken precautions not to get pregnant.

She was at ease again and had almost managed to convince herself that this was nothing more than another pregnancy scare . . . until the positive sign on the EPT said otherwise.

Chapter 26

"Apollo?" Amari banged on the hotel door. "Apollo, baby, are you in here?"

After the shock of failing the pregnancy test wore off, Amari hightailed it to Apollo's hotel room. She had no idea what her next move would be; much of it was riding on Apollo's reaction to hearing that he was going to be a father.

She was as apprehensive waiting for him to come to the door as she was waiting for her pregnancy test results to be confirmed. It was another minute before he responded to her knocking. He appeared disheveled and unhappy to have his night disrupted. "You should've called first," growled a shirtless Apollo, standing at the front door of his hotel suite.

"I know it's late, but you said I could come anytime." Amari shrugged and pasted on a smile. "So here I am!"

He wiped sleep from his eyes. "Yeah, but I didn't think you'd drive across town in the middle of the night without a phone call or some advanced warning, not at two in the morning."

"Well, I'm here now. Are you going to let me in?" She peered inside.

He positioned his athletic frame firmly in the doorway, blocking the entrance. "This isn't a good time."

"Why not? What's going on?" she asked, trying to peek into the room.

"I'm working," he answered callously. "I told you that I write songs late at night."

"I remember. I'm not here to disrupt your creative process. The reason I came over is because I have something to tell you."

At that moment, Amari heard something fall and hit the ground with a low thud. Its contents scattered onto the floor. A silver tube of lipstick rolled out into the hallway and halted when it bumped against the toe of Amari's shoe. She picked it up and examined it. A horrified look swept over her face as it dawned on her that Apollo wasn't alone. "What's going on, Apollo? Is someone here?"

"Sweetheart, I just knocked over my purse. Can I take off this blindfold and turn on the lights?" called a female voice from inside the hotel room.

"You have company?" asked Amari. "Who's that?"

"A friend. It's no big deal." He turned to address the voice in the darkness. "Yeah, baby, hit the lights." The room illuminated, but Amari didn't see anyone.

Amari crossed her arms in front of her. "I thought you said you were working."

"She's helping me out," finished Apollo in a controlled and annoyed tone.

"In a blindfold?" she asked incredulously.

Apollo didn't bother responding. "What's the problem? We said that we could see other people, right? This ain't no love thang."

Amari stood cemented in the doorway unable to move or speak. She realized that it was naive and plain stupid of her to think that she was the only one Apollo was bedding. She had broken her own cardinal rule of letting her guard down and trusting him.

"I . . . I . . . just . . ." Her eyes dropped to the floor. "I came because I had something very important to tell you."

A blond woman in hot pink boy shorts, a matching bra, and knee socks appeared at the door. "Sweetie, the bed is so lonely without you." She pouted. "When are you coming back?"

"In a minute, all right?" Apollo pulled her into a long, passionate kiss, caressing the small of her back as she moaned softly. Amari was sickened having to witness it.

"Oh, hey," said the woman to Amari once she pulled her lips away from Apollo. "Who are you?"

"Brooke, this is Amari. She writes for a magazine. She did a story on me a few weeks back."

"That's nice," Brooke replied drily, then shot Amari a cold, threatening look, sensing there was more between them than an article.

Amari quickly decided that Brooke wasn't worth expelling the energy required to affirm or deny whatever suspicions she had about Amari and Apollo's relationship.

"I really need to talk to you, Apollo," insisted Amari. She cut her eyes to his female companion. "Alone."

He sighed and opened the door all the way, moving aside to allow Amari to pass through. "Brooke, can you wait in the bedroom for me? I'll only be a minute."

"Sure." Brooke kissed him again. "Don't take too long, okay?"

"I won't." He patted her on the behind as she walked off.

After a few intense moments of silence, Apollo prompted Amari to speak. "Okay, what's this about? What was so important that it couldn't wait until tomorrow?"

Amari tottered into the room still dismayed by what had just transpired. "I'm sorry for interrupting your night. You were obviously very hard at work doing *something*."

"Why are you here?" snapped Apollo. "And next time, call before just dropping by. I'm very busy, you know that. I go on tour in a few weeks; I'm trying to get this album together. I can't get distracted like this!"

"I'm sorry. Really, I should have called. Just . . ." She paused, building the courage to ask. "Is that woman your girlfriend?" His relationship status never mattered before, but seeing as how this blond Becky could be the future stepmother to her unborn child, Amari felt like she had a right to know whether she was dealing with a random groupie or the main chick.

"No, she's not my girlfriend," replied Apollo, agitated. "Look, Amari, I'm really busy. As you can see, I have company, so I'd appreciate if you get on with telling me what you needed to say."

"Then I'll make it quick." Amari cleared her throat. "Apollo, I'm pregnant."

He registered no reaction. "Okay, and . . . ?"

Amari was stumped. She felt like her life as she knew it was unraveling and Apollo was acting like she'd just told him that the sky is blue.

"And you're the father," she told him.

He laughed a little. "Yeah, right."

"I'm serious, Apollo. I'm pregnant with your child. Calculating from my last period, I think I'm about four weeks along." She paused. "I'm pregnant. We're having a baby."

Apollo brushed it off. "Am I supposed to believe that considering how much you sleep around? You can miss me with that BS."

His accusation riled her with fury. "I haven't been with anyone other than you in months, and you know that!"

"How am I supposed to know that? Don't you have a boyfriend?"

"I *had* a boyfriend. It's over now. He dumped me once I told him about us."

"Oh, I get it now." Apollo nodded slowly. "So when you couldn't pin the baby on that dude, you decided to come to me. Nice try, now get up out my hotel room! I've got things and people to do."

"Apollo, do you think I would go through the trouble of coming here and humiliating myself if I weren't one hundred percent sure this was your baby?"

He grunted and cussed under his breath. "How do I know you're even pregnant? Where's the doctor's report?"

"I don't have one. I took an at-home pregnancy test."

"Well, where's the pregnancy test?" prodded Apollo.

"At home on my bathroom counter. I'm not lying, Apollo. Trust me, you're the last person I'd choose as my baby's father, but what's done is done. I'm pregnant. I have no reason to lie to you. You know that."

"I don't know squat!" He turned around and faced Amari. Looking in her eyes, he could tell she wasn't lying. He softened his stance a little. "How much?"

"I just told you, four weeks."

"No." He took a few steps toward his sofa. His jeans were sprawled across it. He reached into his pocket and pulled out a wad of cash. "How much do you need to go get rid of it?"

Amari narrowed her eyes in anger, furious that he'd attempt to buy her and their child off. "What did you just say to me?"

"I know you're not seriously thinking about keeping this baby, are you?"

"Why wouldn't I?"

"Look, Amari, I didn't sign on for all this with you!" Apollo looked toward the bedroom and lowered his voice. "We said we were keeping things light and fun, just sex, that's all."

"That's all it takes to make a baby!"

"Then how much will it take to get rid of one?"

His words pierced her in the heart. "What?"

"Amari, don't stand there looking all bugged out. You knew what this was right from jump!"

"Screw what it was!" she shrieked, not caring if Apollo's jump-off heard her. "There's a baby involved now—a baby I fully intend to keep!"

Apollo shook his head and pleaded his case. "I've got a top-five single out. I'm about to go on tour. I'm twenty-six years old. I don't have time to be a father right now."

"I don't have time to be a mother, but I'm making the time. I have to."

"You do. I don't." Seeing her sad brown eyes and helpless expression sent the wave of guilt through his body that he'd been fighting to suppress. Determined to suppress a little longer if he could, Apollo fumbled around in the pocket of his jeans again and pulled out another hundred dollar bill. "This is all I have on me. If you need more than that to handle the problem, I'll get it to you, but I can't have a kid right now. I'm sorry."

Her eyes welled with stinging, hot tears. "So I'm just supposed to give up my baby so you can go on tour and live out your rock star fantasy?"

"It's not a fantasy. It's what I was created to do. You've even said it yourself. Things are just really starting to take off for me. I can't have that kind of dead weight holding me down."

"Dead weight?" echoed Amari. "Is that all our baby is to you?"

Apollo exhaled. "Not just the baby."

Amari bit her lip. "I see. You mean the whole package, mother included." There was nothing more to say. "Thank you for letting me know where we stand."

"This ain't about us," clarified Apollo. "But if we're honest about it, you wouldn't even be here if ol' boy hadn't curved you or if you weren't pregnant. I'm just some young buck giving you the business. Why would we bring a child into that?"

"We don't have to be in love to love this child."

"I ain't never loving a child I didn't ask for, especially if I don't love the mother. Keep this baby, and you'll be another baby mama and a Double A groupie. Is that what you want?"

Being the host mother to a twenty-six-year-old rapper's spawn was definitely not in Amari's life plan. Having Apollo around would be the equivalent to having two children for the birth of one. She wasn't sure she was willing or ready to deal with that.

"Amari, getting rid of the kid is for the best. Be grateful that we have enough resources to throw money at the problem and move on," resolved Apollo. "I mean, with your hectic schedule and lifestyle, what are you going to do with a baby? Honestly, what kind of mother do you think you'd be? This child deserves better than either one of us could give it."

"Maybe you're right," she conceded. Amari couldn't argue with him. She was barely a decent human. How could she possibly expect to be a good mother? The most she could be expected to do was screw up her baby as badly as she did everything else. No child deserved that, and no innocent child deserved to have her as a mother.

He walked over to her and slid the money into her hand. "Just take the money and run," he implored, hoping to placate her and his guilty conscience. "I'll send you a cashier's check for a couple of thousand tomorrow. You said that you need a vacation. Use that to go relax on the beach for a week or two after you take care of the problem. I'll even go with you to the doctor to get it taken care of if you want."

She shook her head. "That won't be necessary."

"Amari, you know this is the right thing to do for everyone involved. How many times have you told me that you like your life the way it is and how having kids would complicate it? Think about it; am I really the kind of man you want to have a kid with?"

"Considering that you have a half-naked woman waiting for you in the bed in the next room, I'm inclined to say no."

"Neither one of us ever intended for this to be more than sex. Let's just deal with the situation at hand and get it over with. Six months from now, you'll forget this ever even happened."

Chapter 27

Amari came home to her empty apartment. It seemed colder and more desolate than usual. She didn't have Mandrel. She no longer even had the piece of relationship that she had with Apollo. Her parents couldn't be counted upon, and her brother had his own life and problems. She had no one . . . except her baby.

And there was God. How many times had Mandrel and Armand told her that God was ever present and would never forsake her?

She had never prayed, but that was because she never had anyone that she felt the need to pray for, but her baby was helpless, and to a larger extent, so was she.

"Ugh!" she cried out in frustration. "What am I going to do?" She flopped onto her sofa. "Maybe I should take the money and run to the nearest abortion clinic. Apollo was right. No one would know, and in six months, it won't even matter."

She knew that was a lie. There was no way she could forget about the child growing inside of her regardless of the circumstances.

She rolled over several possible outcomes in her mind. She thought about begging Mandrel to take her back and two of them raising her child together, but it didn't take much deliberation to know that wouldn't work. If he couldn't get over her cheating on him, he definitely wouldn't accept the evidence of her betrayal.

She thought of adoption and how some people might consider it noble of her to provide her baby with a better, more stable home environment with two loving parents like the Christophers had been to her mother. Then she remembered the outcome of that decision and the irrevocable domino effect it had on her entire family. She knew the chances of her child falling in love with his or her cousin were extremely slim, but she didn't want her child to grow up with the stigma of not being wanted.

There was also the issue of the child's father. She believed that Apollo honestly meant it when he said he wasn't ready for children. In all fairness, he was practically a kid himself, at least compared to her. Did she really want a child with a man who was eleven years her junior and basically the same age as her fetus in terms of being responsible and able to put someone else's needs ahead of his own? Would her baby end up like her and Armand, only knowing the father through pictures and other people's stories about him? How could she knowingly resign her child to that fate, especially after experiencing firsthand how devastating it could be?

Amari felt like an even bigger complication than having Apollo as a father was having her as the child's mother.

"Sorry," she told her baby. "Fate wasn't on your side in the parenting department."

There was nothing about Amari that screamed "good parenting material." She was always on the go. She couldn't cook. She liked sleeping until noon. She hated changing diapers and being responsible for anyone other than herself. She was faced with the truth more and more every day of how flawed she was. With so much stacked against her, how could she expect to raise a mentally sound, productive child?

She realized that she couldn't, not on her own, and there was only one person who could help steer her in the right direction.

Amari kneeled down in front of her sofa. She wasn't sure why she felt compelled to do it aside from having seen it done that way on television. She assumed it couldn't hurt though. She needed every advantage she could muster.

"Um, God, it's me, Amari." She shook her head. "Shoot, that sounds corny, like I'm about to whine about boys and cry about my period like that insipid book character Margaret. Let me start over."

She cleared her throat. "Okay, it's me, God, but you already know that, don't you? Just like you probably already know what I'm going to say, so why bother praying?" She sighed. "I guess you want me to say it anyway, huh? Okay, here goes. I know I've messed up . . . a lot. And I know I haven't come to you for much of anything. I've always had my money or my connections to depend on.

"But those things won't help me now, God. There isn't anyone I can call on to fix this, so I need you to bail me out here. I would promise to be perfect and say I'm not gonna lie or drink again and I'll go to church every Sunday. We would both know I'd be lying, but, God, I'd give anything for you to help me be a good mother to my baby. I'm not totally sure what that looks like because I didn't see much of it growing up. I didn't see a good father either. I don't know how to give this child what he or she needs. I just know I can't raise this baby by myself and if I'm going to do this, I need your help.

"Then again, Armand grew up the same way I did, and he's turned out to be a terrific parent. If you can give me some of what you gave him, I think I'll be all right. While we're on the subject, let things work out between Armand and Nia. He loves her and those kids so much.

"Watch over my parents, too. God, you know they're both totally screwed up, but they're not bad people.

Maybe one day, we can get together and act like a real family again the way they do in sappy Christmas movies. If not, I don't want anything bad to happen to them. I pray they can find peace, maybe even find you.

"I would ask for something for me, but I'd rather you save up all your blessings for this baby, unless you insist on sending me the Tori Burch purse I saw in the window last week, which, as a side note, can double as a very cute diaper bag. Let this baby be happy and healthy and be brought up in love. I guess you know by now that I've decided to keep it. I'm keeping Apollo's money, too, by the way!

"Okay, that's all I really wanted to say. Um, keep doing your thing, Lord! Oh, all of this I pray in the name of Jesus. I think that's what I'm supposed to say. Thank you . . . or bye. No, wait, I should say 'amen,' so amen."

She peeled herself off the floor with no concrete evidence that her prayer would be answered or if it was even heard, but she felt deep in her heart that God not only heard her but that He also understood her.

Chapter 28

Amari strolled down the aisle in a long blush-colored Grecian grown, carrying tea lilies tied together with a long ribbon. She smiled at the debonair groom to assure him of her love and that he was doing the right thing before taking her place in front of the altar. She was followed by her nephew Trey, who waddled down the aisle as the ring bearer, and his sister Jaycee, who showered the runaway with white rose petals in preparation for her mother's walk down the aisle of Armand and Nia's vow renewal ceremony.

Armand's stoic expression dissolved into tears the moment he saw Nia, beautiful in an ethereal column wedding gown, walking toward him. He met his bride, and they faced Pastor Campbell hand in hand.

The pastor addressed the happy couple. "Armand and Nia, I wasn't there when you first joined hands and hearts in marriage all those years ago, but I imagine you did it surrounded by as much love and support as you have today. While you took each other as man and wife with the best, most honorable intentions, no one could've accurately predicted where life would lead you.

"On that day, you took vows and promised to love, honor, and cherish one another for the rest of your lives. Each day and each year has brought with it wonderful blessings along with heartbreaking trials over the course of your marriage. In this day and time when it's so easy to give up when the going gets tough, you persevered, and here you are today, still honoring those vows you took six years ago. You are leaving a legacy of love and commitment for your children. This marriage is pleasing in the sight of God.

"As we all stand in celebration and solidarity with you this afternoon, do you now wish to reaffirm the vows you took six years ago?"

They both replied, "We do."

"We have our own vows," spoke up Armand.

"By all means, brother." The pastor stepped aside and gave him the floor.

Armand cleared his throat and faced his wife. "In Colossians 3:12, God's Word commands us, as 'the elect of God, to put on tender mercies, kindness, humility, meekness, longsuffering; bearing with one another, and forgiving one another.' I can honestly stand before you today and say that you have not only upheld your vows to me, but you've also kept that promise to Him. I know I haven't always made it easy to love me, especially over the past couple of years, but I told God if He allowed our marriage to be restored, I'd spend the rest of my life being the best husband I can be.

"Nia, I promise to love you and our family for the rest of my days. To honor and protect you and to nurture our marriage. You have my heart, my fidelity, and all that I am. I want to make you feel the way I feel when I hear your voice or see your beautiful face. When I look at you, I see the essence of God and why He created me in the first place. My heart beats because you breathe, and I now know what it means to love someone else more than I love myself.

"God is real. God is love, and my love for God allows me to love you completely and eternally."

"Well said, brother." The pastor turned to Nia. "Nia, do you have vows prepared for Armand?"

She nodded and wiped away a tear. "Armand, my love, my heart, my soul's joy. Colossians also tells us that above all things is love, which is the bond of perfection. Our bond has been tested. It bent, but it did not break, and I thank God for that. I'm so thankful that we have another chance, and I will cherish you and our family every day of my life. I vow to listen and respect you and support you in your position as head of our household. Never again will I take you or what we have for granted. I'm yours now, forever, and always. I love you with everything I have in me to love. I vow to fight for you and for our marriage and family until my dying day. I give myself to you fully. All I have is yours. And whatever we do in word or deed, do all in the name of the Lord Jesus, giving thanks to God the Father through Him."

At the pastor's request, they recommitted their pledge to one another by exchanging rings with each other and their children.

Pastor Campbell faced the congregation gathered in the church. "Armand and Nia, you have again pledged to uphold the vows you made on your wedding day in addition to new promises made on today. You have symbolized this renewal of marriage by the joining of hands, taking of vows, and by exchanging rings.

"May you forever be joined as man and wife. It is my prayer and the hope of all here today that God will continue to bless this family and uphold this union.

"Armand, you can salute your lovely bride!"

The guests erupted in applause as Armand and Nia fell into a loving kiss. Amari wiped away tears of joy before hugging and congratulating the happy couple.

"It can still happen for you, sis," Armand whispered to her. "Don't give up!"

Amari caught up with Armand while the rest of the guests ate, danced, and fawned over Nia's dress. "Hey, you got a sec?" Amari asked her brother.

"For you, I've got at least three. What's up?"

"Those were some really beautiful things you and Nia said to one another up there. I didn't know you had it in you!"

"Never underestimate me, young lady. I've got game for days! I just choose to use my powers for good instead of evil these days."

"Don't talk that talk if you can't back it up!" she warned him.

"We meant every word of it, Mar. I'm gonna get it right this time. We both will."

"Aren't you scared of messing up again?"

Armand shook his head. "Nope. That's not to say we'll never do anything to hurt each other again because I'm sure we will, but I'm confident that we can work through it. We have God on our side, so we can't go wrong."

Amari was still skeptical. "You really have that much faith in Him?"

"I do," he maintained. "God wouldn't have allowed us to find our way back to one another if it wasn't His divine will for us to be together. And what God puts together, no man can put asunder."

"I hope that's true."

"Why? You thinking about trying to work things out with Mandrel?"

"No, there's someone else."

"Dang, girl, you don't waste any time! Who is he now?"

"I'm thinking about calling him Eric. Chanel if it's a girl."

"Huh?"

"Armand, I'm pregnant."

He froze. "I don't think I heard you right. Can you repeat that?"

"You heard me right. I'm pregnant. It's Apollo's baby."

His eyes bulged. "Whoa! Does he know?"

She nodded.

"Is he happy about it?"

"I have his abortion money burning a hole in my purse as we speak, so what do you think?"

"Are you happy about it?"

"Happy? I'm terrified!" confessed Amari. "I can't even keep my plants alive. What am I gonna do with a kid?"

"What concerns you the most right now?"

"Not being a good mother to this child. I don't want him or her to grow up the way we did. Ashamed, feeling different, and unwanted. I want to love this baby, but I'm not sure if I'd even know how. I've never really had to love anyone before, never had anyone completely dependent on me."

Armand blew out a deep breath. "Dang! What you gon' do?"

"I was going to take the money and run to the nearest clinic! Then I thought about you and Nia. If God can help the two of you make it, maybe He'll do the same for me and my baby."

"God can do anything," he assured her. "Have you been to the doctor yet? Is everything okay with you and the baby?"

She nodded. "I had my first appointment two days ago. The baby and I are both fine. I'm almost six weeks. He or she should be here right around Christmas."

"I can't think of a better Christmas present," said Armand. "You said everything is okay, but you still look worried. It doesn't sound like you're going to get a lot of support from the kid's father. Are you going to be okay with that?"

"Of course not, but what can I do? I can't make Apollo step up to the plate and be a real father. The most I can do is hit him up for child support."

"Well, no matter what happens, you know you have Nia and me. We'll help you out any way we can. Your child will have a father figure regardless."

"I appreciate that. I couldn't ask for a more positive male figure in my child's life." She broke into a smile. "You're going to be an uncle, can you believe it?"

"I thought I had a better chance of being a monkey's uncle than a real one!" he joked. "But this baby will turn out to be a blessing. You'll see."

"I prayed the other day," revealed Amari.

Armand reared his head back, astonished. "Really?"

"Yeah, it was the first time since . . . probably ever."

"What did you pray about?"

She exhaled. "The baby. You. Our parents."

"What was your prayer about the baby?"

"Just that God would keep him or her safe and that I do right by this child, whether that means raising it or giving it up."

"That was mighty big of you. And don't underestimate yourself, Mar. I know I tease you all the time, but I think you'll be a great mother. Everybody makes mistakes and no parent is perfect. Any kid would be lucky to have you."

"Thank you." She smiled. "You have no idea what it means to me to hear you say that."

"What about our parents? What did you pray about for them?"

"I prayed that one day we can all act like a real family. I want that for this child. Even if it doesn't happen, I asked God to give them peace and health. I also told Him that I forgive them."

"Wow! I'm proud of you, Mar. It sounds like you're ready to take this Christian thing seriously."

"I am. I know I slacked off a little with going to church after Mandrel and I broke up, but I'm coming back. I want this child to be raised in the church. It's like I said after Ro's funeral. I want to do something different and be a better person. I've even been thinking about seeing that therapist you keep talking about. I think I may have some issues that I could use some help sorting through."

Armand pointed toward her stomach. "Now you have a good reason to go."

"Yeah—me! I tried to be someone I wasn't for Mandrel, and I tried to be the person I've outgrown for Apollo. Now I just want to be what God wants me to be." She placed her hand over her stomach. "Even if that means being a mother."

Chapter 29

"How do you feel? Do you think you're equipped now to make better decisions in your life?" posed Dr. Nelson.

Amari sat up straight. "I think I'm getting there," she declared with confidence.

"Do you still feel caught between two worlds: your old life and the new one you were trying to carve out?"

"I think for me, the key is trying the balance the two, at least right now it is. I'm not going to be running around the city in miniskirts, chasing fun and men. At the same time, I'm not ready to join the deaconess board either! I can't deny that some of the old me is still there, but it's a day-by-day process. Even though it's in baby steps, every day I get stronger in who I am in the Lord. I'm confident that one day, I'll be in the place He wants me to be.

"In the meantime, I'll keep going to church, maybe not every Sunday but most. And I'll keep reading the Bible." She grinned from embarrassment. "Probably not every day, but a lot of days. Regardless, I'm not going back to the way I used to be. I couldn't."

Dr. Nelson closed her notebook and smiled. "I think that's enough for today. I think you made a lot of progress for this session, don't you?"

Amari nodded. "I feel good."

"What have you learned today?"

Amari took a moment to think before answering the question. "I've learned several things. I learned that I have to value myself and that includes valuing my body.

I've learned that I have to live in my truth and that it's not always pretty, but I have to be strong enough to face it."

"Anything else?"

"I have to own up to my mistakes and hold other people accountable for theirs. I know I have choices now. My relationships weren't screwed up by accident. It was the result of decisions I consciously made. In the same vein, I have to accept my dad wasn't around because we were cousins. He wasn't there because he didn't want to be. Not having his presence definitely skewed the way I see men, but I do have another Father who will never let me down, and He's God. Because He accepts me unconditionally, I can accept myself."

Dr. Nelson was pleased. "Very good. I couldn't have said it better myself."

"Is this what they call having a breakthrough?"

"Yes, it is." Dr. Nelson stood up. "Oh, before you leave, tell me about this new relationship."

"Right now, it's wonderful. Perfect, really." Amari beamed while looking back at him. "For the first time, I feel like we'll be all right. I don't think I'll mess up with him the way I have in the past. He means everything, and nothing is more important than making sure he feels loved, safe, and happy."

"I don't think I received a formal introduction," noted Dr. Nelson.

"We can fix that right now." Amari bolted to her feet and approached the person behind her. "There's someone here who wants to meet you." She reached down in the carrier and pulled out Eric, who was just waking from his nap. She cradled him in her arms and faced her therapist. "Dr. Nelson, this is Eric Christopher. Eric, this is Dr. Nelson."

"He certainly is an adorable baby," cooed Dr. Nelson, moving in close enough to get a good look at him. "And a good baby, too. He didn't make a sound the whole session."

"I think he slept through most of it, but he's a good baby, aren't you?" Amari kissed her son on the forehead.

Dr. Nelson reverted to her therapist role. "I suppose next session we can delve into your relationship with his father."

"Oh, Lord!" cried Amari. "We may be here all day discussing that one, but Apollo is coming around. I think he's warming up to the idea of being a dad. I'm not going to let him worm out of being in his son's life though. I'm going to make sure Eric doesn't grow up without a father the way Armand and I did."

"That's good to know. What about you? How are you coping with motherhood?"

"I love being a mom," boasted Amari. "I never thought I'd say it, let alone live it, but I've finally found what I was looking for. I wanted my life to have meaning and purpose. Now it does. Raising my son to be a man of God is my purpose, one of them anyway."

"What about the rest of them?"

"I'm figuring it out, slowly but surely. I guess that's what those remaining sessions can be for." Amari glanced at the clock. "I hope you don't mind that we went a little over an hour."

Dr. Nelson shook her head. "No, not at all. I think you needed it."

"I agree." Amari gathered the baby bag and her other belongings. "I'm sure I'll feel differently once your bill arrives."

Dr. Nelson laughed. "It won't send you into financial ruin, I promise."

"Thank you, and thanks for today, too. You're a good therapist, Dr. Nelson. I feel like I can tell you anything, and you'll listen without judging me."

"That's what I'm here for." She squeezed Amari's hand. "Until next time, take care of yourself, Amari, and that beautiful baby of yours."

"I will, and I'll be sure to schedule our next session with your receptionist on the way out. While we're on the subject, how many more of these sessions do you think I'll need anyway?"

"I'll be here until you no longer need me," replied Dr. Nelson.

Amari turned around before leaving. "You know I used to think all of the counseling stuff was a bunch of fluff, something that weak people do who can't figure out their own problems."

"And now?"

She smiled. "And now I no longer believe that."

"Seeking help is never a sign of weakness. Remember that. Even the Bible says that there is wisdom in those who seek counsel." Dr. Nelson opened the door to let Amari and Eric out. "Have a good afternoon, Miss Christopher."

Amari gave a slight nod. "You have a better one."

Four months later, Amari returned to Dr. Nelson's office for her final counseling session. Whereas she started out dreading their sessions, she now looked forward to them. It had been two months since their last appointment, and she couldn't wait to tell Dr. Nelson about all of the progress she was making. She could finally report that Apollo had stepped up and started spending more time with Eric. Even though she and Apollo were no longer romantically involved, they maintained a cordial relationship for their son's sake. She was still attending church service and Bible study and had even joined one of the church's ministries. Mandrel had moved on to another woman, but he and Amari managed to forge a friendship from the rubble of their doomed romance. Amari had found a healthy balance among work, play, and family life. And, for the first time, Amari felt fulfilled in every area of her life, including her growing relationship with God. She no longer felt rejected. She knew God loved and accepted her just as she was, so did her child.

Amari entered Dr. Nelson's office building and approached the receptionist's desk. "Hi, my name is Amari Christopher. I'm here for my two o'clock appointment with Dr. Nelson."

The receptionist seemed confused. "Who are you here to see again?"

"Dr. Denise Nelson."

"Oh, I'm sorry." The receptionist reddened. "I guess no one called you."

"Called me about what?" asked Amari. "Does Dr. Nelson want me to reschedule?"

"No . . ." She pursed her lips together. "I apologize for not informing you sooner, Miss Christopher, but Dr. Nelson no longer works here."

Amari was dumbfounded. "What?"

"She's been gone about two months now. Don't worry, we have several highly qualified therapists on staff." She handed Amari several business cards. "I'd be more than happy to schedule an appointment for you with one of them."

"That won't be necessary. So what has happened to Dr. Nelson? Was she let go for some reason?"

"No, she left on her own. Quite frankly, we were all surprised. We thought she was happy here."

Amari was still in shock. "I was here not that long ago. She didn't say anything about leaving."

"When was your last session with her?"

Amari thought back. "I guess it was around the end of April."

"That's when she left. After her appointment that day, she packed up her office and told us that she was learning."

The timing of Dr. Nelson's departure rattled Amari. "Did she say why she was leaving or where she was headed to?"

"No," answered the receptionist. "All she said was that her work here was done. She didn't leave a forwarding address or anything."

"What about her patients?" asked Amari. "Were they all assigned to new therapists in the building?"

"Actually, you were her only client at the time, so there was no one else to reassign."

"Her only client?" echoed Amari, puzzled and trying to make sense of it all. "How was she earning money? I know she didn't earn any from me because she never sent me an invoice. I haven't paid for a single session since I started."

"Really?" The receptionist wrinkled her nose. "That's odd. We bill immediately after each session."

"Is there any kind of paperwork detailing what I owe?" asked Amari, even more confused. "I'd like to settle the bill if I can."

The receptionist rose from her chair and pulled open the file cabinet backed against the wall behind her desk. "Let me check her files."

As the receptionist rummaged through the file folders, Amari grew more concerned. She prayed that no harm had come to Dr. Nelson, but she also started to have doubts about who her therapist really was.

"Nope!" exclaimed the receptionist and held up an invoice from Dr. Nelson with Amari as the recipient. "It says here that you don't owe anything. It says paid in full." She handed the paper to Amari.

Amari shook her head in disbelief. "I don't understand. I've been seeing her for weeks, and I never paid for a single session! Why would she say I've paid in full?"

"I don't know what to tell you, but I'd sure love to get a receipt like that!" stated the receptionist. "I'd give anything for the good Lord to come out the sky and pay a bill for me!"

"Can you tell me anything you know about Dr. Nelson, like where she's from or does she have any family around here? Any insight you have would be helpful."

The receptionist returned to her seat. "I just started working here three months ago, so I never knew much about her or how long she'd been here. She's a very nice lady as far as I can tell, always nice to me and had an encouraging word and a smile. No matter what day it was, she'd be the first one here and the last one to leave. You were her only official client, but she accepted walk-ins. People came in off the street to see her all the time. Regardless of how down they were when they came in, they always seemed happier after talking to her."

"Has anyone moved into her office yet?"

"No, and I'm not sure anyone will. The other therapists are talking about using it to store their records and files, things like that."

"Is it okay if I look around in there for a second? I don't want to take anything. I just want to see if she left anything that may be a clue as to what happened to her."

The receptionist hesitated but relented. "I guess it's all right." She pulled a ring of keys out of her desk drawer.

"Thank you so much!" exclaimed Amari and followed her down the hall to Dr. Nelson's office.

She inserted the key. The locked clanked and she pushed open the door and flipped on the light switch. "I don't think you're going to find anything. She took almost everything with her and left the office spotless."

"I see." The light illuminated the sparse office. The walls and fixtures had been stripped, and dust had already begun to settle Dr. Nelson's desk and chair. "You don't have to stay. I'll just be another minute."

The receptionist ducked out, leaving Amari alone in the office that was now eerily vacant. Nothing remained except the Bible Dr. Nelson kept open on the desk. Amari picked it up. It was turned to Isaiah 9:6.

"For unto us a Child is born. Unto us a Son is given; And the government will be upon His shoulder. And His name will be called Wonderful, Counselor, Mighty God, Everlasting Father, Prince of Peace," she read aloud. She reread a portion of the last line. "And His name will be called Wonderful, Counselor."

She set the Bible back in its place. None of it was adding up. She didn't understand why Dr. Nelson would leave so abruptly without so much as a note or an e-mail to explain her exodus. Why was Amari her sole client and why hadn't Dr. Nelson charged her for the sessions? Where had she gone? Would she ever come back?

Amari needed answers, but she suspected she'd gotten all she was going to get from that receptionist. She pulled out her cell phone and called Armand.

He answered after the second ring. "What's up?"

"Nothing much. Armand, have you seen Dr. Nelson lately?"

"Nah, I haven't gone to her since before Nia and I reconciled. Why?"

"We had an appointment today, but she resigned. She's gone, just up and vanished like a thief in the night."

"Really? That's strange."

"She didn't even call to cancel our appointment."

"She probably got a better position and relocated. I'm sure a woman with her credentials is in high demand. I bet she got an irresistible offer and followed the money."

"Yeah, maybe." Amari still wasn't persuaded. Dr. Nelson didn't seem like the type who'd be motivated by money. Her bargain basement outfits were proof of that.

Amari pushed Armand for more answers. "How did the two of you meet again?"

"It's weird because it was right around the time I started praying and going to church. Nia had left with the kids, and I was at my lowest point. Dr. Nelson just kind of popped up out of nowhere during one of my runs in the park. She said she had been watching me and could tell I was going through something major. She told me she was a counselor and that I should come by her office one day for a session."

"And you went, just like that?"

"Pretty much. I have to admit that I thought she was some sort of nut job at first, but I was desperate for help back then. Something told me go and see what she was about. Turns out, she was legit."

"Why did you stop seeing her?"

"Well, really she stopped seeing me. After our last session, she said that her work was done and that I didn't need her anymore. I haven't heard from her since."

"That's the same thing she told the people here before leaving," recalled Amari. "Something else is bizarre too."

"What is?"

"She didn't charge me that whole time I was seeing her. In fact, my invoice says that I'm paid in full, but I never shelled out a dime. What do you make of that?"

Armand was quiet.

Amari was alarmed. "Are you still there?"

"Yeah," he replied. "I was just thinking."

"About what?" asked Amari, hoping it might be a clue.

"You may not believe this, but I don't remember paying her either."

"Armand, how many people do you know who work for free like that?"

"None."

A hush fell over both of them.

Amari felt an inexplicable chill in the air. "I wonder where she came from and how she ended up in Atlanta."

Armand sighed. "Beats me."

"Beats you and me both." Amari stared at the bare walls, which once housed Dr. Nelson's many awards and degrees. "I guess we'll never know. Whatever the reason is, I'm glad she came. She helped me work through a lot of issues. I hate I won't have the chance to thank her."

"Same here," said Armand. "I'm just glad we had a chance to meet her while she was here. She was a godsend to both of us."

"Yeah." Amari looked around at Dr. Nelson's now vacant office. Her eyes landed on the open Bible. "I was just thinking the same thing."

Book Discussion Questions

1. Does Amari represent the majority or minority of successful single Black women today? Explain your reply.
2. What about Amari do you think attracted Mandrel to her? Was it a doomed match from the start? Why or why not?
3. Were Mandrel's expectations of Amari (i.e. salvation, conservative dress, no makeup, etc.) unreasonable or for her good? Explain.
4. Do you think Amari really loved Mandrel or did she have a void in her life that he fulfilled?
5. Why do think Amari reverts to her old habits once she meets Apollo?
6. Do you think Amari and Apollo could've forged a real relationship? Why or why not?
7. As a Christian, should Mandrel have given Amari another chance after she confessed to cheating?
8. Considering her family baggage and tumultuous relationship with Apollo, do you think Amari can be a good mother to Eric? Why or why not?
9. Do you think Dr. Nelson was an actual therapist or a celestial being? Why?
10. What did Dr. Nelson represent in Amari's life? Would she have recognized the need for change without her?

UC HIS GLORY BOOK CLUB!

www.uchisglorybookclub.net

UC His Glory Book Club is the spirit-inspired brain-child of Joylynn Ross, Author and Acquisitions Editor of Urban Christian, and Kendra Norman-Bellamy, Author for Urban Christian. This is an online book club that hosts authors of Urban Christian. We welcome as members all men and women who have a passion for reading Christian-based fiction.

UC His Glory Book Club pledges our commitment to provide support, positive feedback, encouragement, and a forum whereby members can openly discuss and review the literary works of Urban Christian authors.

There is no membership fee associated with UC His Glory Book Club; however, we do ask that you support the authors through purchasing, encouraging, providing book reviews, and of course, your prayers. We also ask that you respect our beliefs and follow the guidelines of the book club. We hope to receive your valuable input, opinions, and reviews that build up, rather than tear down our authors.

What We Believe:

—We believe that Jesus is the Christ, Son of the Living God.

—We believe the Bible is the true, living Word of God.

—We believe all Urban Christian authors should use their God-given writing abilities to honor God and share the message of the written word God has given to each of them uniquely.

—We believe in supporting Urban Christian authors in their literary endeavors by reading, purchasing, and sharing their titles with our online community.

—We believe that in everything we do in our literary arena should be done in a manner that will lead to God being glorified and honored.

We look forward to the online fellowship with you.

Please visit us often at:
www.uchisglorybookclub.net.

Many Blessing to You!

Shelia E. Lipsey,
President, UC His Glory Book Club

ORDER FORM
URBAN BOOKS, LLC
97 N18th Street
Wyandanch, NY 11798

Name (please print):_____

Address: _____

City/State: _____

Zip: _____

QTY	TITLES	PRICE
	3:57 A.M.: Timing Is Everything	$14.95
	A Man's Worth	$14.95
	A Woman's Worth	$14.95
	Abundant Rain	$14.95
	After the Feeling	$14.95
	Amaryllis	$14.95
	An Inconvenient Friend	$14.95
	Battle of Jericho	$14.95
	Be Careful What You Pray For	$14.95
	Beautiful Ugly	$14.95
	Been There Prayed That	$14.95
	Before Redemption	$14.95

Shipping and handling-add $3.50 for 1st book, then $1.75 for each additional book.
Please send a check payable to:
Urban Books, LLC
Please allow 4-6 weeks for delivery.

ORDER FORM
URBAN BOOKS, LLC
97 N18th Street
Wyandanch, NY 11798

Name(please print):_____

Address: _____

City/State: _____

Zip: _____

QTY	TITLES	PRICE
	By the Grace of God	$14.95
	Confessions Of A Preacher's Wife	$14.95
	Dance Into Destiny	$14.95
	Deliver Me from my Enemies	$14.95
	Desperate Decisions	$14.95
	Divorcing the Devil	$14.95
	Faith	$14.95
	First Comes Love	$14.95
	Flaws and All	$14.95
	Forgiven	$14.95
	Former Rain	$14.95
	Humbled	$14.95

Shipping and handling-add $3.50 for 1st book, then $1.75 for each additional book.
Please send a check payable to:
       Urban Books, LLC
Please allow 4-6 weeks for delivery.